# THE OUTLAWS OF MAROON

# THE OUTLAWS OF MAROON
a novel

## JOHN CURL

In gratitude for your insights, Andy, Bryn, Fletcher, Karen, Kristina, Nancy, Martin, Robin.

Cover by John Curl.

ISBN-13: 978-0-938392-04-0

Homeward Press, Berkeley, CA

# THE OUTLAWS OF MAROON

# CHAPTER ONE

Gabe and Henry set out the food near the garbage cans. Henry knew where all the strays lived. The cats, always on the watch for danger, crept cautiously out of the shadows when they saw him. The most skittish ones peeked from the alleys until the boys retreated far enough away, then darted out and scarfed it all down. Henry fed the neighborhood strays a couple of times a week, with kibble from a lady in his building, and Gabe often went around with him. Gabe hated fourth grade, and so did Henry.

After school and on weekends they hung out in the little park, Bennett Park, usually down at the far end by the granite rock, where the bushes and weeds were thicker. But some kids from Broadway started coming around and bothering everybody, so instead they started hanging out in the big park, Fort Tryon Park, which was further away, but had isolated corners and nooks to hide in.

Then they discovered the Little Woods. That's what Gabe and Henry called it. It didn't really have a name. People in the neighborhood sometimes called it *that empty lot*. Some said it was part of Fort Tryon Park, even though you couldn't get there by any of the paths, and it was separated from the big park by a high chain-link fence. Other people said that Mother Cabrini's Church owned the lot, even though Cabrini Boulevard separated it from the main church grounds.

The Little Woods started a ways up from Columbus School, across the street, beyond the last apartment building. Very few cars drove this way, because the street led only to the park entrance; and few people walked this way because of its isolation: it felt a bit dangerous. At the outer edge of the sidewalk was a black iron fence, and beyond that a sheer drop, over twenty feet down in some places. When you looked down, you could see the granite retaining wall holding up the edge of the sidewalk. At the bottom of the wall, a steep hill thick with trees and bushes tumbled down to a meadow at the West Side Highway. Closed off at the south end by apartment buildings, at the north by the park, on the east by the wall, and on the west by the highway, the Little Woods was almost inaccessible, a wild space right in Manhattan. That's the way it was back in 1951.

Gabe and Henry found two ways to get down into the Little Woods. The short way was straight down, at a spot they called The Place, where a star maple tree grew close to the wall. Here they jumped the cast iron fence at the outer edge of the sidewalk, and lowered themselves down between the tree and the granite rocks, holding onto the branches, climbing down rock to rock. That was the shortcut from school. The long way was through Fort Tryon Park, which was pretty roundabout, but safer in terms of not being seen. Beyond the neat lawns and beds of flowers, winding macadam paths and old people on benches, under some bushes and dense undergrowth, the hooks that held the chain-link wires onto the metal post at the bottom were broken, and they pushed it aside enough to crawl under.

Now that spring was here, almost every day as soon as school let out, and on weekends, Gabe and Henry would slip down the wall and run around in the Little Woods. They didn't have a lot of time on school days, because they had to be home by 5:30 at the very latest. None of the other kids ever went there or even knew that they went there. The teachers all said it was forbidden.

8

Once they were down there, nobody could see them, and they could run like crazy through the trees. Lots of birds and wild animals lived there. Squirrels and chipmunks and salamanders and sometimes raccoons or possums. Blue jays, red-tailed hawks, even an occasional hummingbird, and a couple of times at dusk they saw a big snowy owl. Once they watched a groundhog, with little oval ears and a round flat tail, sitting on a branch eating green unripe wild cherries. Occasionally they smelled a skunk. Henry saw a coyote there once, but Gabe didn't see it. They got down on their hands and knees and howled like coyotes, but no real coyotes ever answered them. A few stray cats lived there too. Down towards the highway, the Little Woods leveled off into the meadow where a rainbow of butterflies—tiger swallowtails, mourning cloaks, painted ladies and numerous others—flitted from flower to flower, along with bumble bees and honey bees and dragon flies, and an uncountable number of other insects. In the middle of the meadow, at a distance from other trees, stood a majestic elm.

They would stretch out on Bear Rock, and talk and talk, overlooking the Hudson River and the bridge, gazing across at the cliffs and beyond that toward Maroon hidden from view somewhere past the line of trees.

At twilight, the lightning bugs came out in the meadow, and sometimes Gabe and Henry ran around catching them in nets they'd made from old pillow cases and wire clothes hangers. They put the fireflies into jars to make lanterns, used them to light their way along the paths, then always let them fly away free.

.

All spring Gabe had been telling Henry about Maroon and showing him pictures. Henry wanted to hear about it over and over. He was coming to Maroon with Gabe for two whole weeks in July, during summer vacation. They couldn't wait. Every day felt like forever, school was never going to end.

Maroon was just seven acres, but behind the old chicken coop was the stream and the pine forest, and to Gabe it was a whole vast world. Almost every day he met up with the local farm kids, who had chores in the morning but could usually roam unconstrained until dusk, when the crickets started singing and the whippoorwills began to call. Mom grew up there in New Jersey a long time ago, back before the Great Depression when Grampa was trying to be a farmer. Grampa still lived part of every year there, and the whole family went there every summer from as far back as Gabe could remember. Well, Dad still had to work at his job in the city, but he came out for one whole week and on weekends.

The little clapboard house had only three small rooms, but to Gabe it was perfect, or almost perfect. They got their water from an outdoor hand pump, used kerosene lanterns for light, had an old ice box instead of a refrigerator, and an outhouse which Gabe didn't much like. Beyond in back was the old chicken coop, now a storage shed, and beyond that the pine forest, the wild huckleberry bushes, the gurgling brook, the little pond with frogs and water skeeters. Down the road was the secret swimming hole on Metedeconk Creek. In the forest you almost never saw the bigger animals, but you heard them rustling, and sometimes caught a glimpse of one through the underbrush, or saw their paw or hoof prints.

When people asked why they called the old farm Maroon, even though the house was yellow and the roof was red, Grampa Benjo always explained that it wasn't maroon the color, but maroon like when your boat hits a rock in the middle of the ocean and you're marooned on an island. It didn't make a lot of sense to Gabe, but Grampa didn't exactly understand some words, since English wasn't his first language.

10

Because of Maroon, Gabe knew both country and city, but Henry had lived his whole life in the big city. He had never been to the country, or even away to summer camp. Gabe tried to describe to him what country life was like, but could never quite explain it, just like he couldn't quite explain to the farm kids what city life was like. But Henry still knew an awful lot about birds and animals and bugs, usually even more than Gabe, but he got it from hanging out in the parks and from books.

Washington Heights was a pretty diverse neighborhood. You could hear many accents and languages on the street. Almost all of the kids in Columbus School belonged to one ethnic group or another. But each group mostly hung out by itself, and Gabe didn't quite fit into any of them, and neither did Henry. In class, Henry usually spoke with his school voice, but outside, or when he was worked up about something, he spoke more like his family, but the teachers always corrected you when you spoke that way in class. When anybody asked Henry what he was, he never really answered. He was sensitive about it. Henry's mom and gramma and the man he called Pimple Simon all looked different from him. Gabe never saw Henry's dad. It didn't really matter to him. Gabe's own family was pretty mixed too, and he was sensitive about it too. When he started kindergarten a long time ago, Mom said, "If they ask what you are, tell them you're an American."

For Gabe, summer in Maroon meant feeling happy and free. In contrast, winter in Manhattan was bleak, and meant being constricted and confined. Whenever he looked out through his bedroom window, tucked up alongside the George Washington Bridge, he imagined Maroon out there, across the river, waiting for him.

•

The sidewalk was filled with kids funneling in from the surrounding blocks. Every morning they gathered outside the gate in front of Columbus School, and waited until the second bell rang and the doors opened.

Today was assembly day, and everybody had on their assembly outfit. The boys wore white shirts and blue ties, and the girls wore white middy blouses with gold scarves. Blue and gold were the school colors. At ten o'clock the whole school would be marching down to the auditorium.

That morning, as soon as he got out of the house, Gabe pulled off his tie and stuck it in his pocket. Gabe hated wearing a tie. It made him feel like a dog on a leash. Henry hated ties too. Gabe's mom always remembered when it was assembly day, and made sure that he was dressed properly.

Gabe saw Henry coming toward him in the crowd, in his green corduroy pants a couple sizes too big, worn in the knees, suspenders, and his sky blue cap with a little hummingbird embroidered on it. Not only did Henry have no tie, but he was wearing his flannel shirt with red, white and black cross stripes, kind of frayed in the elbows. He was a little shorter than Gabe, more wiry. His ears stuck out of a shock of brown kinky hair that Gabe's mom always said needed cutting.

When Gabe saw Henry, he remembered his tie, stuck his hand in his pocket, but it wasn't there.

Henry whispered, "After you left yesterday, I found something amazing."

"What?"

"This is top secret. You won't snitch about this ever, right?" Henry looked him in the eye.

"I'm in on this. I won't tell."

"I'll show you after school."

"Show me now."

"It's not here. It's down in the Little Woods."

When they finally got to class, they separated, each to his seat. Miss Odelia had seated them on opposite sides of the room.

Miss Odelia began, "Today as you know is assembly day. I'm very pleased to see that almost everyone has remembered to wear your assembly outfits. Everyone except for Gabriel and Henry. Would you two please come up here."

They slunk up to the front.

She opened a desk drawer and pulled out a white shirt and two bow ties, the baby kind you clip onto your collar with a metal snap. "Put these on."

No matter how much Gabe hated ties, clip-on bow ties were the worst of the worst.

She handed him a bow tie, and Gabe scuttled back to his seat.

Henry stood there looking up at her.

Miss Odelia said, "Take off that shirt."

"Here?" Henry asked.

"Right here." She was trying to humiliate him in front of the class.

A nervous giggle circled around the room.

Henry unbuttoned his flannel shirt while the class tittered. He pulled it out from under his suspenders, and let it fall to the floor. His sleeveless undershirt had holes. Miss Odelia shoved the white shirt at him. He grasped it reluctantly.

"Put it on."

Gabe could see that Henry now had the problem of putting on the white shirt without taking off his suspenders, which were holding his corduroy pants up. He started but got self-conscious and couldn't quite figure it out, so he just put it on over his suspenders. It was several sizes too big and looked ridiculous on him.

"Don't leave it hanging out," Miss Odelia said. "Tuck it in."

He couldn't tuck it in without unhooking his suspenders. Henry got flustered, and just stood there, looking pained. The giggling died out. Most of the kids felt sorry for him, realizing that they could be next. Except for Jim Stoloff, who had an oily grin on his face, and so did Rory Golman, they were loving it.

"Go into the clothes closet," Miss Odelia finally muttered. "Here, take the tie. And pick up your shirt from the floor."

Henry slunk off and disappeared into the closet, which was on one side of the room, with sliding doors.

"Now, has everybody done your assignment?" Miss Odelia asked. "Has everybody memorized the words to the fourth stanza of 'The Star-Spangled Banner'?"

A few voices in unison, "Yes, Miss Odelia," while the rest of the class mumbled nonsense syllables.

"Now, today at assembly," Miss Odelia went on, "we are going to be singing the fourth stanza of 'The Star-Spangled Banner' for the first time. I hope you are all prepared, I hope you all did your homework and now you have the last stanza memorized as well as the first stanza. I gave you this assignment last Friday, so you had ample time to do it, and I have reminded you several times since then."

"Yes, Miss Odelia."

Henry emerged from the closet, the shirt tucked into his pants under his suspenders, and the bow tie in place. Gabe saw the defiance in Henry's eyes.

"Did anyone not do their homework?" Miss Odelia gazed around the room.

Roco raised his hand.

14

"Francisco, you didn't do your homework?"

The teachers called him Francisco, but the kids called him Roco.

"My cousin was having a baby."

"You gave that same excuse last month."

"That was a different cousin."

"You shouldn't let that stop you from doing your homework. You'll need to catch up."

"She didn't have one hair, the baby, not my cousin, she looked like a egg, and it was soft on top, like you could stick your finger right into her brain. I'm not kidding."

The class tittered. Miss Odelia ignored it.

"Anyone else not do your homework? Excellent. Then everybody else has studied the words to the last verse of 'The Star-Spangled Banner' at home, and has come prepared with questions about anything you didn't understand."

She stepped toward the large poster pinned to the board, with a bald eagle scowling at the top, above all four verses.

"So what are your questions?" She scanned the room. "No one? Surely someone must have a question. Everybody understands every single word in the song? Arisu."

Ari said, "What's a hireling?" She was slight, one of the smaller girls in the class, but knew how to use her tongue.

"Let's look at those lines. They're in the third stanza." She stood at the board with her pointer. "Please read that line out loud."

Ari read, "No refuge could save the hireling and slave."

"Does anybody know what a hireling is?" No one raised their hand. She went on, "A hireling is a soldier who fights for money. Another word for that is mercenary." She wrote both words on the blackboard. "In the American Revolution, there were mercenaries fighting. Which side were they fighting on, Arisu?"

15

"The British?" she answered uncertainly.

"That's right. German mercenaries, called Hessians, were fighting with the British, trying to stop the Americans from gaining our freedom. Does that answer your question, Arisu?"

"What about the slaves?" Ari replied. "What were the slaves doing there?"

"Oh yes," Miss Odelia said. "Well, those were still the days of slavery, before the Civil War."

"Who were the slaves fighting for, the Americans or the British?"

A puzzled expression came over Miss Odelia's face. She gazed at the words on the poster as if she had never actually thought about it until now.

Then she said hurriedly, "That's in the third stanza, and we don't have time today for a full discussion of all four verses. Today, we're focusing on the fourth verse, because that's the one we'll all be singing today in assembly. Does anyone have any questions about the last verse? How about you, Henry?"

He just shook his head.

She gazed right at Gabe. "Gabriel, did you do your homework?"

"Yes."

"Do you have a question?"

*Two days before, Gabe had been studying at his little table, when Grampa Benjo came in, yawned and stretched his arms wide. "What a day!" "Grampa, I'm trying to read." "Sorry for breathing. Stop burying your nose in those books once in a while, run around the block a few times. It'll do you good." "I'm doing my homework. I've got to get it done." When he needed help with homework, Mom usually helped with arithmetic and Dad with writing. Once in a while he asked Benjo, but he usually wasn't much help, and*

16

*often left Gabe more confused, so he just asked him when nobody else was available. Benjo came around and looked over his shoulder. "What's that?" "It's The Star-Spangled Banner. I've got to read it for school." "Oh, say can you see..." Benjo began to sing, then trailed off. Gabe said, "That's not even the right melody." Benjo stared at the page. "Look at this: Then conquer we must. That's what the politicians always say: then conquer we must. Why? Why do we always got to conquer?"*

So when Miss Odelia asked Gabe if he had done his homework and if he had a question, first he drew a blank, and then he found himself saying, "Why do we always got to conquer?"

"Read the line to us."

"Where it says, Then conquer we must."

"Yes, that is in the fourth stanza, the one we have been memorizing. That line goes together with the next one. The whole thought is, *Then conquer we must, when our cause it is just.* Does that answer your question?"

"It still doesn't make sense to me."

"What part of it doesn't make sense to you?"

"What's *our cause*? And what does that mean, *when it is just*? When it's just what?"

Jack raised his hand. "When it's just a joke?"

"Kelly."

"When it's just an excuse." Kelly had thick glasses and was left handed. He was notorious back in second grade for being on TV on Howdy Doody in the Peanut Galley, and getting kicked out by Buffalo Bob.

Miss Odelia flashed a tense grin and glanced around the room. "What is a *cause*? What is a *just cause*? What does that mean? Elkie?"

Elkie replied, "Just is like justice. Because of justice." Elkie had come into their class a few weeks after school started last fall. She must have been new in the neighborhood. Her clothes were somewhat different from the other girls, and she pronounced some words with an accent, just certain words.

"Good answer. Very good, Elkie. Because of justice. We must conquer because of justice. Does that answer your question, Gabriel?"

"Kind of. I'm not sure. I've got to think about it."

Henry's hand shot up. Miss Odelia reluctantly called on him again.

"How do we know?"

"How do we know what?"

"How do we know when our cause it is just?"

Miss Odelia set her jaw. "America's cause—our cause—is justice. Americans believe in justice. Don't you, Henry?"

Henry said, "What is justice?"

She glared at him. "That's more than we have time to get into today."

The bell rang twice. The speaker above the door crackled and Miss M. Drannily's voice echoed through it. "Time for assembly."

"I'm afraid we don't have any more class time this morning." Miss Odelia sighed. "Everyone line up in size place with a partner, boys with boys and girls with girls."

In the midst of the shuffle, Gabe and Henry met at that back of the room.

Henry said, in a low voice, "That's it. I had it."

"What do you mean?"

"They want to break us like ponies, ride around on our backs. Not me. I'm not taking this junk any more. I'm out of here. I'm quitting this stupid school."

"Where are you going to go?"

"To Maroon."

"But that's just for two weeks."

"I'm sure not coming back here to this junk. No way. I'm not coming back. I'm not living in this jail my whole life, that's for sure. I'm breaking out. Want to break out? Want to stay in Maroon with me?"

Before Gabe could answer, the line started to move out the door. They scrambled to find their size places.

Gabe wound up with Jim Stoloff as his partner, and Henry wound up right in front of Rory Golman. Jim poked Gabe in the back.

Gabe turned. "Don't do that."

"Do what?"

"You know what you did."

"Nobody touched you."

Miss Odelia said, "Is something wrong, Gabe?"

"No, nothing's wrong."

For some reason they both hated Gabe and Henry. They lived in Monarch Towers, a group of tall buildings set off from the rest of the neighborhood by fences and guards, with clipped rolling lawns and patches of multi-colored flowers in neat rows, that seemed to be always in bloom. Gabe had to walk past there every day on his way to school, and he always crossed the street when he saw Jim and Rory and Jim's big brother. Monarch Towers had an elaborate kids' play area with monkey bars and slides and tunnels and see-saws, but only kids who lived there could use it, and it was usually empty, because only a few kids lived there. Gabe and Henry snuck in a few times, but the gardener chased them out. Once they tried to slip into the building through the delivery entrance, to see what was inside, but the doorman grabbed them. The super recognized Henry because Pimple Simon—Henry's gramma's husband—was a super too, and

19

Pimple Simon hit Henry for it, and said he would hang him in the closet if he ever did it again.

All the classes marched through the hall, down the stairs to the auditorium, a big theater with a stage in front, a flag, an upright piano, and a podium. On the stage were Principal Hopper and the Drannily sisters. While they entered the auditorium, the junior sister—Miss C. Drannily—played her usual marching music on the piano. Each class filed into a different section, and each kid stood in front of a seat. They had to wait to sit down until the senior sister—Miss M. Drannily—told them to. Mrs Hopper, with her big bush of blue-white hair, was planted next to the flag on the stage, and Miss M. Drannily stood at attention by her side.

Together the Drannily sisters taught the upper grades Language Arts, which consisted of Miss M. focusing on grammar and Miss C. teaching composition and literature. In those days Columbus School was kindergarten to sixth grade. The lower grades stayed with their homeroom teachers all day, except for lunch and recess, while the fifth and sixth graders had special teachers for different subjects. Miss M. looked a little older than Miss C. They wore similar long brown dresses but M. kept her hair pulled back into a bun, while C. wore hers down. M.'s tiny waist was cinched by a black belt, and C.'s by a pink one. Miss M. doubled as the vice principal and school disciplinarian, and was always mad about something. Miss C. taught art and music appreciation, and was the school librarian. The kids mostly liked Miss C. She always had a pained smile in her eyes. Nobody in the school ever called her Miss Drannily, because Miss Drannily always meant her sister, Miss M. Sometimes Gabe saw the Drannily sisters striding in and out of Monarch Towers, so he figured they must live there.

As always, when everyone was settled and seated, Principal Hopper shuffled to the podium, told everybody to face the flag, place your right hand over your heart, and recite the Pledge of Allegiance.

Then Miss M. Drannily took center stage, her back ramrod straight, and declaimed, "From now on in every assembly we will be singing both the first and last verses of our national anthem. Today is the first time. I assume everyone is prepared." She raised her hands like an orchestra conductor.

Miss C. struck a chord on the piano and began playing, Miss M. started waving her hands and singing, the kids joined in. It actually sounded pretty good.

Then Mrs Hopper said, as always, "I will now read the Twenty-third Psalm." Gabe knew the psalm by heart, from having heard it so many times. Mrs Hopper must have had it memorized too, but still always read from the open Bible on the podium, which she probably just used as a prop.

"Yea, though I walk through the valley of the shadow of death..." She began to hack and covered her mouth with her embroidered hanky. Her cough had gotten worse as the school year progressed, and she had begun to lisp and stammer. "*Ththurely...*" She screwed up her face and moved her jaw from side to side, then tried again, "Surely goodness and mercy *ththall...*" It turned into a wheeze, almost a whistle. It was like she was losing control of her jaw or her tongue. With a determined expression, she continued, "Surely goodness and mercy shall follow me all the days of my life: and I will dwell in the *houth* of the Lord for ever. Amen." Mrs Hopper hacked a few more times, shut the Bible, stepped back from the podium, shuffled over to Miss M., whispered something through her handkerchief, then dropped into a folding chair next to the flag, Bible in her lap, looking somewhat crestfallen.

Miss M. said, "Mrs Hopper is not feeling well today, and asked me to give the talk that she planned." Drannily cleared her throat. "Those who have been in my grammar class know that I always assign a word of the day. Every day, never miss a day. That way we grow our vocabulary, one word at a time. Today's word is vigilance, v-i-g-i-l-a-n-c-e,

21

vigilance. This afternoon when you go back to your homeroom, every class will have a discussion on vigilance. Does anybody know what that word means? Hands?"

A couple of hands shot up and a few others tentatively raised. Drannily, as was her practice, didn't call on anybody but answered herself in her high-strung tone, "Vigilance means being always watchful, alert, wary, keeping a careful eye out for danger. It comes from the Latin *vigilare*, to keep awake. Sometime this afternoon—and I won't say when—Columbus School will have a duck-and-cover drill, so we will all be vigilant and prepared for the nuclear threat that all Americans are concerned about. And we must also be vigilant and prepared for another threat, one perhaps even more alarming because it is insidious, like a snake in the grass. The very foundations of our freedom and democracy, the envy of the world, are under threat from enemies right here in America, un-American calumniators who hate freedom and democracy, and want to take them away from us. These are new and different enemies, perhaps even more treacherous because many of them may look just like ordinary people in our neighborhood. But we do not need to be afraid: we need to be alert, vigilant. We can all help catch them. This afternoon, third graders and up will receive a special VIP Vigilance note pad and pocket pencil, which we call V-Pads. Your homeroom teacher will explain all the details, what entries are appropriate, and what are not. Columbus School is honored to be selected for this pilot program. Do the work carefully, because in one week all the pads will be collected and handed in to our friends at the Internal Protection Agency. So who is going to be vigilant? Hands?"

Again, several of the same hands shot up. Miss M. ignored them and continued, "We all are. Each of us. It's up to all of us. We keep our eyes open, our ears peeled. Vigilance! V-i-g-i-l-a-n-c-e! Vigilance!"

Her sister Miss C. punched some chords on the piano, they led the kids in singing 'O Columbia, the Gem of the Ocean' and few more songs, then marched everybody back to their homerooms.

•

# CHAPTER TWO

Miss Odelia's class filed quietly two-by-two up the stairs and down the hall, but as soon as they stepped past the threshold of their homeroom, a murmur went up, everyone broke ranks and scrambled about, chattering and joking.

Shaking a ruler, Miss Odelia enunciated in her firmest voice, "Come to order. Now. Everyone take your seat." She banged the ruler on her desk.

Henry and Gabe were in the back with a few of the other kids. They hadn't taken their seats immediately because they were on opposite sides of the room.

Henry whispered to Gabe, "The word of the day is burp, b-u-r-p, burp."

"No, it's fart, f-a-r-t, fart." Gabe whispered back.

Miss Odelia said sternly, "Gabriel, perhaps you can share what's so funny with the rest of us."

"Sorry."

"Share your joke with the rest of the class."

The room was suddenly silent.

Gabe thought fast, but drew a blank. "There isn't any joke."

"Henry, tell us all Gabriel's little joke."

Henry glanced at Gabe, then back at Miss Odelia, and spelled, "N-o-w-a-y! No way!"

Everyone burst out laughing.

Miss Odelia's eyes narrowed. She snapped, "Both of you, to the principal's office."

Henry said, "We were just kidding."

"Now!"

Henry and Gabe looked at each other again, then both slunk toward the door.

Miss Odelia said dourly, "Anybody else want to join them?" Her eyes darted around the room, pausing at each face to make sure that all expressions were somber and all eyes downcast.

The first door to the office opened into the secretary's alcove. From there doors led to the principal's and the vice principal's adjoining offices. From the hall, as they approached, through the textured glass Gabe could see the secretary, Miss McKlosky, broken up like in a kaleidoscope.

She told them to sit on the big wooden bench, one at each end, separated from each other. Miss McKlosky wore a phone headset, and kept talking into it in a low voice. Gabe could tell that she was trying to make it sound like she was working but was really chatting with somebody.

They had to wait a long time. Henry rolled his eyes. Gabe almost cracked up, but bit his lip and stared at the wall.

Gabe could hear muffled voices coming from the principal's inner office.

Finally Miss McKlosky said, "Mrs Hopper will see you now."

They reluctantly stood.

Principal Hopper was at her desk, the corners of her mouth turned down. She looked enormous. The buttons tugged against the buttonholes of her white blouse. Glowering next to her like a lamp post alongside a house, was Miss M. Drannily. Her pointy black shoes were highly polished.

25

"Shut the door," Mrs Hopper said.

They were alone in the room with Hopper and Drannily.

Gabe fidgeted, feeling very small.

"Don't look down," Hopper commanded. "Look at me."

Through her thick bifocals, Mrs Hopper's eyes looked like the polar bear at the zoo who wants to bite your face off. Gabe wondered if those glasses gave her the power to see right into his brain.

Hopper said, "Why did Miss Odelia send you here?"

After a pause, Henry responded, "We were joking around."

She swung her gaze to Gabe. "And *what'th... what'th...*" She began to hack into her handkerchief, then pulled herself together. "And *what'th* your version?"

Gabe's throat was dry, and at first he couldn't get any words out. "We were joking around."

Hopper's eyes narrowed. "Is that what your parents *thend* you here for?" She began wheezing and coughing again.

Neither boy responded.

"*Thpeak* up."

An awkward silence.

Drannily leaped in. "Speak up. Mrs Hopper can't hear you. Is that what your parents send you here for, to joke around?"

"No," Gabe said mousily.

"*No, Mrs Hopper,*" Drannily corrected.

"No, Mrs Hopper," the boys repeated in unison.

"They've been here before," Drannily said to Hopper. "Both of them. This isn't the first time."

It actually was the first time for Gabe, though she was right about Henry.

26

Drannily riveted her gaze on them. "But I assure you, it better be the last time. This is going down on your permanent records, you know that, don't you? Are you sorry? Say it. Mrs Hopper wants to hear you say it. Say, *We're sorry, Mrs Hopper.*"

In unison, the boys repeated, "We're sorry, Mrs Hopper."

Drannily said, "Now grow up become real boys, like Pinocchio, and starting acting your age."

A hint of a smile appeared briefly in the center of Hopper's red lips. "Now back to your *clathroom.*"

In the hall, Henry whispered, "Pinocchio? Real boys? Who does she think she's kidding? They're the ones who aren't even real people."

"If they're not real people, then what are they?"

"Trilobites. Those two, Odelia, Pimple Simon. And Jim Stoloff and Rory Golman. They just pretend they're people. They think they got us fooled. They're not fooling anybody. They're really troglobites."

"What?

"Troglodytes, trilobites, something like that. Look it up. It's in all the books. They crawl out of sink drains, and now they're all over the place. They're taken over the whole city. They were never kids. They're born old."

"If they're born old and were never kids, what about Jim and Rory?"

"They're just pretending they're kids, they're in disguise. They're not fooling anybody."

"You're just making that up."

"No I'm not. It's real. Look it up."

"How do you know if somebody's one of them?"

"You just know," Henry replied.

"How do you know for sure?"

"Because troglodytes got claws on one of their feet instead of toes. That's how you know for sure, when you seen their claws." Henry hooked his fingers. "I seen Pimple Simon's claws all the time, whenever he takes off his smelly socks."

•

As they re-entered Miss Odelia's classroom, she shot them a steely glance. "Take your seats. Quietly." On the blackboard behind her was written VIGILANCE.

Jim Stoloff and Rory Golman were standing in the front of the class, beaming.

Odelia held up a little spiral-bound note pad, with a black cover and a gold emblem. "Along with your V-Pad, you will receive an information sheet for your parents or guardians. Jim, take the pads, Rory the sheets. One to each pupil."

Jim tossed a pad on Gabe's desk. On the shiny black cover was a big gold V, in its center an official-looking emblem. A sharpened little pencil with the same V insignia was stuck into a plastic sleeve on the binding.

"Open your V-Pad to the inside cover. Write your name on the line, and below that our classroom number and grade. Now we are going to read this together, so we all understand what to do. Jim, read the first paragraph."

"This is your Vigilance Pad. By accepting this V-Pad, you are officially en..." He stumbled over the word.

"Enlisted," Miss Odelia said.

"...enlisted in the Student Vigilance Project of the I.P.A. Keep it with you at all times, so you are always ready."

Miss Odelia said, "Does everyone know what the I.P.A. is? Jack?"

"I didn't raise my hand."

"What is the I.P.A.?"

"Why are you always asking me?" Jack curled his lip. "Ask Miss Drannily."

"Does anybody know? The Internal Protection Agency is one of the parts of our government that keep us safe. Rory, continue."

"If you see or hear anything sus..."

"Suspicious," she said.

"...write it down. If you see question..."

"Questionable."

"...activity, such as someone who is saying sus..."

"Suspicious."

"...things or is carrying a sus..."

"Suspicious."

"...package, or who leaves a bag off on the sidewalk, or who is dressed in..."

"Inappropriately," she said. "That's enough, Rory. Thank you." Her eyes scanned the room. "Henry, have you been paying attention?"

Henry gave her a bug-eyed look.

"Finish reading this to the class." She cracked a little smile.

He began, "...inappropriately for the weather, such as wearing a coat when it is warm, or taking pictures in an unusual way, or who is unnaturally loitering or abnormally nervous or staring or watching for no good reason or who is in a forbidden place or somewhere they should not be, or who is saying things that arouse your suspicion: if you see any of these, take notes in your V-Pad. Report them! Write them up!"

"Thank you, Henry. Very good. Any questions?"

Elkie said, "My mom is always nervous, I think that's what made her sick. Should I write that up?"

Kelly jumped in, "My mom is nervous too. She always thinks she's fat." He was a little chubby himself.

"Many mothers are nervous," Miss Odelia said.

Jack said, "What if you know somebody who wets their bed?"

Everybody giggled.

Miss Odelia responded, "I don't think so."

Roco said, "I got a cousin who always wears his coat in the house, even when it's sweating in there, and says freaky things. I'm not kidding."

"Use your judgment."

Ari said, "My uncle acts weird. I wish he didn't live with us."

Miss Odelia looked flustered. Suddenly she said, "Duck and cover."

It took an instant to sink in. They all scrambled and crouched under their desks. Gabe stuck his nose into the crock of one arm, and held his other hand behind his neck.

"Very good, class. Very well done. If this had been a real nuclear attack, you would have all been safe. All clear. You can come up now."

Everybody got back up into their seats.

She stepped to the blackboard, took a piece of chalk, underlined the word VIGILANCE. "As Miss Drannily explained at assembly, we are now going to have a discussion about this word."

She went on and on.

Gabe opened his V-Pad and wrote, LET'S WRITE UP MISS ODELIA.

He tore out the page, folded it into an airplane, wrote HENRY on the front, waited until Miss Odelia turned around again, then sailed it across the room toward him.

Miss Odelia turned back around just as it missed Henry and landed on the floor near Elkie's feet.

"Elkie, what are you doing?"

"Nothing, Miss Odelia," she said.

"What is that? Bring it here. Give it to me."

When Miss Odelia saw Henry's name on the front, she shot him a riveting glance. When she opened it and read what was inside, she was fuming. "Elkie, did you write this?"

"No, Miss Odelia."

"Then who did?"

Gabe hesitated, then raised his hand.

"Gabriel," she said in a slow deep voice. "Report to Mrs Hopper's office again. Take your things with you. You too, Henry. Both of you. Out. I don't want you back here today."

A few minutes later they were sulking again in front of Mrs Hopper and Miss M. Drannily.

Hopper rolled her eyes. "Miss Drannily, what do we do with boys who..." She broke off, hacking into her handkerchief. "...who *refuthe* to *liththen*?"

Drannily said, "They don't belong in fourth grade. They have not yet learned how to act like big boys. Because they are still babies." She pointed a wrinkled finger at them. "You will go back into kindergarten, with the other babies. You will both stay there until your parents come in and talk with Mrs Hopper. You go to room 201. And you to room 203."

They crept silently back down the hall.

"I don't care," Henry whispered.

"I don't either," Gabe whispered back.

"We just got to make it till summer, then we're off to Maroon. I can't wait."

"I been thinking," Gabe began tentatively, "about what you said before, about staying there and not coming back, and I don't think it's going to work."

"Why not?"

"My mom won't let me," Gabe said.

Henry shut his eyes and took a deep breath. "So, don't tell her."

"You mean, like, run away?"

"Yeah."

"Where would we stay? In the house? In the chicken coop? They'll just find us."

"There's a big forest right behind the house in back, that's what you said, right?"

"Yeah, the big pines start right on the other side of the old chicken coop. There's miles and miles of pines. You can hike all day and never get to the end of it."

"Then we'll go live there in the forest."

"Where will we sleep?"

"We'll find a cave way deep in the woods where nobody can find us."

"I never saw a cave out there."

"Then we'll build ourselves a house, a tree house."

"How will we get food?"

Henry said, "We'll be pirates."

"We can't be pirates. Maroon's in the country. Pirates can't live in the country."

"Why not?"

"They can only live by the seashore."

"Pirates can live anywhere they want."

32

"No they can't."

"Then we'll be outlaws. Outlaws live in the forest all the time, and they get food. What's the problem? Don't you want to go?"

"I want to go more than anything, you know I do, and I want to go there with you."

"You're the one who's always saying it's full of food out there."

"Well, it is," Gabe conceded. "There's farms all over the place, and they've all got plenty of food." It was almost starting to sound feasible to him. "And there's a store up on a hill a ways away down the road, and they've got lots of food there too, and you can ride there on your bike. Everybody's got bikes out there. The store lady knows everybody, and if you don't have money, she lets you take things anyway and pay some other time."

"And the kids you know out there, they're not jerks, right? They won't snitch on us, will they?"

"The farm kids? No. They're cool. They'll help us for sure. Everybody helps each other out there. Nobody ever even locks their doors most of the time. Sure, they fight once in a while, but then they always make up." Gabe thought a moment. "But wouldn't you miss your mom and gramma?"

"Maybe a little."

Gabe knew that Henry wouldn't miss his gramma's husband.

"I'd miss my family too. A little, I think. And what about the Little Woods? And the strays. I'd miss them, wouldn't you?"

"Well, we can come back and visit," Henry said. "I been looking at that bridge ever since I can remember, but I never been across it, not once. I never even knew what was out there on the other side, until you told me. All we got to do is get through two more months in this jail, then we're off to Maroon."

"I think it's more than two months," Gabe said cautiously.

"Not much more. Then we won't have to go to stupid Columbus School ever again. And never see Miss Odelia's dumb face, ever again."

"Never again."

From down the corridor came a teacher's voice, "What are you two doing in the hall?"

Gabe turned the handle of room 201 and looked around at all the little kids. This had been his room in kindergarten, and the familiarity felt somewhat comforting.

"Can I help you?" This teacher was new in the school. His old kindergarten teacher was gone.

"Mrs Hopper and Miss Drannily told me to come here."

"Why?"

"They just told me to stay here until my parents come and talk with them."

"I see. What grade are you in?"

"Fourth. Miss Odelia's class."

She shook her head. "Just take a seat in the very back of the room, and do not disrupt the class. I'm Miss Prince."

Gabe wracked his brain all afternoon for a convincing story to tell Mom and Dad, but couldn't think of one.

At the end of the day, he met Henry in the hall.

"How was it?" Gabe asked.

"It was fun. They just let me sit in the back of the room and do anything I want. How about you?"

"They just left me alone too. What did you do all day?"

"Nothing," Henry replied. "I just fooled around. I drew pictures."

"Can I see?"

Henry showed him his notebook, filled with birds and animals.

"What are you going to tell your mom?" Gabe asked.

"Here's what I'm going to tell her." Henry cupped his hands together, then opened his empty palms.

"What?"

"Nothing. I'm not telling her nothing."

"Then what are you going to do, just stay in kindergarten?"

"Why not? Who cares? It's fine with me. I like it a lot more than fourth grade. I hate Miss Odelia. I don't want to be in her stupid class. Besides, we just got to hold out till summer, then we're off to Maroon. I'll just stay in kindergarten. I'd rather be in kindergarten."

Gabe had not considered that as a possibility. "Maybe I'll stay in kindergarten too."

"Let's get out of here. Let's go to the Little Woods."

•

Outside of school they circled around the block, as they always did when they headed toward the Little Woods, to avoid attracting attention and to cover their tracks, in case somebody was spying on them or following them.

When they got to The Place, two old people with dogs were standing there chatting while the dogs sniffed each other's tails. They waited impatiently behind a car across the street, while the people blabbered on and on.

When they finally left, they threw their bookbags over the fence and climbed down the wall. A few paths, rough from disuse, followed the slope of the hill. Gabe and Henry called them deer trails, and that's what they might have been, a long time ago.

They ran down the hill to Bear Rock, a giant boulder about halfway down, that looked like a sleeping bear with a few smaller rocks around it, and a nook between the rocks, filled with a bed of old pine needles and dried leaves, which was fun to sit on or roll around on.

Squirrels chased each other through the white oaks and star maples and pitch pines, leaping from branch to branch. Gabe and Henry crept up to the top of Bear Rock.

Henry motioned toward a nearby horse-chestnut tree, where they'd been watching birds build a nest of twigs and grass. At first Gabe had said they were thrushes, but Henry pointed out their long beaks and yellow eyes, and said they were brown thrashers. When it came to birds and bugs, Henry was usually right.

One of the birds was sitting on the nest. An almost identical thrasher, brown with a speckled breast, hopped onto a nearby branch. The first spread her wings and moved off the nest. Gabe glimpsed four new small spotted eggs. The other bird replaced her on the nest, and she flew away.

Then Gabe remembered what Henry said that morning on the sidewalk before school.

"Is this what you meant this morning? When you said you found something amazing down here? The eggs?"

"This isn't it. It's something else. You're not going to say a word about it to nobody else, right?"

"Just tell me what it is."

"This is no joke. This is serious. This is just between me and you," Henry said. "Our secret. Do you swear until the day you die?"

"I swear."

"Until the day you die."

"Until the day I die. Now show me. What is it?"

"Follow me."

Henry jumped up and scampered away along a trail.

They ran down to where the land leveled off near the highway, but not so close that the drivers could see them. The trees here thinned out into the meadow, with tall weeds and flowers. The backsides of the high brick buildings extended out over the slope of the hill, in some places on concrete stilts twenty feet high. Their front entrances faced the street at the top of the hill.

They snuck along carefully from tree to tree and rock to rock, so they wouldn't be spotted by a driver or by someone looking out a window. They really didn't have to worry much, because they were mostly concealed from the cars by the high weeds, and people in the apartments above almost always looked out at the river and the bridge and the sunset, and almost never down at where they were.

They crouched behind a big rock. They were in a more open space, where there were just scattered trees, between the last regular apartment building and the back side of Monarch Towers. The hill became very steep here, almost a cliff with a retaining wall. Gabe had never come this far down, and had never seen Monarch Towers from the back side.

Henry pointed with his chin to the back of the building. "The secret entrance. Do you see it?" He was whispering, although no one else was there to overhear him.

Gabe saw the big metal door on the side of the building, but there was nothing secret about it.

Henry glanced around. "Come on. Stay close to the wall." He sprinted. Gabe followed.

Their backs against the corner of the building, Henry said, "Now walk real slow. Don't startle the bees. They're guarding the secret entrance."

Henry hunkered beside an old log lying on the ground. Through a crack at one end, a steady line of bees entered and exited. Henry put his hand up, a bee climbed onto his finger and walked up his palm. He turned his hand over, the bee maneuvered between his fingers back up to the top side. Henry held his hand out. Gabe placed his own hand on top of Henry's. The bee climbed onto Gabe's finger, up his arm, and flew away.

Then Gabe saw the secret entrance. At the base of the metal door, the earth had eroded away, the cement was cracked, and a chunk of concrete had slipped down the hill, leaving an opening underneath the metal door frame, an opening just big enough for a kid.

They knelt together in front of it. It looked dark and scary, with cobwebs in the corners.

Henry crawled in. Gabe watched him disappear under the building's foundations. Then Henry stuck his head back out. "C'mon."

Gabe held his breath, closed his eyes, and crawled gingerly inside.

It was a large open space under the back part of building, like a cave. The dirt floor was flat at the bottom, then sloped steeply up in back to the big cement slab ceiling twenty feet above their heads. The lower walls were concrete, with rough surfaces and metal bars sticking out in some places. Six concrete pillars were spaced across the central area, like giant legs holding up the back side of the building. A ways up, the outside walls became red brick, like the rest of the building. Light came in through several series of open slits high up in the brick, that must have been put there for ventilation. A sparrow perched in one of the high ventilation slits, eyeing them.

A shadow moved. Gabe jumped. "What if there are bats in here?" he blurted. "Or rats?"

"Bats would be hanging from the ceiling sleeping right now, and we'd see rat poop all around."

"What's that then?" Gabe pointed.

"That's squirrel poop, not rat poop. I know rat poop." He lived in a cellar apartment.

Henry fiddled with the latch mechanism on the big metal door, a handle connected to long steel rods fitting into holes in the top and bottom of the steel frame. Nothing moved when he tried to turn the knob, wedged and corroded in place from long disuse.

Henry picked up a long rusty spike that was lying on the ground, and shoved it into the latch mechanism. "Now it's jammed with our special secret lock. Now nobody else can get in, even if they got a key. Nobody can get in here except us."

"Nobody except us," Gabe echoed. He felt in awe and a little scared.

"We can do anything we want in here. And nobody can tell us nothing."

"Nobody can tell us nothing."

"Now we got a hideout."

•

Around the neighborhood they found good junk that people put out on the curb, old folding chairs, a rug, a broken ladder, a shovel without a handle, boards, wooden fruit crates, some blankets and bed sheets. They dragged it all down to the hideout. They had to dig out the inside of the secret entrance a little, to get some of the things to fit inside. They rolled the rug out over the flat part of the dirt floor.

They snuck lots of good stuff out of the storage rooms in Henry's basement, where Pimple Simon kept things that people tossed. On the way to the hideout, they avoided passing in front of certain buildings, because the neighborhood supers were suspicious and got drunk together and acted stupid, that's what Henry said, and they all knew Pimple Simon.

In the toy store on 181st Street, they picked up handfuls of crayons and chalk, but they didn't have money, so the clerk made them leave it all on the counter, even though Henry told him they would pay when they got money. But the next day Henry came into the hideout with handfuls of crayons and chalk anyway, and they decorated the walls with drawings.

Pimple Simon kept careful track of his paint, and had all the cans labeled, so they went to the paint store on Broadway, and the man gave them two big cans from their back room that had been mixed the wrong color. Henry found brushes in Pimple Simon's stash, and they painted the walls, splashed some, started painting each other, and got into a fight about it. Henry was on top and held Gabe's wrists, but then they were rolling around in the dirt, first one on top, then the other. Gabe grabbed Henry's collar, pulled his shirt up over his head, and tickled him in the ribs.

"Stop it," Henry yelled, but Gabe didn't pay any attention.

They ran around in circles, up and down the slope, arms open like they were flying, with old towels tied around their necks for capes, then leaped, tucking in their shoulders, landing, spinning and laughing in the dirt. They rolled around tickling each other, they couldn't stop laughing, and just lay there gasping for breath.

They set up a bug zoo. They had plenty of jars of all sizes, holes poked into the metal lids so the bugs could breathe. Gabe and Henry went out on safari and collected skeezixes, with long crazy legs, and glazering greens, leaf hoppers, and even walking sticks. Some of these were not the names in the bug books they had, but the names Gabe

40

and Henry gave them. They knew the book names for skeezixes and glazering greens, but they liked these names better. Caterpillars too, and they kept fresh leaves in the jars for them to eat. They kept some of their bug books down in the hideout, and looked them up and read about them. They turned over rocks in the Little Woods and found grubs and earthworms and centipedes and click beetles you flip over on their backs, and with a snap they hurl themselves into the air and usually land on their feet, and when they don't, you give them a little nudge. They caught a bunch of bugs whose names they didn't know, and weren't even in the bug books, maybe they were bugs that nobody had ever seen before. They would gaze at them in the bug jars, and think about what it would be like to be a bug. They never kept a bug in the zoo for more than a few days, then they let them all go, and started catching new ones.

Sparrows were regular visitors to the hideout, and squirrels and chipmunks. Occasionally a pigeon would peek through the slits in the brick, but pigeons were too fat to fit through.

They set the ladder up against the wall by the open slits in the brick overlooking the highway and the river, and took turns being lookout, watching for trouble coming from the road or from boats or a helicopter or a plane or a blimp that flew by. When the sun was low in the sky over the Palisades cliffs, they sighted through the slits towards the river, and flashed sunlight rays off mirrors to the passing boats. Grampa Benjo had taught Gabe the trick. You stick up two fingers like a V to aim through, flash the sun off your little mirror, and shoot a sunbeam a long ways, to warn about danger or signal for help or flash it in a bad guy's eyes and blind him while you get away. They carried the little mirrors around with them in their pockets, and signaled each other when they were in different parts of the Little Woods.

Up on the higher rungs of the ladder, peering through the slits, it almost felt to Gabe like he was in a medieval castle and those were the slits they shot arrows through at bad guys in armor who were attacking them. Through the slits you could see the highway almost all the way down to the apartment building where he lived, tucked up right alongside the bridge. Lines of cars and trucks streamed under the span toward them. Gabe flashed a sunbeam at the windshield of an oncoming car on the highway. The car swerved, almost hit a truck, then straightened out and continued past. Gabe felt shaken, frightened by his own power.

•

# CHAPTER THREE

The sun crept toward the horizon across the river, the crickets started chirping, the fireflies flashing. Gabe and Henry reluctantly left the hideout and started back through the Little Woods.

Henry stopped short. "Snake."

Gabe jumped. "Where?"

Henry pointed toward where some tree roots disappeared into the ground like giant fingers. "He just crawled down that hole."

Gabe peered cautiously. "What did he look like?"

"He's just a little guy. He's striped. Probably a garter, a baby garter. I didn't get a good look at him."

"They got garters out in Maroon too."

"Let's wait here and watch a while, see if Uncle Wiggly comes back out."

Gabe followed Henry to some bushes a ways away, where they hid and watched for a long time.

"Out in Maroon," Gabe said, "sometimes the country kids bring along a snake stick in the woods."

"What's a snake stick?"

"It's got a little fork in one end, to pin him down."

"They got rattlers out there?"

"I never seen one. Just garters and brown snakes. The kids don't bother them. They're kind of like pets. They hang around the barns and eat mice."

A flock of tiny black-capped chickadees fluttered and tittered back and forth through the branches.

Henry said, "Those birds are really hopping. They're all worked up about something."

Finally the little snake face appeared near the tree roots, the thin greenish body about ten inches long, with light stripes, narrowing at the tail. The snake stayed close enough to duck into his hole at the first sign of danger.

"He's a little garter, all right," Henry whispered. "He's looking for food."

"What do you think he eats?"

"Mostly bugs. He's too little to swallow a mouse."

Out of nowhere a flurry of brown and red feathers. A large red-tailed hawk swooped down, sunk its talons around the snake, grasping the snake's head in its curved beak, shook him, spread its wings, lifted up into the sky, holding the writing snake, but just as it did, chickadees surrounded the hawk, darting and pecking. The hawk dropped the snake and flew off, the chickadees following him a ways.

The snake landed hard on a rock, bounced, and lay there squirming, twitching, and bleeding, a few feet from his hole.

"Why do you think the chickadees did that?" Gabe asked.

"They were probably just protecting their nests."

They watched the snake for a while, until he stopped squirming.

"Do you think he's dead?" Gabe said.

Henry poked him with a branch. "He's dead."

"We can't just leave him here. Maybe we should stick him back in his hole."

Henry said, "That's too weird. Let's bury him."

They rolled over the rock he fell on, dug out a hole in the moist earth with sticks, dropped the snake into the hole, covered him over.

They rolled the rock on top of him.

Gabe said. "Do you think we should say a prayer?"

"I don't think they usually do it for snakes," Henry replied.

They walked quietly along the trails to the granite boulder wall, and scaled the wall out of the Little Woods, back to Cabrini Boulevard.

Leaning against the chain-link fence near the schoolyard gate across the street, stood Jim Stoloff and Rory Golman from their class. With them was Jim's big brother, Preston, who was in fifth grade. Jim and Rory always acted even worse when Preston was around. Preston was sleeping a red yoyo with a spinning green star.

The school yard was always left open until six o'clock, but it was just a long stretch of concrete with a few basketball hoops without nets. After school the bigger kids took over, and some of them liked to fight, so Gabe and Henry mostly stayed away.

Jim pointed at them, and said, "There they are, Preston, those fruits we told you about, the ones they kicked back to kindergarten. We own them."

"You two," Preston yelled at them. "Hey you."

With a flick of Preston's wrist, the yoyo rushed down the string, then bounced back up. He grasped it in his fist.

"What do you want?" Henry stopped short.

"Come over here. I want to talk to you."

"About what?"

"Let's get out of here," Gabe whispered.

But Henry just stood there, so Gabe stood there with him.

Preston moseyed across the street toward them, doing a walk-the-dog with his yoyo. At the row of parked cars, by the open space beside a fire hydrant, he stopped. Behind him, Jim and Rory spread out a couple of car lengths up and down the block, then strode onto the sidewalk, cutting off escape in both directions. They were cornered.

Preston stepped from the gutter onto the sidewalk near the fire hydrant.

Gabe backed away toward the building. Henry held his ground.

Preston was a head taller than Henry, and towered over him. "What did you bad little puppies do to get yourselves kicked back into kindergarten?"

"Ask your brother." Henry replied. "He knows so much."

Jim made a fart sound. "They pooped their pants, they're always stinking up the room. They get down on all fours and smell each other's butts like the little poopy dogs they are. That's why Odelia kicked them out."

Preston bared his teeth. "Want to get back into fourth grade? Maybe somebody can fix it for you."

"How are you going to do that?" Henry queried.

Preston said, "Don't worry about that. We got ways."

"We run this school," Rory interjected.

Henry said, "We don't need your help. Nobody asked you for it."

Preston said, "You don't got to thank us. We like to help out our friends."

"Since when are you our friends? You're always giving us a hard time," Henry came back. "What do you want?"

Jim said, "Lend me a quarter. I'll give it back tomorrow."

Gabe said, "Leave us alone. We don't have any money."

Rory said, "Stop lying. You got money."

"C'mon," Jim said, "empty your pockets."

"Nobody's giving you nothing," Henry said.

"Hold up," Preston enjoined. "We don't want your money." He spun the yoyo up and down the string.

"Then what do you want?"

"We just want to be friends." Preston smiled.

"Well, I don't want to be your friend, because you're just a bully," Henry said.

Jim said, "Don't fool around with them any more, Preston. "These guys are punks. They're sock puppets. They're chickenshit. They're little poopy dogs. We own them." He crossed his arms.

"Really?" Preston said, "Little poopy dogs? Show me."

"Want to see? We can do anything we want with them. We can make them smell each other's butts. Want to see?"

"You better leave us alone," Gabe said.

From either side Jim and Rory took a slow step toward them.

"Hold up," Preston said.

Rory and Jim stopped short.

Preston said, "Don't be scared, little pups. Nobody's going to make you do anything you don't want to, not while we're around."

"Nobody's got to make them," Rory said. "They do it all the time, when they think nobody's looking."

Jim hooted with delight. "Both of you, down on all fours."

"Run, Henry," Gabe cried, and tried to duck away, but Rory grabbed his arm, twisted it behind his back, and pushed him down over the hood of a car. Gabe's shirt ripped at the shoulder.

Jim shoved Henry from behind.

Henry stumbled onto the pavement, his hummingbird cap and bookbag flying, scraping his hands on the sidewalk.

Bent over the car hood, unable to move, Gabe stopped struggling and watched helplessly.

Jim picked up Henry's cap, tossed it to Preston.

Henry pushed himself to his knees, gazed at his bleeding palms. He looked like he was going to cry.

Preston towered above him, lifted the sky blue cap high in the air.

Gabe held his breath.

"Give me my cap," Henry said in a shaky voice, still on his knees.

"Out of the goodness of our hearts, we offer to get you back into fourth grade, and you don't even appreciate it. You sure are thankless little puppies."

"Give me my cap," Henry said. "Give it to me."

"What'll you do if I don't?"

"I'll call our gang. You think it's just us two. It's not. Want me to call them? I'll call them."

Preston sniggered. "The only gang you got is a gang of poop in your pants."

Jim and Rory guffawed.

Henry climbed to his feet, raised his arms above his head, gazed at the sky. From deep in his throat rose a growl like a wild animal, growing louder and louder, until he was howling at the top of his lungs.

Kids ran toward them from down the street and from the schoolyard, and suddenly they were circled by a crowd.

Preston looked stunned.

Henry's howl trailed off. He paused. "Here's my gang. Now give me my cap."

Preston glanced warily around at the crowd.

Henry made a sudden movement.

Preston flinched, took a step backwards, tripped over the fire hydrant, stumbled off the curb and fell into the gutter. The cap went flying.

He glanced around at the circle of kids, confused and rattled.

Then he scrambled to his feet and spat out, "This isn't the end. Watch your back." He spun, burst through the crowd, stormed away down the block. As he ran, the yo-yo bounced along the sidewalk behind him, the string still attached to his finger.

Jim stood there frozen. Rory let go of Gabe's arm.

Then Jim and Rory both broke and sprinted down the sidewalk after Preston. Halfway down the block they turned and shouted that they were going to kill Henry and Gabe. All three ducked around the far corner.

A kid who got there late asked, to nobody in particular, "What happened?"

"A fourth grader just beat up a fifth grader."

"Who got beat up?"

"Preston Stoloff. He's in my class. His dad runs the PTA."

Henry picked up his cap and bookbag, and muttered to Gabe, "Let's get out of here."

As they shambled away, Gabe said, "My shirt's tore." He bit his lower lip. "My dad's going to be really mad."

"Come over my house. I'll give you one of mine. He'll never know the difference."

"Now they'll get all their friends together and really beat us up. They've got a lot of friends."

"We got friends too," Henry said.

"I never heard you yowl like that."

"I did it once before when Pimple Simon was punching me. That shut him up for a while."

They walked quietly down the block.

The front way into Henry's basement apartment, on Fort Washington Avenue, was right past the garbage cans, past the furnace room, where in winter you could feel the heat radiating through the metal door with DANGER painted on it, past the elevators, past the washing machines that were always making a racket. Henry's apartment was partly below ground. Out of his windows you could see the low shrubbery around the building. There were all kinds of places in the basement where you could go, and Henry came and went pretty much as he pleased. His family seemed to have almost given up trying to track him. When they complained that they couldn't find him, he claimed he was right there in the building all the time. There were three ways out of his apartment, the front door, the back door, and the casement window in his room. Pimple Simon had two big mongrel watch dogs that were always growling and barking and snapping, and sometimes he hit them with a leash and they whined.

They tried to duck past the kitchen to get to Henry's room.

"Come here," his gramma called.

Henry slunk into the kitchen. "Gabe is with me."

Gabe didn't see Henry's mom anywhere around.

Henry's gramma scowled at Gabe, then gave Henry one of her long-suffering looks. "Where have you been?"

50

"Nowhere."

"It's late. You're a mess. What did you do in school today?"

"Nothing."

"You'll be the death of me, and that's a fact. It's almost dinner time. Don't your friend have to go home?" She shook her head in dismay.

"He's just going to be here for a few minutes. I got to show him something for school."

"Don't you have homework? Don't lie. You don't want me telling Pappy you been lying again."

"They didn't give us any homework. They never give us homework on Wednesday. And he's not my pappy!"

"A few minutes. No more."

Pimple Simon burst into the room. "Stop pampering that kid!"

"Back off," his gramma said. "Go back to your beer and sit down."

He had a red nose and smelled funny.

"The worse he gets, the more you pamper him. That's why he is the way he is. And that daughter of yours. Where is she? She's supposed to be here taking care of her kid, but she's out God knows where, with God knows who."

"She's working."

"Ten years old and already a loser." He scowled and shook his head at Henry. "You'll never amount to nothing."

"Stop drinking that beer!" his gramma said.

"This is my house, I'll do whatever I want."

"Nobody can stand to be around you when you get like this!" she shouted.

"Nobody can stand to be around you too!" he shouted back.

Henry nudged Gabe with his elbow and whispered, "Let's get out of here."

They hurried into Henry's tiny room, in the back of the building, cluttered with stuff. He had a few tropical fish. The air smelled stale. The small casement window above his bed let in some light, and he propped it open with a book.

Henry opened his dresser drawer and slipped Gabe a shirt. It was a little short in the sleeves.

"Why did he say you're ten years old?" Gabe asked Henry. "You're still nine."

•

The next morning before school, when Gabe arrived at the usual place outside in front of the gate, he noticed that a lot of kids kept staring at him and whispering to each other. Henry wasn't there yet.

Roco emerged from the crowd. "What happened after school yesterday?" Roco walked with a slight limp, he more loped than ran, but he was still fast.

"Nothing." Gabe shrugged.

"Why'd Henry beat up Jim's big brother?"

"Nothing like that happened."

Jack and Kelly joined them.

"I heard those guys were messing with you again," Jack said.

"We were just fooling around. Nothing happened. It wasn't a big deal."

Kelly said, "You guys better watch out. Their dad is a wheel, and so is Rory's mom."

Jack said, "Did you do those divisions? Can I see?"

"Remember, I'm still in kindergarten," Gabe replied. "I don't have to do homework now."

"I forgot. Lucky dog."

Henry appeared through the crowd. A murmur went up. Everybody turned and looked at him.

Roco grabbed Henry's sleeve. "So why'd you beat up Jim's brother?"

"I didn't beat anybody up."

Jack said, "We heard you two are in a gang."

"There is no gang," Henry responded.

"Who else is in your gang?"

"Honest, we don't have a gang."

Jack smirked, "Then why is everybody talking about it?"

The second bell rang, the school doors opened. The kids pressed inside.

•

Gabe's family's apartment was right next to the bridge. It wasn't very big, and he shared his room with Grampa. Each of them had one side of it, and they put dressers in the center of the room for a divider. Through his front window, Gabe watched the sunset behind spectacular red clouds across the river toward Maroon.

A long time ago, before Gabe was born and before they built the bridge, this was a more upscale block, a choice location, because of the river view. When they started to build the bridge, it became noisy and dirty, so many of the tenants moved out. Then when the war started, everybody was scared they were going to bomb the bridge, so most of the rest moved out, and the rents became very low. It was rent controlled. That's how Grampa Benjo and Gramma

53

Fannie, despite not having much money, got to move into an apartment overlooking the river. Then when Gramma died, Mom and Dad and Gabe moved in with Benjo. Grownups were always telling Gabe how lucky he was to be living here, at the fringe of the more upscale neighborhood, and being able to go to one of the city's better public schools.

Benjo spoke with an accent, which made him sound dumb sometimes. And sometimes he did do dumb things, like sleeping with his head out the window, running into the freezing ocean at the beach in the middle of winter, just eating vegetables and never any meat, making wild black cherry wine in a big smelly jug under the sink, and arguing that the world is flat, which he mostly did just to annoy Dad. He often said things that didn't make sense, at least not at first. But Benjo really wasn't always that dumb. He understood sundials. Sometimes he took Gabe on the train to Point Lookout Beach, way out on Long Island, when almost nobody else was there. That's where Benjo always made a sundial in the sand with a stick in the middle, and they'd follow the shadow so they knew when to catch the train back home. It was still a wild beach at that time, and they'd always take long walks, collect shells, and build a driftwood fire between the dunes. Gabe was happy spending all day watching and tending the fire, listening to it snap and crackle, gazing spellbound into its heart, where some spirit seemed to inhabit the flames. The beach was fun in winter, when it was mostly just Gabe and Benjo and the water and the waves and the sand and the seagulls and the sandpipers and the sky.

Gabe must have dozed off, because it was dark. Outside, the streetlights were on. He pulled the covers over his head. Finally he decided to get up, and opened the door to the living room. He could hear his parents in the kitchen. The tension in their voices caused him to stop.

The kitchen was tiny. Squeezed into it were a stove, a sink, a few cabinets, a small table and two chairs. If more than two were eating at the same time, they had to go into the living room. The kitchen window looked out on the side of the bridge.

Mom was saying, "We can't tell him what to do."

"Why not?"

"This was his place. He took us in."

They were talking about Grampa.

Dad said, "He's got to stop being involved with those people."

"He's not going to stop. He's always been like that."

"The world's different now. He could get away with it before. He can't get away with it now. They're going after everybody."

Gabe decided he'd heard enough. He stole back to his bedroom and shut the door loudly, to make it sound like he'd just come out into the living room. His parents' conversation abruptly stopped.

Mom stuck her head out of the kitchen. "Hi, honey." She looked stressed.

They both came into the living room. Gabe didn't like the look on their faces.

"Daddy and I need to talk to you."

"About what?"

They sat on the sofa. "Come here," Dad said.

He stood in front of them.

They both seemed fidgety, like they didn't know what they wanted to say.

Finally Dad began, "I don't know how much you know about this. A lot of bad things have been happening."

Mom cut in, "Not at home. Out in the world."

"Do they talk to you about these things in school?" Dad asked.

"No."

"Well, they should. That's what school is for."

"They talk about stuff sometimes," Gabe said, to be agreeable.

"Good," Mom replied.

"What do they talk about?"

"Different things. I don't know."

"Well..." Dad fidgeted. "What we want to tell you is..." He just trailed off.

Mom said, "Don't ever repeat anything outside the house, anything you hear somebody say at home."

"That's right," Dad jumped in. "Not at school. Not anywhere outside the house. Anything you hear anybody say at home, they're just saying it to the family, and it's not anybody else's business."

Mom continued, "So never repeat anything you hear at home to anybody outside the house, at school, anywhere. Do you understand?"

"Yes."

"What do you understand?"

Gabe didn't say anything.

"Never repeat outside anything you hear at home," Mom repeated.

"I won't."

Mom leaned toward him and said, almost in a whisper, "We're not going to Maroon."

"What do you mean?"

"We're not going this summer."

"We're not going?"

"Maroon is gone. It's gone. They're taking it away from Grampa, they're taking it away from us, they're taking the land away. They're taking it all away. We probably can't go there ever again."

"Why?"

"They're giving it to somebody else. They're going to knock it all down with bulldozers and build a mall there."

"A what?"

"A shopping center."

"Why?"

"Because they can. It's hard to explain. They're doing it because they can. It's gone. Maroon is gone. That's just the way it is. That's just the way it is. We just have to accept it. Tell Henry we're not going. I know you two were so looking forward to it. I'm sorry."

At first Gabe couldn't wrap his head around it. Maroon was gone. It was like saying the sky is gone.

He slunk back to his room, confused.

Late that night Gabe woke again to the sound of muffled voices in the living room. Grampa Benjo was out there with them.

Gabe stole to the door.

Mom said, "You don't need to be involved with those people."

"Those people are putting themselves on the line."

"But you don't need to be involved. Do you want to be a dead hero? You're retired now."

"I'm not involved. They're just old friends now."

"What if they take away your retirement?"

"They can't. That McCarthy's just blowing air. If FDR was still alive, him and his goons would be still hiding in some drain pipe."

"They're coming after you. That's why they're taking the land."

"Maroon's got nothing to do this. The land is just business as usual to those blood suckers. We're going to knock their blocks off."

"It's more than just a coincidence," Mom said. "They're going after everybody. What if they go after the whole family? We could be evicted."

"They can't do that," Benjo replied curtly.

Dad, who'd been sitting quietly, burst out, "For crying out loud, don't you understand? Everybody is being blacklisted. I could lose my job,"

Mom said, "We could all wind up on the street."

"Do you eat to live or do you live to eat?" Benjo replied.

•

The next morning, as soon as Gabe met Henry in front of the school gate, the words burst from his throat. "We're not going."

Henry stopped short. "Not going where?"

"To Maroon. We're not going."

"Don't joke."

"I'm not joking. My mom just told me last night. We're not going to Maroon."

Henry looked dumbfounded. "Why?"

"It's not even there anymore, that's what she said. It's gone," Gabe replied.

"How could it not be there?"

"I don't know. That's what she said."

"She's lying to you. They just don't want us to go."

"Why would my mom lie?"

"That's what grownups do, they lie. How stupid do they think we are? What is it now, just a big hole in the ground? Like all of a sudden it's disappeared?"

"How should I know?"

"What did she say? Exactly."

"She said they're taking it away from my grandpa, they're knocking it all down with their bulldozers and giving it to somebody else."

"Why?"

"They're going to build some shopping stores there."

"Why would they do that?"

"How should I know?"

"Did you ask her?"

"Yeah."

"What did she say?"

"First she said she couldn't explain. Then she said something weird."

"What? Tell me exactly what she said."

"Something like, *They're doing it because they can.*"

"Is that everything she said?"

"She also said, *That's just the way it is.* She said it two times. *That's just the way it is.*"

"What do you think she meant by that?"

"How should I know?"

"It don't add up. It's not gone. It's still there. Even suppose they knocked down the house and the chicken coop, they can't knock down the whole forest, can they?"

"They better not."

"So let's just go see for ourselves."

"But how could we even get there? We always drive there in my uncle's car. Maybe we can ask him to drive us."

"We don't need him. You said it's not far, that's exactly what you said. We'll walk. We'll just walk across the bridge and keep on walking till we get there."

"Okay, but it's not right across the bridge, and I'm not sure if I remember the whole way. I usually fall asleep in the car, and they wake me up when we get there."

"You said your grampa showed you a map, right?"

"Yeah."

"Do you know where it is?"

"Probably in his drawer."

"Can you get it?"

"I'll ask him."

"Don't ask."

•

After a week in kindergarten, Gabe could barely stay awake, although it really didn't matter, because the teacher just ignored him. All the little kids in the class looked at him like he was an idiot. And maybe I am one, he thought. Gabe wondered what they were doing back in Miss Odelia's class. When he walked through the halls now, everybody seemed to be staring at him.

Late in the afternoon, Miss Prince told him to report to the principal's office. On the bench sat Henry.

The inner door opened. A weird metallic taste came into Gabe's mouth. Everything moved very slowly. Inside were Mom, Grampa Benjo and Henry's gramma. Mom gave Gabe a look that made him sink through the floor. Mrs Hopper sat at her desk. Miss M. Drannily stood shaking her head.

"Now we're all here," Mrs Hopper began, then cleared her throat and rolled her eyes toward Drannily.

Drannily riveted her gaze at Gabe, then at Henry, then back at Gabe again. "The last time you two boys were in this office, Mrs Hopper instructed you very clearly to have your parents contact her. Did she not?"

"Yes, Miss Drannily."

"Yet neither of you followed instructions. Why? Speak up."

"I forgot," Henry said.

Henry's gramma said, "He didn't forget." She grabbed him by the collar and shook him. "Stand up straight."

Mom said, "What about you, Gabriel? Why didn't you tell me and Dad?"

"I thought you'd be mad at me," Gabe replied.

Drannily said, "Mrs Hopper was forced to contact your families herself, because neither one of you followed instructions. Neither one of you has a proper attitude. Neither of you has learned to pay attention or to take responsibility for your actions. That is unfortunate."

Henry's gramma said, "He's been a handful from the day he was born. Makes us all a nervous wreck. We don't know what to do with him."

Gabe's mom said, "What shall we do with them, Mrs Hopper?"

Hopper coughed into her hanky. "I believe they are *thtill* correctable, and I think *Mith* Drannily can *thraighten* them out."

Drannily glared, lips pursed. "Out of consideration for your families, starting tomorrow Mrs Hopper is letting you return to Miss Odelia's class. But because of your misbehavior, you will have to work ten times as hard to catch up on all you have missed. And starting tomorrow, every day instead of going to recess and playing in the yard with the obedient children, you will report to me in my office, right next door, and there you will learn good work habits. I'll take good care of you two." She shifted her gaze to the grownups. "I assure you, when I'm through with your boys, they will have benefited from my supervision, they will have learned to behave and make their families proud. When they learn to obey in small things, they learn to obey in all things."

By the time they left the principal's office, the cleaning people were in the halls, and all the other kids were gone.

Very subdued, Gabe and Henry slouched down Cabrini Boulevard a few paces in front of Mom, Benjo, and Henry's gramma.

"I'm sorry to be seeing you under these circumstances," Mom said to Henry's gramma.

"Yes, all this is trying, to say the least."

"Now that Principal Hopper has the boys under her wing, I'm sure a problem like this will never happen again. I hope Gabriel hasn't been a bad influence on Henry."

"Lord, no. Your Gabriel's very polite, not like some of those others Henry's brought home."

"How is Henry's mom? I'm sorry, I've forgotten her name. We've seen each other so rarely."

"Gloria is just fine. Busy, overworked, two jobs."

"I'm sorry it didn't work out for us to take Henry with us to the country this summer. We've been having legal problems about the land, that's why we're not going."

"Oh? He didn't tell us about that."

"I'm sorry for the disappointment."

"To tell you the truth, I'd forgot he was going."

"We'd love to have your whole family over for dinner sometime."

"I'll tell Henry's mom. I'm sure she'll be pleased."

"Do you have a phone? We don't have one yet, but we're getting one real soon. Now we use our neighbor's, but only when we really have to."

62

"We're getting one real soon too. Henry's grandpa needs it for work. He's the super of our building, you know, and supers have got to have a phone these days."

"That's a fact," Mom said.

Henry's gramma turned to Benjo. "So you know the principal from outside of school?"

"A little. From the old days," Benjo replied. "I used to work with her husband."

"Was he a principal too?"

"Electrician. Must be ten years since he passed. She's not the same, not that any of us are. She looked under the weather. What do you think?"

"In low spirits." Henry's gramma sniffled.

"The principal did seem not well," Mom said.

Benjo bit his lower lip. "I still see some of our old friends once in a while. I'm going to check in with them about her. I hope somebody's been keeping tabs on her. And something about that vice principal—what's her name?"

"Miss Drannily," Mom said.

Benjo shook his head. "Something about her makes me wonder."

After Henry and his gramma cut off onto Pinehurst, Gabe, Mom and Benjo continued down Cabrini, turned onto 181st Street, and slogged down to Riverside Drive.

When they got home, Gabe scooted right to his room and shut the door behind him. Dad was not home yet. Gabe dreaded having to explain everything to him and watch him shake his head. He lay down on his bed, feeling sad and beat.

•

# CHAPTER FOUR

All the way to school the next morning Gabe fretted about what awaited.

As they entered the classroom, Miss Odelia looked very annoyed to see them. Some of the kids giggled. They crept around the back of the room to their old seats.

They were totally behind and a little lost. It was hard to focus on what anybody was saying.

The recess bell finally rang. While the rest of the class bustled downstairs to the yard, Henry and Gabe slunk toward Drannily's office.

In the hall Gabe muttered, "What do you think she's going to make us do?"

"I don't care what she makes us do. I know what I'm going to do."

"What?"

"Write her up. I'm going to write up Hopper too. I'm going to write them all up. Want to do it with me?"

"What do you mean?"

"They gave us those V-Pads. They told us to write everybody up. Isn't that what they told us to do? So let's do it. Now that we're stuck in the office, let's find out what's really going on, snoop them out and write them up."

"If we do that, it's going to make them awful mad. We already know they hate to get wrote up. That's why Odelia kicked us out. Remember that paper airplane? And I was just kidding."

"Well, I'm serious."

"We're just going to wind up in more trouble."

As soon as they got inside, Drannily pointed them to two small tables against opposite walls, stacked with books. "You, sit over there. You, over there."

The door was ajar between Drannily's office and Mrs Hopper's. Gabe could see the principal's desk, piled with papers, but nobody was there.

Drannily said, "No talking. Not a peep. I will be working at my desk on very important business and I don't want any interruption. Today you will begin work on a project that will require your full attention. Those books on your tables are from our school library, and every one of them has been written in. I'm sure your teachers have instructed you to never, ever write in a book. However, some pupils do not pay attention, and write in books. Your job for the rest of the school year, will be to go through every page of every book in the library, and when you find any writing or underlining, you will erase it, being very careful not to damage the page. When you run out of books on your table, take more from the cart." She indicated a rolling cart piled high with books. "And when you run out of books on the cart, refill the cart from the library. Now, in front of you are your erasers. Any questions?"

"What if it's written in pen?" Gabe asked.

She shuddered. "Make a note of it, including page number, and set the book aside."

Drannily rummaged through some papers at her desk. Gabe watched her through the corner of his eye. Atop her desk was a box with switches and wires. Drannily pulled over a microphone, blew into it with a little hissing sound, and it amplified.

So this is how they do it, Gabe thought. The office made announcements, sometimes to the whole school and sometimes to a particular class. There were speakers in all the classrooms, the halls, and even in the yard.

"Attention. All-school." Over the speaker Drannily always paused between words. "This—is—a—reminder. Tomorrow is assembly day. White shirts and middy blouses. Also, very important: third grade and up, do not fail to bring in your completed V-Pad. Tomorrow all V-Pads will be collected."

She pushed the mic away, put on headphones, listened for a while, flipping switches on the box, making funny faces, then set the headphones down. She glanced at her watch.

A small bulb flashed on the electrical box.

"Yes?"

Miss McKlosky's voice said, "Mr Blinka is here."

"Send him in."

Into the room stepped a man with a neat pencil mustache and muttonchop sideburns, in a tweed blazer with elbow patches and brown-and-white wingtip shoes. It was hard to read his expression.

"Good day, Mr Blinka."

"Good day, Miss Drannily. I see you've got company."

"These are my assistants Gabriel and Henry. This is Mr Blinka, from the Internal Protection Agency, who is directing the V-Pad program in our school. You boys have the privilege of meeting a real live P-man, like the ones I'm sure you've seen in movies and TV. You must be very excited."

"Consider yourselves Junior P-Men," he said.

"Boys, tell Mr Blinka, *Pleased to meet you, sir.*"

"Pleased to meet you, sir," they repeated.

66

Blinka said to Drannily, "Now show me the problem."

She directed him to the box with the microphone. The two of them poked around in it and spoke in low tones.

Blinka put on the earphones, then took them off. "I'll have it all tested. It'll be set right."

Drannily said, "Now boys, go to the library, pick up two empty book carts and meet Mr Blinka in front of the elevator. You will be helping him bring up some boxes from downstairs. It is a special privilege when fourth graders get an opportunity to ride in the school elevator." She kicked off one of her pointy black shoes, bent forward and rubbed her foot. Gabe could barely believe his eyes. Her toes were hooked and bent over like claws. He shuddered.

Out in the hall, on the way to the library, Gabe whispered, "You were right, she's one of them." He made a claw with his hand.

"Trilobites," Henry replied. "I told you. That Blinka guy's one too. He was at my house last week, plotting with Pimple Simon."

"Mr Blinka? He's one too? What were they plotting about?"

"The same stupid stuff. He's going around the neighborhood telling all the supers to spy on everybody and write them up."

"Did he recognize you?"

"He just looked at me a little funny. Kind of like he was looking at a dog."

"He looked at me like that too."

"Come over to my house later, and I'll show you some stuff he left." Henry pulled a few V-Pads out from his pocket. "Want some?"

"Where'd you get those?"

"From a box in the office. There's lots." He handed some to Gabe, who stuffed them in his pockets.

The school library was just down the hall. Gabe opened the door a crack and peeked in. Miss C. Drannily glanced up from her desk. No one else was in the room.

"Can I help you?" She looked a lot like her sister, but the lines were softer on her forehead, at the corners of her eyes, and around her mouth.

"We're supposed to get two book carts, Miss C." Gabe said.

She always told the kids to call her Miss C.

"Who sent you?"

"Miss Drannily sent us," Gabe replied. "We're helping Mr Blinka in the office."

"So you're the two from Miss Odelia's class working in the office now?"

"Yes, Miss C."

"I remember you from library class. I know your names. Don't tell me." She paused and took a little stubby pencil out from behind her ear. "Gabriel and Henry, right? Take those two carts over there. Empty them first. Pile the books on the table. What do you boys think about those V-Pads?"

Gabe and Henry looked at each other.

She played with the pencil. "I'm just curious. I'm always interested in what pupils are thinking."

"They're okay," Henry replied cautiously.

"I guess," Gabe said.

"What have other students been saying? What's something some other pupil said to you about the V-Pads, anything?"

"I don't know," Henry said.

Gabe added, "Nothing much."

"How about your parents? You gave them that note, didn't you? What did they say?"

"Nothing," Henry said.

"They didn't say anything," Gabe replied. Actually he had lost the note.

"Well, I hope you buckle down and make good constructive use of your time in the office. Part of growing up is learning how to take responsibility for your own actions. Don't hold yourself back. Always say what's on your mind. If you need to talk about something, about anything, you know you can always come here. I'm a good listener, they tell me. You know where the library door is. And we always have good books around."

They rolled the two carts into the hall and found Blinka waiting by the elevator. Gabe actually was a little excited, since he had never been in the school elevator or to the basement, and legends about both circulated through the school. As they slowly sunk to the basement, those words of Miss C. kept bouncing around in his head: *Don't hold yourself back. Always say what's on your mind.* That seemed the opposite of what everybody else was telling him to do. He felt confused. They rolled the carts out onto the concrete floor of the basement and peered around, fascinated.

Mr Grayley, the custodian, slouched in a chair near the furnace and coal pile, in bib overalls, leaning on a push broom. The brim of his Yankee cap was pulled down, almost covering his face.

"Grayley, wake up, it's me, Blinka."

Mr Grayley lurched forward and almost lost his balance. "Blinka. What brings you here today?"

"We've still got a wire problem upstairs. When will it be fixed?"

"Next week."

"We need it Monday. I don't want to come back here and find that same problem."

Grayley stood. "It'll be taken care of."

"How are things on this end?"

"Maybe we shouldn't be talking about this around here." Grayley tilted his chin toward the boys. "Too many flies on the wall."

"It's not your job to worry about that."

"They understand more than you think."

Blinka rubbed his mustache. "Don't insult me, Grayley. I understand exactly what they think. Every IPA agent is a highly trained psychologist."

"And I was a kid once." Grayley ambled toward the corridor. He beckoned at Blinka. "I got to show you something down the hall."

"What?"

"C'mon. It's down the hall." Mr Grayley winked at Henry and Gabe. "Wait here, boys. I just need your boss for a few minutes."

The two men disappeared down the corridor.

As soon as they were alone, Henry started exploring the room, jotting notes in his V-Pad. Gabe waited near the cart, keeping one eye on the hallway.

Footsteps coming down the hall. Henry tucked the pad into his pocket and scooted back to the cart.

Blinka and Grayley re-emerged. Gabe smelled whisky.

Blinka said, "C'mon boys, let's go get those boxes now."

He led them out into the schoolyard, where his car was parked. They loaded the boxes from his trunk while he watched. Then they rolled the book carts back inside, past Mr Grayley, who was slouched in his chair again, leaning on his broom. As they passed, Grayley raised an eyebrow, shook his head and shrugged.

Upstairs they wheeled the carts into Drannily's office.

Drannily and Blinka talked quietly some. Then she said, "Boys, Mr Blinka and I need to go into Mrs Hopper's office for several minutes. Listen carefully. I will only say this once. Do not leave your seats while I am gone. You are not to talk. Not a peep. Not one peep. Although I will be out of sight, I will be able to hear every word you say, even if you whisper, and there will be consequences, I assure you. I always keep my ear up to the wall."

The two disappeared into Hopper's adjoining office, and shut the door behind them.

As soon as they were gone, Henry caught Gabe's eye. They made funny faces, then got bored and began leafing through books. Gabe found one that was kind of interesting, erased a few things, and started reading it. Then he remembered what Drannily had said about being able to hear them talking, even though she was in the other room. Gabe wondered if she really kept her ear up to the wall.

He happened to be sitting next to the wall adjacent to the door they had gone through. On the other side of the wall was Mrs Hopper's office.

He put his ear up to the wall and, to his surprise, he could actually hear their voices in the other room. They were a little muffled, but he could make out most of what they were saying.

Drannily said, "We've been barraged with complaints from parents, but that can be contained. The problem is that Mrs Hopper still opposes extending it through the end of the year."

"That is not optional."

"And the same teachers are putting up a fuss."

"You'd think they'd be afraid to expose themselves."

"They're a brazen bunch. Never miss an opportunity to undercut the standard lesson plans, insert their own pernicious ideas."

"Do you want Hopper out sick again tomorrow?"

"Absolutely. Keep her out the rest of the week, if you can. Next week too. We need to get the program solidly in place."

"We can have the hospital call her back for more tests."

"By the way," Drannily asked, "if I may be so bold, how is the investigation progressing?"

"This is off the record of course."

"Of course."

"We've already got enough to remove her whole cadre."

"I knew it."

"You were right. Her husband was one of the worst. The unions were their cover. Still are."

"You *will* wait till summer to remove those teachers, won't you? To remove them all during the school year would be terribly disruptive. When school is out it will be just picking rotten fruit."

"I wish that was for me to decide, but it's above my pay grade."

"Tell me what to expect."

"Whenever it happens, it won't be pretty. They'll probably come in the middle of the day. Expect officers escorting them out of the building."

"Why would you disrupt the school like that?"

"The Agency has to act. Show we mean business. This is going to make headlines."

"Oh my goodness, I wasn't expecting it to be so public."

"This is a matter of national security."

"You know best, of course. I don't want to pry, but may I ask which teachers are on the list?"

"This is strictly confidential."

"My lips are sealed."

"Batra of course, Grainger, Daumer, Larrosun. There's one more. We decided to go for five."

"Talavera?"

"No, I don't think so. O' something."

"Not Odelia?"

"That's right. Odelia."

"She's one of them? Oh, that is news to me. Odelia!" she sighed. "I suppose you know best."

"One final problem I want to touch on with you, Miss Drannily. Your sister."

"What about her? Surely you haven't been monitoring my sister along with those others."

"Just tell her to watch her words, and she won't have anything to worry about."

The bell rang twice.

Blinka continued, "I think we've finished our business. I'll be back tomorrow."

The door between offices opened, and Drannily and Blinka stepped back in.

Gabe quickly opened a book and started erasing some scribble in the margin.

Drannily tucked a few loose strands into her bun. "Now I am going to do something that I hope you boys will give me no reason to regret. I am going to give you both a very responsible assignment. Every boy in Columbus School would die to get this job. I am making you the V-Pad monitors." She paused for it to sink in. "Tomorrow you boys will be collecting the V-Pads handed in from the entire school. This is a test of your maturity. Understood?" She nodded affirmatively in answer to her own question, then repeated, "Understood?"

They responded almost in unison, "Yes, Miss Drannily."

"I expect you will not disprove my judgment of your character."

As soon as Gabe and Henry left the office and were in the hall, Gabe whispered, "I could hear them, Drannily and Blinka, right through the wall."

"What did they say?"

"Really weird stuff. I couldn't understand it all."

"Write them up."

"I didn't think to do it."

"Do it now. Write up what you can remember."

"I'll try." Gabe rummaged in his pocket, pulled out a V-Pad, slid the little pencil out of its holder, but didn't know what to jot down. "What are we going to do with these V-Pads once we got them all written up? We can't just hand them in to them. Then they'll know that we know."

"We'll figure that out. Let's both write them up, then we'll compare. Tomorrow let's change seats."

"I like that seat."

"We can take turns."

•

# CHAPTER FIVE

The 3 o'clock bell rang, the kids broke toward the door. Gabe met Henry at the back of the room. Out in the hall the walls echoed with laughter and chatter, the crowd pushed in waves toward the stairs.

Gabe noticed Preston Stoloff leaning against the wall a ways down the corridor. He elbowed Henry. As they made their way to the stairwell, Gabe watched Preston from the corner of his eye.

Gabe and Henry ducked into the alcove and down the staircase with the push of kids.

At the bottom landing, Jim and Rory stepped in front of them, blocking their way out the exit door into the lobby.

Gabe glanced back over his shoulder. Preston was on the steps right behind them.

"Get out of the way! Out of the way!" voices exclaimed.

The momentum of bodies funneling down the stairs, pushed Gabe and Henry away from the exit, off to one side.

The noisy stream of kids poured past them and out, through the lobby, toward the street.

Preston, Jim, and Rory backed Henry and Gabe up under the stairwell.

Preston said, "So now you're Drannily's wusses."

"No, we're not," Henry said.

"She made you two the V-Pad monitors. We know everything that goes on in this school."

Henry said, "You want the job? You can have it. We don't even want it."

"We want you to keep it. But now you owe us big time."

"Nobody owes you."

"We got you out of kindergarten."

"Go pick on somebody else."

"We're trying to do you a favor but you're too dumb to see it," Preston said. "Want to go back to kindergarten? We can arrange that too. Wipe those stupid smirks off your faces. We rather play nice, but we got kids from Broadway who'll rub your noses in the dirt, any time we give the word. You're working for us now."

"No, we're not."

"Yes, you are."

"What do you want from us?" Gabe said.

"We need you to do something in the office."

"What?"

"Meet us after school in the yard."

"No."

Just then a deep voice rang down from the landing above. "What are you boys doing there?" Mr Daumer, an upper grade teacher, poked his head out over the stairwell.

"Nothing," Preston answered.

"Get going. Time to go home."

Preston flashed a look to kill. "Be there in the yard, or we're coming to collect."

Preston nodded at Jim and Rory, and the three slunk off, out the doorway, leaving Gabe and Henry standing there, silent, shaken.

76

They were the last kids to leave school. As they stepped outside, they both glanced warily about.

Henry said under his breath, "So, what are we going to do?"

"I'm not meeting them in the yard, that's for sure," Gabe said. "Do you think they really got those kids from Broadway, or he was just talking?"

"He was probably just talking, but who knows?"

"What do you think he wants us to do in the office?"

"I don't even want to find out. I'm not going to do his dirty work," Henry said.

"Me neither."

"Maybe we should just get out of here now."

"What do you mean?"

"At this rate we're not going to make it till summer. Let's just get out of here now."

"You mean, go to Maroon? Now?"

"We got no reason not to. Why wait till summer?"

Gabe said, "I got to think about that."

Henry said, "Sometimes you think too much."

"I just don't want to do something stupid."

"What are our options here?. You want to get stomped by the Stoloff gang? My bear howl's not going to work again."

"That was a bear howl?"

"Yeah."

"Bears don't howl like that."

"Then how do they howl?"

"They don't howl at all."

"Anyway, it's not going to work again, and we can't fight them. How can we fight them?"

Gabe said, "Maybe we can get some kids to help us."

"Like who?"

Gabe said, "I don't know."

Henry said, "How about Roco? And what about Jack?"

"Are you serious?"

"Yeah, I'm serious. So when those jerks mess with us again, we'll have some kids watching our backs."

Gabe said, "Why would Roco and Jack help us like that?"

"Because then we'd watch their backs too. We wouldn't really have to fight, just scare them away."

They were both silent for a moment.

Finally Gabe said, "Okay, Roco and Jack."

Henry said, "What about Kelly?"

"Kelly's not going to scare anybody."

"He always hangs with Roco and Jack."

"Sometimes he's annoying," Gabe said.

Henry shrugged. "Everybody's annoying."

"Am I annoying?"

"Sometimes."

"How am I annoying?"

"You're annoying right now."

"You're annoying now too," Gabe said. "And what about the hideout? We can't bring them down to the hideout."

Henry said, "Why not?"

"If we do, it'll be the end of everything. The whole school's going to find out. Remember when we said we wouldn't tell anybody else, nobody in the whole world?"

The next day in the far corner of the lunchroom, which doubled as the gym, Gabe and Henry huddled around one of the long folding tables with Roco, Kelly, and Jack. They spoke in low tones, drowned out by the din around them.

The lunch matron, in her funny white hat, pushed her cart up and down the aisles, handing out box lunches to kids who didn't have anything. The cardboard boxes always contained a cheese or peanut butter or bologna sandwich on white bread, a hard-boiled egg, a small red apple and a half pint carton of milk.

"We don't go messing with anybody, you know that," Henry said. "We're not a gang. We don't like to fight. We're more like a club. A team. It don't matter what you call us."

Jack said, "Everybody says you're a gang."

"Where do you hang now?" Roco asked, "We never see you guys hanging around Bennett Playground any more."

"Some place where there's no jerks bothering everybody," Henry replied.

"Where's that?"

"A good place. A really cool place. Nobody knows except members."

Kelly opened his school lunch box and wrinkled his nose at what he saw inside. "What do you do there?"

Gabe said, "We just fool around and have fun."

Jack took a bite out of his apple, and rolled the rest under the table and across the floor. "Are there, like, rules?"

Roco blew into his straw. The paper cover flew across the room. "I hate rules," he muttered.

Henry replied, "There's only one rule: we stick together, we watch each others' backs."

"That's right," Gabe said. "And the other rule is, Nobody can make nobody do nothing they don't want to do."

"That's two rules," Kelly said.

"One rule or two rules, it don't matter," Henry said, "because that's what clubs do, and gangs and teams do too, they stick together, they watch each others' backs, and that's why nobody can make them do nothing they don't want to do, no matter what. That's why nobody messes with them. That's what it means to be in."

"What if somebody wanted to join?" Roco said.

"First they got to pass the installation."

"What's that?" Jack said.

"That's what clubs and gangs and teams do with new members. They call it the installation."

"Okay, let's do it," Roco said. "Let's do it right now."

"We can't do it here," Henry replied. "We can only do it in a special secret place. If you want in, meet up with us after school."

"Where?"

"By the benches just inside Fort Tryon Park."

After school let out, the five gathered by the benches.

"Everybody still wants in, right?" Henry looked at them one by one. "If you don't, leave now."

They exchanged glances.

Henry led them into the bushes near the chain link fence.

He said, "Everybody down in a circle."

When they were settled in, he took a pine branch and touched them on the head one by one. "Swear by all the trees in the woods. Swear you will never ever tell nobody else about this. Swear by your mother. Not a word. Say it. Say, I swear by my mother. I swear by all the trees in the woods."

The three boys repeated, "I swear by my mother. I swear by all the trees in the woods."

Henry unhooked a safety pin that was holding his shirt together at a missing button, and held it up. Gabe watched his face as he slowly stuck the point into his fingertip. He looked so strangely calm. A drop of blood oozed out. Henry handed the pin to Gabe, who shut his eyes and plunged. He felt nauseous as it penetrated his skin, and grimaced. He passed it to Kelly, who repeated the ritual, then handed it to Roco, who did the same, and passed it to Jack.

Henry extended his bleeding thumb into the center of the circle. Gabe pressed his against Henry's. Roco and Kelly and Jack held out their bloody thumbs and all five pressed and smeared their blood together.

"Now we're all in this together," Henry said. "Forever."

Henry rose, led them under the chain link fence, along the deer trails through the Little Woods, to Bear Rock, then took off down the hill. They followed in a line, slipped past the bees, crawled through the secret door, and stood inside.

Henry said, "This is our hideout."

They gazed around. Gabe couldn't tell whether they were spellbound or shocked. "What do you think?"

Roco threw up his hands. "This is amazing."

"Wild!" Jack shouted.

Kelly gasped. "This is the greatest place in the world."

•

Every day after school, they brought more stuff to the hideout and made themselves at home. With five of them in the group now, the shortcut down the wall was too risky, so they only used the long roundabout way through Fort Tryon Park under the fence.

Until now Gabe mainly knew the three just from school and the street, but now he was getting to know them better.

Roco and Jack were pals most of the time, always joking around, but also kind of rivals, bickering about stupid stuff, always taking each other down a notch. Kelly was their favorite audience, and also their foil. Henry mainly just ignored their banter.

They tied a rope around a steel rod sticking out from one of the concrete beams going across the ceiling, and swung around and around. They made bows and arrows out of sticks and twine and had shooting contests. Jack brought down a little red bike but wouldn't tell where he got it from. They dug out ramps and mounds, made a bike park, with hills and curves and jumps, and had jumping contests. Kelly had never ridden a bike and kept falling over, but he kept trying, until he could coast down the hill a ways before he crashed. They set up a two-by-four board between two mounds of dirt for tightrope walking, and rode the bike across it. Roco was best at it, despite his limpy leg. They played dodge ball, giant steps, blindman's bluff, tag, red rover, handball against one of the foundation walls. They played stickball down at the far end, although Gabe and Henry and Kelly weren't much good at it. The others didn't have the slightest interest in the bug zoo or in bugs, and that was fine with Gabe. It was his and Henry's special project.

Everybody complained about their families, and competed with stories about how weird their families were, but Gabe also understood that they were partly just talking.

Roco was hot one minute, cold the next, always busting out with whatever came into his head, even when it was just the opposite of what he said a minute before. He always thought everything was his own idea. Roco's step uncle always gave his allowance to his aunt, and she always kept it and charged him for everything, so there was never any allowance money left to give him. Another aunt threw him against a wall or something when he was little, that's why he

82

had his limp. Some guy with skull tattoos, who was always hanging out at his house, took him to somebody's backyard somewhere, and let him drink beer that smelled like pee, and their dogs got into a fight and bit each other's ears off. Then his mom called the cops on his real pop, and they put him in jail, and Roco only saw him one time since then, and his real pop got a scar on his face in jail that went right across his lip and his eyebrow. Roco always wanted to have peeing and thumb wrestling contests, because he had fast thumbs and could really pee a long ways. Jack was the only one who would ever take him up on it. He also had fast thumbs, and could pee a long ways too.

Sometimes Jack sulked in a corner by himself and bit his nails. He made stuff up, and insisted it was true even when everybody knew it wasn't. He hated to lose at anything, even tic-tac-toe. He was always breaking things. He had a baseball signed by Johnny Mize, but his dad got mad about something and threw it at the TV and it broke and he blamed Jack's mom for it, and he kicked Jack and it hurt for a long time, and everybody was mad at everybody at his house. His uncle used to live with them, and had a truck, but somebody stole it, but it was really Jack's uncle who stole his own truck, and tried to get money for it, then he rolled it over on the highway and after that for a long time he couldn't poop. Jack would spend hours drawing airplanes, but he keep erasing until the paper tore, then he'd tear it up and throw it across the room. But he never stayed mad long, and he could be fun when he wasn't moody.

Kelly was kind of a softy, though he tried to hide it. He'd usually agree with whatever Roco or Jack said. He was always expecting the worst to happen. He seemed more himself when he was just with Gabe one-on-one. Kelly liked to talk about spooky things. He would wait for the right minute, then recite "The Hearse Song" in an eerie sing-song voice. The performance never failed to draw laughs, at least from Roco and Jack. He also sang funny songs like "The

Woody Woodpecker Song" and "Aba Daba Honeymoon". To Gabe's surprise, Kelly had a really nice singing voice; he wished he could sing like that. Kelly's sister always locked herself in the bathroom and barfed and they kept a lock on the refrigerator, so Kelly couldn't just eat when he was hungry. In spite of that, he was kind of chubby, so he must have got food from somewhere. His dad and stepmom called each other bad names, and once his stepdad choked his real mom and she fell down, and sometimes she lived someplace else. Some man who stayed with them a lot, who wasn't Kelly's dad, hit him with his belt for nothing, even though he didn't do anything.

# CHAPTER SIX

Saturday finally arrived. Gabe planned to meet Henry early, as they usually did on Saturday mornings, to feed the strays. But he overslept, and then Mom insisted he eat breakfast, and it took forever.

He rushed over to the alley near the garbage cans, where they usually met, but Henry wasn't there. He wound his way up Pinehurst Avenue past the candy store.

He just felt lazy. That's all it was. As he approached The Place, Gabe just didn't feel like walking the whole roundabout route through Fort Tryon Park and crawling under the fence to get into the Little Woods. He thought, It's just me. Why not take the shortcut, jump the fence and climb down the wall? Nobody'll see me.

He threw his bookbag over the wall, and was just about to jump over and climb down, when he heard a voice.

Almost hidden between parked cars across the street, were two girls. His heart stopped.

It was Elkie and Ari, from his class. They were sitting on the curb with their arms around each other. They often hung out together. Although both Ari's and Elkie's desks were not far from his, Gabe had hardly spoken with either of them.

Ari said, "Why'd you throw your bookbag over the wall?"

"Mind your own business."

"We saw you throw your bookbag over the wall. And we saw Henry do the same thing, and we saw him climb down there."

"He climbed over the wall? You saw him?"

"Why are you going down there? You know we're not supposed to go there. What are you doing down there?"

"Have you been following us?"

"We haven't been following you. We've just been just sitting here."

"Is that where you meet with your gang?" Ari smirked.

"We don't have a gang."

"Everybody knows Henry's got a gang and you're in it."

"Why don't you go home?"

"We can't."

"Why not?"

"We just can't," Ari said.

"So you just sit on the curb?"

"We used to go to Bennett Park playground, but now those boys charge you to play there."

Ari said, "Elkie, let's go climb over the wall and see where Henry went."

"Okay," she replied.

The girls stood.

Gabe folded his arms. "Wait a minute, you can't do that."

"Why not?"

"Because I said so."

"Nobody needs your permission."

"Why do you want to go down there?"

"To meet up with Henry and your gang. Take us with you."

The seriousness of the situation hit him. Gabe considered his options, then finally said, "You better not tell anybody about this."

"We won't."

"You better not."

Ari was smaller, kind of wiry, and squinted through her glasses. The teacher called her Arisu. Elkie's cheeks were kind of olive tan. Her wavy hair was always falling in her face and she was always pushing it back.

When the three arrived at Bear Rock, Henry was the only other one there. He was startled to see them.

"Sorry," Gabe muttered quickly.

Henry pulled him to one side and whispered, "Why'd you bring them here?"

"It was really dumb, I didn't feel like walking all the way around, so I threw my bookbag over the wall, and they saw me. But before that they saw you climbing down too. They were right up there watching you."

"They saw me?" His face fell.

"We were both being dumb and lazy."

Henry said, "Now the guys are going to kill us."

"We got to shut them up, or they're going to tell the whole school."

"This really sucks."

They returned to Bear Rock, where the girls were waiting.

Henry scrunched his face. "You've never been down here till now, right?"

"We didn't even know that you could get down the wall," Elkie replied. Her eyes were brownish-green. Gabe tried not to stare.

Henry said, "Swear that you'll never tell nobody that we come down here or how to get down the wall. Do you swear?"

"I swear."

"So do I," Ari said. She looked a little like somebody from some faraway place, with straight dark hair, defined lips, and almost black eyes that shined. She spoke like a regular neighborhood person, but there was something about her that wasn't like the other girls in his class. Gabe couldn't quite put his finger on it.

"Who else is in your gang?" Elkie asked. "Any other kids from our class?"

Ari added, "Are there any girls?"

"Only members know that," Gabe replied. "It's a secret."

"We know how to keep secrets," Ari responded.

"Do you?" Henry said.

"Try us and see."

"Where's the rest of your gang?" Elkie asked. "Or is it just you two?"

"Don't worry about it," Henry replied.

They sat cross-legged in the nook of dry maple leaves and pine needles that had a special scent that Gabe never noticed anywhere else.

"What does your gang do?" Elkie asked in a low voice.

"Anything we want to do," Henry said.

"You just hang out here?"

Gabe said, "Yeah, mostly we just hang out here in the Little Woods."

"What do you do if it rains?"

Henry said, "If you're scared of a little rain, you shouldn't be in a gang. Go hide under a tree."

"We're tougher than you think," Ari said. Her glasses, held together at one hinge with a paper clip, slipped down her nose.

"Want to see a bird nest?" Gabe asked.

Elkie said, "Where?"

"You can see right down into it from the top of the rock."

They climbed up Bear Rock and watched the brown thrashers feeding their nestlings.

Ari laughed. "Let us join your gang."

"It's not that easy."

"Why not?"

"It's not just up to us."

They climbed back down to the nook and sat on a fallen locust log.

Ari said, "I bet it's just the two of you. If it's just the two of you, you're not even a gang."

"No it's not just the two of us. When somebody wants to join we have an assembly."

"An assembly? Like in school? Do we have to wear middy blouses and white shirts and ties?"

"That's not funny," Henry replied. "This kind of assembly's when the whole gang gets together and decides important stuff, like who's in and who's not."

"And if you take somebody in, then what?"

"Then you got to pass the installation."

"What's that?"

"You got to take it to find out."

"I bet it's something you read in a comic book." Ari said.

Gabe lifted a stone. The millipedes, worms, beetles, and other small creatures living under it froze at the sudden light.

Then the worms started squirming, and the ones with legs scurried away.

Henry said, "Here come the chipmunks." They always came hopping out of their burrows if you didn't scare them away. Henry pulled out a sunflower seed. A chipmunk cautiously took it, leaned back on its haunches, held it in its tiny fingers, opened the shell with its long front teeth, and munched down the seed.

Gabe picked a long brown bug off of a weed.

"What's that? Elkie said.

"It's a walking stick."

"He's strange looking," Ari said.

It kept wiggling its legs.

"There's more of them around here."

Elkie said, "He doesn't like you holding him like that. Let him go."

The bug strolled down Gabe's arm, jumped off and disappeared into the weeds.

They followed the trails through the pines, to the grassy slope. They laid on their sides and rolled all the way down to the meadow in the flatlands. At the bottom, they staggered and teetered about, wobbly and dizzy from rolling, near the tall, stately elm with branches sprouting clusters of tiny pink flowers.

Among the meadow wildflowers, the air was balmy. In the distance, light glistened off the river currents. The highway was near, but the tall weeds hid them from the drivers. They stretched out in the bed of clover. Ari picked a dandelion and watched a ladybug crawling around on the golden petals. She blew on it and the little red spotted beetle spread its wings and flew away.

Elkie said, "This is a special place."

Ari said, "And it's always been right here in front of us. All we had to do is climb over the wall."

An orange and black butterfly fluttered past.

Henry said, "That's a painted lady."

It flew to a nearby stand of Queen Anne's lace, settled on a cluster of tiny white flowers atop a green stem.

Ari tiptoed over, and Henry followed. They gazed from a few inches away as the butterfly slowly flexed its wings.

"Those spots look just like eyes," she said.

Elkie and Gabe sat cross-legged in the purple clover. She placed a blade of grass between her thumbs, held it taut and blew through it. It whistled with a raspberry sound.

She laughed. "My mom taught me how to do that when I was little." She was wearing white socks with rolled down tops. "Before they took her to the hospital." She had a few faint freckles. She picked a clover, brought it to her nose, then slid it behind her ear.

"You and Ari live together now?" Gabe asked.

"Just till my mom is better. I'm just staying with Ari till she's better."

"How come you said before that you can't go home? Why were you were sitting there in the street?"

"Ari's auntie works and we can't go to the house until she's back."

"Don't you have the key?"

"We just can't go there when her auntie's not there. I can't explain. Her cousins are weird. I wish we could just stay here like this forever, and I didn't ever have to go back."

Sunlight flashed in Gabe's eyes. He looked up toward Bear Rock, where the mirror signal was coming from.

"That's them," Gabe said. "That's the gang." The others were up there, and had seen them. He pulled a little mirror out of his pocket and flashed them back.

Henry said, "Wait here." He took off running in a crouch, and disappeared into the tall weeds toward the hill.

"Who's up there?" Elkie asked.

"Do we know them?" Ari said. "Anybody from our class?"

"You'll see." Gabe shook his head. "They're not going to be glad to see you."

Gabe and the girls waited for what felt like a long time.

Finally the sunbeam signal came again, and Gabe led them up the trail to Bear Rock.

"This is the rest of the gang," Henry said.

Roco, Jack, and Kelly were fuming.

"Hi," Ari and Elkie uttered cautiously.

The three boys grunted in reply.

Roco shook his head. "This is not cool."

Jack said, "This is the dumbest thing anybody's ever done."

Kelly pushed his glasses up. "They're going to ruin everything. Girls are mean."

"Okay, it was dumb," Henry said.

"We can't let them in," Roco said. "They're going to drive us crazy,"

"You're already crazy, Roco," Ari said.

Henry said, "Think about it like this: with them in, we can have some fun in that stupid class. We can run rings around Odelia."

Roco stuck out his chin. "Not with those two. They're always trying to be teacher's pet."

"We're not," Elkie responded.

"Why do you say that? Because we do our homework sometimes?" Ari said.

Jack said, "Will you do ours?"

"Do your own homework," Ari rejoined.

Jack said, "That's what we do in this gang, we help each other out. Do you want to be in or not?"

Elkie said, "We want to be in. We'll help you out if you need it, but nobody has to do your homework."

There was a long silence.

Finally Gabe said, "Let's just do it and see what happens."

Henry said, "We got to take them in now."

Gabe said, "We got no choice."

Henry looked around. "Everybody agree?"

Nobody said anything.

"Ready?" Henry continued. "Then we're going to do the installation. Everybody down."

They settled cross-legged in a circle, Henry lifted a pine branch with long needles and small green cones. "Say what I say." He shook it at each of the girls in turn and said, "By the sun and the moon and the stars, by all the trees and animals in the Little Woods."

Ari and Elkie repeated, "By the sun and the moon and the stars, by all the trees and animals in the Little Woods."

"By my mother."

"By my mother."

"I will never reveal these secrets until the day I die."

"I will never reveal these secrets until the day I die."

Henry unhooked his safety pin, pushed it slowly into his thumb, until it dripped blood, then passed the pin to Jack, who in turn drew blood, then handed it to Roco, who handed it to Kelly, who handed it to Gabe. Gabe braced himself, pressed the point into his skin and watched the red liquid appear. He passed it to Elkie, and as he did their eyes met.

She took the pin and, without changing expression, embedded it into her fingertip. Blood spread over her skin. She passed it to Ari, who raised the pin toward the sky, moving her lips a little like she was praying or something, then brought it firmly into the flesh of her fingertip, the skin quickly turning crimson.

They all touched thumbs, smearing their blood together.

Henry stood and nodded. They followed him along the deer paths, down and around, until they reached the back of Monarch Towers, by the bee log and the metal door.

They crawled one by one through the secret entrance, through the hole beneath the metal door frame, into the hideout.

The girls stood silently, gazing around.

Nobody said anything Their expressions were hard to read. Gabe was going to say something, but didn't.

Finally Henry said, "Well, what do you think?"

Ari hesitated, then said, "It has possibilities."

"What do you mean by that?

"It's a mess. Don't you ever take out your garbage?"

"It's not so dirty," Henry muttered.

"Where are the brooms?" Elkie asked.

"We don't have any brooms," Gabe replied. "Why do we need brooms?"

"To sweep up the mess."

Gabe said, "It's just going to get dirty again."

Roco and Jack and Kelly walked away, shaking their heads, and began fooling around at the other end of the room.

Gabe said quickly, "Let's just have fun today. We can clean it up some other time. Want to play a game? We got all kinds of games. What do you feel like playing? We can sit on the rug. It's pretty clean. We've been fixing this place up. We started to paint that wall. Look." He motioned toward the concrete foundation.

"If we're going to play in here," Ari said, "we've got to make it neat first. I don't feel comfortable playing in this mess."

"I don't either. Somebody has to go out and get some brooms," Elkie insisted.

"And dustpans," Ari added.

"What's wrong with you girls?" Henry exclaimed. "This is a hideout! Nobody ever heard of anybody having to be neat in a hideout."

"We don't agree," Elkie said.

"If you don't like it," Henry said, "go clean it up."

"We like it," Ari said, "Don't we, Elkie?"

"Of course we like it," Elkie agreed.

"But don't expect us to clean it up for you," Ari went on. "Nobody's going to be your maid."

"That's a really dumb thing to say," Henry replied.

She folded her arms. "It's not dumb."

"Yes, it is."

"Maybe you're not as smart as you think, Henry."

"And maybe you're not as smart as you think either, Ari."

Gabe glanced around. The girls are right, he thought, it's really a mess. The only part that looked good was the bug zoo. They'd just left everything else scattered around.

Gabe noticed the cookie jar sitting there, and unscrewed the top. "Want one?"

"What are they?"

"Oatmeal-raisin. They're pretty good."

"What's in all those other jars?"

"That's our bug zoo."

"That's where you keep the food? With your bugs? It doesn't have bugs on it, does it?"

"I don't think so."

"What else do you have to eat?"

"This is all we've got."

"We need more food down here," Ari said. "Get some more jars for food."

"We've got lots of jars."

"Not bug jars."

"These are clean."

"Get some new ones."

Gabe kicked at some bird poop on the rug, and tossed a few things into piles. It started to look better.

Elkie said, "It's too dark in here."

Ari glanced around. "Where are the lights? Why don't you turn on the lights?"

"It's not dark," Gabe replied.

"How can you say that? It's all dreary and shadowy everywhere. Creepy things live in shadows. Don't you even have lights?"

"Why do we need lights?" Henry jumped in. "We're never here at night. And even if we had them, we got nowhere to plug them in."

Ari said, "What's that over there on the wall? Right over there by the door."

"Where?"

"Those wires coming down from the ceiling."

Sure enough, a metal cable was coming down from the ceiling, which Gabe had never noticed. Right by the upper hinge of the door, was an electrical outlet box with two sockets.

"Let's plug in a light, and see if it works," Ari continued. "Somebody go get one."

Henry said, "I'll get one tomorrow."

"We need it today. We've got to start getting this place cleaned up so we can play in here. Somebody's got to go out and get some lights today."

"And some brooms," Elkie added.

Ari went on, "And we need more rugs in here."

"Okay, I'll go," Henry replied reluctantly.

"I'll go with you," Gabe said.

"But first we got to feed the praying mantis," Henry said. "She didn't eat yet today. This is important."

They all followed Henry over to the bug zoo.

Henry lifted a big jar. Inside, with some leaves and twigs, was a green praying mantis, with claws and crazy eyes. It looked like something from another planet.

"He's ugly," Ari said.

"He's a she," Henry said.

"That's not a girl."

"Yes it is."

"How can you tell?"

"You just can tell."

"Why do you keep that big praying mantis in that little jar?" Elkie asked. "She needs more room."

"That's the biggest jar we got."

"Why do you keep her in a jar at all? She's going to die."

"We're just keeping her for a few days. To look at."

Gabe snatched a hopper from the hopper jar and handed it to Henry, who dropped it in with the mantis.

"She eats grasshoppers? You're feeding her grasshoppers?" Ari exclaimed. "That's cruel. Let them all go."

"That's what mantises eat."

"What makes you think you can decide which grasshopper lives and which one dies?"

Henry said, "She'd be eating hoppers out there in the Little Woods anyway. What's the difference?"

"There's a difference."

"No there isn't."

"Yes there is."

"What's the difference?"

Ari replied, "I know there is one, but I don't know how to explain it."

Elkie said, "If Henry wants to feed his grasshoppers to his praying mantis, he should do it, but he shouldn't do it in here in the hideout."

"Why not?"

"It's too weird."

Henry banged his forehead with his palm. "It's not weird. It's nature."

"Can't you keep that part of nature out there in the Little Woods?"

Henry said, "Okay, I'll take the mantis outside. I'll let her go. But you're not going to touch the rest of the bug zoo."

Gabe walked Henry to the secret entrance.

Gabe said, "Let's run over to Simon's storage room and get that stuff."

"I'll go. You stay here and keep an eye on things."

"You can't carry it all yourself. They'll be okay."

Henry said in a loud voice, "Me and Gabe are going to go get some stuff, so keep it cool, okay?"

"I've got to pee," Elkie said. "Where's the bathroom?"

"Go in the Little Woods."

"I'm not going to do that."

"Well, you can't just pee in here."

"I'll go with you," Ari said. "How do you wash your hands?"

Henry replied, "There's a faucet that works on the back side of one of the buildings. Come with us. We'll show you where."

"Can you drink from it?"

"Yeah, it's good water. Bring a couple of jars."

"I'm not going to drink out of a bug jar."

Henry said, "Not the bug jars. We got some water jars."

"I'll get them," Gabe said.

Gabe and Henry dropped the girls off at the faucet, hurried over to Henry's basement, snuck into Pimple Simon's storage rooms, gathered up what they could find and carry, and came back with a bunch of stuff, including a light bulb in a socket on top of a short metal rod on a round black base.

"You just got one light."

"If it works, we'll get more," Henry said.

Ari asked, "Where's the shade?"

"I can't just wave a magic wand and poof there's a shade."

They gathered around the outlet. Gabe pushed the prongs into the socket. Everyone gasped and laughed when the bulb came on.

"We got a radio too," Gabe said, holding it up. "We don't know if it works."

The radio worked, but as soon as they plugged it in, Roco and Jack started arguing about what station to put on.

The cleanup crew finally got to work. They worked and worked. After what felt like hours, it looked a lot better. Gabe felt a sense of accomplishment. He felt very proud.

•

# CHAPTER SEVEN

Every day when they got together new and exciting things happened. But it was complicated. Gabe couldn't help but notice who hung out and played together more, who got along better. It kept changing.

Roco brought down a bongo drum, then Jack showed up with a kazoo, Kelly had a couple of old tin penny whistles. Ari brought down a beat up ukulele, a small pink xylophone, and some party horn blowers and noisemakers. Gabe brought over his harmonica. Henry scrounged up a tambourine and a little toy piano. None of them really knew how to play, but that didn't stop them. Someone just started playing, and they all joined in. Nobody was playing the same melody or keeping the same time, but it didn't matter.

Almost from the minute they turned the radio on, the radio wars began. The worst was over ballgames. Roco was an avid Giants fan, Jack a Yankee fanatic. Both could reel off baseball statistics, although neither was much at arithmetic. The neighborhood was mostly split between the two teams. Kelly couldn't make up his mind. Gabe didn't really care, and was kind of bored with baseball, although his dad was a Brooklyn Dodgers fan and took him to games once in a while. Henry had no interest in sports. Ari said baseball was stupid, although she liked to play stickball and was pretty good at it. Elkie didn't follow baseball, but wore a Dodgers cap sometimes, which her uncle gave her. No boy could ever have gotten away with walking around the neighborhood in a Dodgers cap, but Elkie did.

Jack turned the Yankee game on loud, then started fooling around down at the other end of the hideout.

Roco turned it down so you could hardly hear it.

"Turn it back up," Jack yelled from the other end of the hideout.

"Nobody wants to listen to this junk except you," Roco proclaimed.

Jack stomped over and turned it back up. "This is an important game!"

"At least turn it down," Ari said.

"It's not that loud."

"It hurts my ears."

"You never tell Roco to turn it down when he's got some stupid Giants game on," Jack protested.

Roco jumped back in, "You always just want everything your way."

"So do you."

"Who made you the boss?"

"I'm just sticking up for myself," Jack said. "If I don't, I get stepped on."

"Poor baby," Roco mocked.

Elkie said. "Put on some nice music."

"The ballgame's not over!" Jack roared.

"You don't have to yell about it," she replied.

"I'm not yelling."

"You were."

"Well, everybody yells."

"No, they don't."

"In my house, they do."

102

"This isn't your house. And what if somebody out there hears you?"

"Nobody's ever out there." Jack waved his hands. "Why are you all always picking on me?"

"Nobody's picking on you," Elkie said.

Gabe said, "Let's all just take turns."

Ari interjected, "You guys always just want to listen to ballgames, ballgames, ballgames."

"That's right," Jack replied.

"Cut it out," Henry said.

"It's not fair."

"Yes, it is."

Ari said, "I don't even want to hear another ballgame the whole rest of my life."

"Let's all just take turns," Gabe repeated.

Roco sprang on it. "Right, let's take turns. You've had your turn, Jack. Now it's somebody else's turn."

"It's only the eighth inning. It's still my turn."

Roco said, "No, it's my turn."

"No," Ari said, "It's Elkie's turn and my turn next. Let's put on some quiet music."

"No way," Jack said.

"How come I never get a turn?" Kelly protested.

Jack said, "Then get another radio. Let's each get one. We'll each have our own radio and then we can all listen to whatever we want."

"Right," Ari rejoined, "all blaring at the same time."

Elkie said, "Let's just turn it off altogether and have some quiet time."

"What is this, nursery school?" Jack sniggered.

"Why do you guys have to always be so noisy?" Elkie went on. "Let's have some time when everybody is just quiet together."

"Yes!" Ari exclaimed.

"That's the most boring thing in the world," Roco said.

Elkie replied, "No it isn't. It's nice."

"I hate it when it's quiet."

"Let's try it and see."

"You try it." Roco said. "I'm not going to."

"It's not quiet unless everybody's quiet," Ari said. "Everybody has to be quiet at the same time."

"The rule of the gang is that nobody can make nobody do nothing they don't want to, right Henry?" Roco folded his arms. "So if you don't like it, too bad."

"Wait a minute," Henry replied. "That's not exactly right."

"What's not right about it?"

"The too bad part. I don't know about that."

"Let's vote on it," Jack said. "Everybody who agrees with me, raise your hand."

"Wait," Gabe protested. "What are we voting for?"

"I'm not voting," Ari said. "It's not fair."

"Why?"

"Because there are more boys than girls, so it's not fair, because then the boys always win."

"That's fair," Roco said.

"You just don't care about fair."

"Yes we do," Jack said.

"Then we need more girls in here," Ari said. "If there are five boys in the gang, there's got to be five girls too, and then it'll be fair."

"No way," Roco replied.

"Then if we're the only girls and the boys get five votes, then we get five votes too."

"No, you don't. There's only two of you. That's not fair."

"You guys just want to keep the hideout like it's Boys House. But it's not all just Boys House now," Ari said in a firm voice.

Elkie said, "Ari, if they don't want to be fair, let's make a little place just for ourselves, where we can get away and be quiet all by ourselves any time we want."

"And boys can't come in."

"Right, unless we invite them."

"Maybe we don't even want to," Kelly said.

Roco jumped back in, "You can't do that. This isn't just yours. This is everybody's hideout. You can't just take a place and say it's yours, and tell us we can't go there. You can't tell anybody where we can go and where we can't go in the hideout."

"Oh yes we can," Elkie replied. "We need to feel safe here."

"You don't feel safe?"

Ari said, "You must think we're really stupid. We know what boys are like. We know how to take care of ourselves. This isn't all just Boys House now. Maybe if you're nice and quiet, we'll invite you in."

"And you have to leave when we tell you," Elkie added.

At the far end of the open space, alongside one of the pillars, the girls set up two chairs, draped a bed sheet across and over, put a blanket on the floor, brought over some games and books, drew a hopscotch design in the dirt outside, and hung up a sign that read Girls House.

The girls disappeared inside.

One game that the hideout was not very good for was hide-and-seek, because there were few places to hide, except behind the concrete pillars or under a chair or the rug or something. They played it anyway.

Kelly was it and found everybody except Jack. He looked everywhere, then gave up and yelled, "Olly olly in free, come on out, Jack."

Jack came running down the dirt hill in back. "You got to see this," he said.

They all clambered up the steep slope that formed the back wall. At the top where the concrete ceiling met the hill, was a low open space full of cobwebs and spiders, where nobody ever went because it was too creepy and dirty. Jack crawled through a gap in the cobwebs, and Roco, Henry, Gabe, and Ari followed. Elkie and Kelly stayed outside.

Tucked into the top far end behind the dirt and shadows, so you could barely notice it, was a boxlike thing made of metal.

Jack pushed on a little bend in the sheet metal. A panel slid to one side, with a scraping sound.

"I was in there," Jack said.

Everybody peered in. You could see inside the box because some faint light was filtering into it from somewhere.

Gabe followed the others inside. Some of the light was coming in through a metal grate above their heads, and more from another grate at the outside wall. Henry pushed up on the top grate. It moved a little. Dust fell down into Gabe's face and got in his eyes.

Henry rubbed some dust between two fingers. "This is coal. That's their furnace room up there," he whispered. "This is an air duct for their coal pile."

"A duct?"

"To keep the coal aired out." Henry knew a lot about basements. "For the fumes."

"Do you think somebody's up there? What if they heard us?"

"Nobody goes in furnace rooms in this weather," Henry whispered. "Not usually. They won't be in there hardly at all till next fall, and then those boilers make a lot of noise. We don't got to worry too much about that. Let's get out of here."

They climbed out, blinking and shaking the coal dust off their faces.

Henry slid the creaking metal door shut. "But we can't take stupid chances. Pimple Simon's got a bunch of insulation. We can stuff it in all around the box. That will take care of it. But we still got to stay away from here anyway. We shouldn't be making a lot of noise up here. It's too risky. We got to make this place off limits. We got to be smart."

Roco said, "What do you mean, we can't make noise? Are you crazy? That's bunk."

Henry said, "Make all the racket you want down there, just not up here."

Jack said, "You're always making a big racket, Roco."

"Not half as much as you."

•

Kelly brought a huge pile of comic books to the hideout. Most of them were things like Porky Pig, but a bunch were Tales From The Crypt and other horror comics.

"Why do you guys read those scary comics?" Ari asked.

107

"I just like them." Kelly replied.

"All they do is kill people."

"You can learn a lot of stuff from them."

"Like what?"

"Like here." Kelly displayed a page. "When ghouls are shooting poison gas at you, and you don't got a mask, you can get your shirt wet in the river and that makes it into a gas mask."

"Nobody's shooting poison gas at us."

"But what if?"

When they got tired of reading comics, Roco and Jack set up one of the ladders over by the metal door, climbed up and started tossing stones through the slits, as Kelly watched.

"What are you guys doing?" Gabe asked.

"Shooting guided missiles," Jack explained.

"At what?"

Roco tossed a rock through the slit. "Those bees."

"Don't do that. They're our friends," Gabe said. He glanced around, looking for support, but Henry, Ari, and Elkie were all down at the other end of the hideout.

Roco threw another stone. "It's a science experiment."

Jack said, "We're just playing with their heads a little."

Gabe said, "I don't think they're going to like it."

"They like it."

Suddenly Jack jumped off the ladder. "Here they come!"

Roco leaped off. "Run!"

The ladder came crashing down, everyone scrambled, tripping and stumbling, to the far end.

Bees poured through the slits, circled and looped around the room.

The group huddled together by the far wall, shuddering and ducking when bees swooped down and buzzed them.

"If they land on you, don't swat them!" Henry said.

After a long while, the bees thinned out.

They cautiously crept back. Roco and Jack set the ladder up again, climbed up and peeked through the slits.

"They're cool," Roco said. " I told you, they like it."

Ari said, "Don't ever do that again."

Jack said, "What are you, our mommy?"

Kelly said, "That was fun."

"We were lucky this time," Henry said. "They were just giving us a warning. They were being nice."

•

It rained hard all night. Enormous claps of thunder jolted Gabe awake. The walls of his bedroom shook in the dark. Out the window, zigzag lightning struck the cliffs beyond the river, brilliant flashes silhouetting the bridge and illuminating the clouds.

It was still pouring the next morning. Gabe splashed through puddles on the way to school. His shoes and socks were soaked. By mid-day the rain had stopped, and through the classroom windows Gabe could see luminous sunbeams breaking through the clouds.

At the end of the day, when they got to the Little Woods, all the bushes were still dripping. Every time a leaf shook, droplets splattered. Mud, pine needles, and dead leaves caked on their shoes as they slogged along the deer trails.

"Just look at those guys." Ari pointed to the sky.

A large flock of birds soared overhead in formation, headed toward the river, the bridge, the Palisades.

Migrating birds were crossing the sky almost every day, now that it was spring.

"I wonder what they are?" Elkie said.

Henry said, "They're not geese, that's for sure, or ducks."

Gabe said, "Maybe some kind of gull."

"Gulls don't fly like that," Henry said. "I never seen birds that fly like that around here before."

They disappeared into the clouds over the Palisades.

Ari said, "I wonder where they're going."

They quietly watched the clouds a while, then continued on along the trail.

Through the branches Gabe's eye caught on a white object down in the meadow.

"Look at that down there, on the ground near the elm tree. Is that an animal?"

Roco said, "Let's take a look-see."

They descended stealthily. The hill was slippery, with rainwater still draining off. The meadow was soggy with puddles. Once they got to the flatlands, they could no longer see through the tall weeds.

They crept cautiously towards the elm, stopped short at the edge of the small clearing. A large bird sat on the ground, salt-white, with yellow patches around its eyes, a long pinkish sack beak.

"He's huge. It's a pelican," Henry said in a low voice. "I never seen anything like him around here."

Gabe whispered, "I seen pelicans on Long Island, where my grampa takes me sometimes, but not like this one. Those other pelicans are a lot smaller and kind of brown and they look really different."

Kelly said, "What do you think he's doing here?"

Although the river was close, few water birds came into the Little Woods.

"Maybe he saw all the puddles and thought it's a lake," Ari said.

"I seen this kind of pelican in a book," Henry said. "They live a long ways away. He probably just got tired of migrating and he's taking a break."

"Or maybe he's lost," Elkie said.

"The rest of his pelican friends are probably waiting for him somewhere. He'll catch up."

"What if he got lost from his friends? He looks so sad. Maybe he's hurt. What if he broke his leg? What if he broke his wing? We can't just leave him here, some animal's going to eat him. Let's bring him to the hideout."

"For what?"

"To fix him."

"We can't fix a pelican," Henry said. "Just leave him alone."

The bird waddled clumsily forward on its webbed feet, spread its enormous wings, exposing a long row of ebony along the outer edges of its snowy flight feathers, then started flapping, raising leaves and dust. The force of the breeze almost pushed Gabe back.

The pelican lifted off the ground, settled briefly on a branch near the treetop, then rose into the air, circled above the highest leaves, tucked its head back into its shoulders, surged high into the sky, and soared toward the river, alternating gliding and flapping, then disappeared into the clouds over the Palisades.

•

Gabe wasn't very competitive in games. Although he liked to play, he got bored quickly, and didn't really care if he won. Jack and Roco, in contrast, hated losing.

If Jack was losing, he would often quit suddenly and walk away, either that or start cheating. He didn't even hide it. He seemed to think cheating was just part of the game. Everybody usually just ignored it. He usually just smiled when he was caught.

Roco cheated sometimes too, but that didn't stop him from calling out Jack about it, not that it ever did much good.

Gabe, Roco, Kelly, and Jack were playing Go Fish.

Roco said, "Jack, stop peeking at Kelly's hand."

"What are you, a cop?" he answered with a sly smile.

"You're always peeping."

"No more than anybody else. No more than you." Jack replied.

"You're a peeper and a cheater."

"Everybody peeks."

"I don't," Kelly mumbled.

Jack said, "If you don't want somebody to see your cards, Kelly, hold them up and stop showing them to everybody."

"You don't have to look." Kelly replied.

"Anybody would look."

"I wouldn't."

"That's why you lose," Jack said, sticking out the tip of his tongue.

"I don't always lose," Kelly said.

Roco said, "Remember that time in second grade you got kicked off Howdy Doody?"

"What about it?" Kelly perked up. He liked to tell the story; it had given him notoriety.

"What really happened? What's the real story?"

"I told you lots of times."

Elkie said, "I never heard it from you. How'd you get on Howdy Doody?"

"My uncle knew somebody."

Roco said, "Some kid peed on you, right?"

Kelly said, "Okay, here's what happened. So my uncle knew somebody, so they got me into the Peanut Gallery, and I told everybody to watch, and there were all these TV cameras and kids, and Clarabelle was nice and let me honk his horn, and then just before they were going to start, this kid next to me peed all over me, and that jerk Buffalo Bob kicked me out. He was a real jerk. That why nobody saw me on TV, but I was really there."

"You know what I think, Kelly?" Jack said.

"No, what do you think?"

"I bet you got scared of being on TV, and you peed yourself."

"That's a lie!" Kelly exclaimed.

Roco jumped in, "Stop getting in Kelly's face, Jack."

Jack fixed his gaze on Kelly. "Am I getting in your face?"

"I don't care," Kelly muttered.

"See?"

"That's not Kelly talking," Roco snapped back, "That's the worm."

"What worm?"

"The one you stuck in his head."

"Did I stick a worm in your head, Kelly?"

"No," he said. "Yes."

Jack said, "Kelly, do that worm song again."

113

"Do you really want to hear it?"

"C'mon, let's hear it."

"Okay." Kelly leaned forward, tried to make a scary face, and recited in a sing-song voice:

"The worms crawl in, the worms crawl out
They eat your guts and spit them out,
They eat your eyes they eat your nose,
They eat the jelly between your toes,
They spread it on a slice of bread,
And that's what you eat when you are dead.
So, do not laugh when the hearse goes by,
'Cause you may be the next to die."

Everybody laughed, although they'd heard it many times.

Roco said, "Why do you like creepy things so much, Kelly?"

"I don't know. I just do."

Gabe said, "Who's turn is it?"

Roco continued, to no one in particular, "Do you ever wonder what it's really like to be dead?"

"Yeah," Jack replied. "Do you?"

"No, I never think about it much," Roco said.

"I don't even care if I die," Kelly said.

"Why not?" Roco said.

"I don't know. I just don't."

"You're weird."

"It's my turn," Jack said. "Kelly, do you have eights?"

Kelly made a face, and handed him three eights. Jack placed the book of four in his pile, then said, "Kelly, do you have sixes?"

Kelly handed him two sixes.

Jack said, "Okay. Gabe, do you have fours?"

Gabe said, "Go fish."

Jack picked a card. "Got it." He displayed the four of clubs. "Roco, do you have queens?"

Roco threw two queens at him. "You're just a cheater."

"You're just a sore loser."

Roco threw the rest of his cards on the ground. "Let's settle this thing, once and for all."

"How are we going to do that?" Jack replied.

"Pissing contest. For the Olympic world championship. Winner take all."

Jack said, "Nobody wants to watch you piss, Roco."

"Cold feet?"

"You just drank a soda."

"Drink ten sodas. It don't matter. I can beat you any time, any place."

"Oh yeah?"

"Oh yeah. I beat you last time."

"In your dreams. You did not."

"How about a rematch?" Roco said.

Jack said, "Kelly, you're judge."

"You coming?" Kelly asked Gabe.

"Not this time."

The three of them scrambled out the secret entrance.

Henry yelled after them, "Don't pee on the bee log again."

•

Elkie and Ari brought a pile of dress-up clothes to Girls House, and the two acted out make-believe stories, some

115

from movies and books and fairytales, others they just made up as they went along. They performed sometimes just for each other, sometimes with the boys as their audience. Little by little they got the boys to join in. The stories usually included some songs and dances. Ari was usually the narrator or the director, because she was good at it. The dress-up clothes were mostly girls' stuff, and the girls usually had the best parts. Gabe and Roco and Kelly got involved sometimes and played roles in the stories. Jack mocked them about it, and was rarely willing to play. Henry usually wouldn't play either, and when anybody asked him why, he said, "I don't like make-believe."

Then Henry started moping. Everybody could see it. Everybody asked him what's the matter, and he just said, "Nothing."

Finally it dawned on Gabe, and he said, "Next week's your birthday."

"No, it isn't," Henry snapped.

"Yes it is. I remember."

Ari overheard and said, "You're going to be ten next week?"

"I don't have birthdays."

"What do you mean?"

"Birthdays are stupid."

"Why do you say that?"

"I don't know. Just leave me alone."

Then Gabe remembered something. "You got kind of weird around your birthday last year too."

"Well, birthdays are weird."

"They don't have to be," Ari said.

"Well, they are for me."

"Why?"

"I don't know why. They just are."

"How was it weird last year?" Gabe asked.

"Stop ganging up on me," Henry said.

"Nobody's ganging up on you," Ari said.

"You really want to know?" Henry said.

"Yeah."

"Okay. It was stupid. My gramma and Pimple Simon decided we were all going to go to a restaurant on Broadway. Them, my mom and me. For my birthday. They never go out to restaurants. It's a big thing to them. They never go anywhere. They wanted to go out to a restaurant for my birthday, and then they got into a big fight about what restaurant to go to. Not my mom. My grandma and Pimple Simon."

"So what happened?"

"They just finally got tired of fighting and decided on a restaurant. Then I refused to go. That made them really mad. That's it."

"Why did you refuse to go?" Ari asked.

"Because they never even asked me. It was my birthday and they never even asked me what I wanted."

"Was your mom there?" Elkie asked.

"Yeah."

"What did she say?"

"Nothing. She never says anything. Okay? Now you know. That's why I don't have birthdays. It's stupid."

Ari said, "It's not stupid."

Later, Ari and Elkie emerged from Girls House in full dress-up clothes and blowing party horns.

Elkie said, "Announcing a special birthday play."

Roco said, "Nobody wants to watch you two play Cinderella and Cleopatra again."

"We will perform..." Ari said.

"Dum da dum!" Elkie exclaimed.

They held up a sign.

"The Animals Picnic," they proclaimed together.

Elkie said, "It's like the Teddy Bears Picnic, only different."

Henry said, "I told you, I don't want a birthday."

"This isn't just for you, Henry," Ari replied. "This is for everybody's birthday. It'll be fun. Everybody's going to get a part. We made costumes for everybody."

"Leave me out," Henry said.

"If you don't want to be in it, you don't have to."

"I want to be the bad guy," Roco said.

"I want to be the bad guy too," Jack said. "Or else I'm not playing."

"You can both be the bad guy," Elkie replied. "Roco, you can be the Sheriff, and Jack, you can be the Wicked Witch."

"No way," Jack said.

Roco said, "You'll be perfect."

Jack said, "I'll be Long John Silver."

Kelly said, "I'll be Jesse James."

Ari said, "They aren't even in the story. First listen to the story, and then we'll decide who's who."

Jack said, "Why aren't they in the story?

"They're just not."

"So put them in," Kelly responded. "You're just making it all up."

"Okay, they're there. They join the Merry Men. You can be Jesse James, Kelly."

"Does he fight with the Sheriff and Long John Silver?"

"Yes."

Kelly smiled. "Good."

Ari said, "Who wants to be Robin Hood?"

"I'll be Robin Hood," Roco said.

"You're already the Sheriff. You can't be both."

"Why not?"

"They have a sword fight. You can't have a sword fight with yourself."

Henry said, "I hate sword fights."

Ari said, "They're just cardboard swords. You should be Robin Hood, Henry."

Henry said, "No, you should be Robin Hood, Ari."

Roco said, "If she's Robin Hood, I'm not playing."

Ari said, "I'm already Cleopatra."

Elkie said, "Now we've got too many parts."

Ari said, "If you don't want to be Robin Hood, Henry, you can be Merlin. Gabe, you can be Aladdin. Elkie is Cinderella. There's still the Good Witch and the Wicked Witch."

"We're going to have to double up. I'll be Cinderella and the Good Witch," Elkie said.

"That makes you the Wicked Witch, Ari," Jack said.

"Why? Because I'm a girl? You make a better Wicked Witch than I do, Jack."

"No way."

"I'll be the Wicked Witch," Roco said. "I'll take both parts. I'll be Long John Silver and the Wicked Witch."

After much discussion Ari agreed to be Robin Hood and Henry agreed to be Merlin.

They all put on their costumes. Roco looked amazing dressed as the Wicked Witch.

Ari went on to tell a wandering plot that didn't make much sense, although nobody expected it to. As far as Gabe could make out, Cinderella and Cleopatra are sisters, and the Wicked Witch puts a spell on the Good Witch and takes her captive, and tries to kill the girls, but they escape into the forest, where they are taken in by Robin Hood and the Merry Men, who are living under some tree roots, hiding from the sheriff, who is trying to kill all the forest animals, who are helping the girls. Robin Hood gets into a stick fight with Long John Silver on a log over a river and falls into the water, but Merlin, Jesse James, and Aladdin rescue him. They go in disguise to a bow-and-arrow shooting contest, where Robin Hood wins the golden arrow and gives it to Cinderella and Cleopatra, which makes the sheriff mad, so Robin Hood and the sheriff fight with swords, the Wicked Witch sends her flying monkeys to grab them all, but Merlin casts a spell and turns the Merry Men into forest animals, they jump onto the backs of giant birds and escape to the Little Woods, where they have a picnic and Cinderella and Cleopatra sing:

> If you go down to the Little Woods
> You'll get a big surprise
> If you go down to the Little Woods
> You'd better go in disguise!
> Beneath the trees where nobody sees
> We'll hide and seek as long as we please
> 'Cause that's the way the
> Animals have our picnic.

The others joined into a circle dance, singing:

> Beneath the trees where nobody sees
> We'll hide and seek as long as we please
> 'Cause that's the way the
> Animals have our picnic.

They danced around and around, laughing and singing the verses over and over again, until they all collapsed on the ground.

After they recovered, they lit the ten candles on cookies, everybody blew them out and sang Happy Birthday to everybody else.

When they were full and relaxing on the rug, Elkie said to Gabe, "Why do you always just move your lips and not ever really sing?"

"I was singing."

"No, you weren't."

Gabe stuck his tongue into his lower lip. "Well, if you know so much, why are you asking me?"

"You don't have to get mad."

"I'm not mad."

"What?"

"Nothing."

"What?"

Gabe said, "I'm just not good at it. I do something wrong. I don't know how. That's what Miss Owens told me in second grade, just to move my lips because I mess up the other kids when I sing."

"She told you that?"

"Yeah."

Elkie said, "Anybody can sing."

"I can't."

"Yeah, you can. Sing something."

"I can't."

"Sing, *Pop Goes the Weasel.*"

"I can't."

"How about, *Sing a Song of Six Pence?*"

"You really want me to sing it?"

"Yeah."

"Okay." He began, "*SING a song of six PENCE...*"

121

Elkie burst out laughing.

"See," he said. "I told you I can't sing."

"I'm not laughing. You have a nice voice."

"Then what's so funny?"

"You go loud and soft when you're supposed to go up and down."

"What do you mean?"

"Listen to the notes: *SING a song of six PENCE...*"

Suddenly Gabe heard it. How could he have missed it? That's what he was doing wrong all this time, he wasn't listening to the notes go up and down. Mom always said she couldn't carry a tune, and neither could Grampa, and they had taught it to him wrong. It seemed impossible, he had always heard melodies of course, but not really. He had always listened to the volume but never really heard the notes before, in all his life, and it amazed him.

Very tentatively, he tried, "*SING a song of six PENCE,*" and heard himself singing for the first time.

Later, finally, as dusk seeped in, they left the hideout and started reluctantly back along the trails.

Halfway to the Fort Tryon Park entrance, Jack said, "I forgot something. I got to go back and get it."

"What did you forget?" Gabe asked.

"Just some stupid thing," he replied.

"Do you want us to wait for you?"

"No, you go on ahead. Don't worry about me." Jack turned and ambled back toward the hideout.

Gabe and the others continued down the deer trail.

But twilight was quickly setting in, and Gabe started to think, maybe they shouldn't leave him alone like that.

"I'm going to go back and help Jack."

"Okay," Roco said.

Henry said, "Catch you in the morning at the gate."

Gabe galloped back down the trail, past Bear Rock, through the tall weeds, past the bee log, under the metal door into the hideout. The light was on, but shadows and twilight enveloped the room. It felt a little spooky. He didn't see Jack anywhere, and shakily called out his name.

No answer.

He heard a rustling noise. "Jack? Is that you?" he called out.

Girls House shook and Jack poked his head out of the old bed sheets that formed the walls and roof.

"What are you doing in there?" Gabe asked.

"Just looking around for something. Why'd you come back?"

"Just to make sure you're okay."

"I'm fine."

"C'mon, let's go."

"You go. Don't wait for me."

"What are you doing in there?"

"Nothing, I told you, I'm just looking around."

Out of curiosity Gabe lifted the sheet.

Jack, dressed as the Wicked Witch, said, "I just wanted to see what it felt like. Please don't tell, OK? Please."

Gabe said, "Jack, I won't tell. I don't care."

"Really?"

"Really."

•

# CHAPTER EIGHT

Gabe noticed Henry and Ari hanging out together in the bug zoo for a long time. He found himself watching them. He couldn't help himself. He had noticed them spending time together in the bug zoo before. Henry kept showing her the jars of bugs and leaves, and she kept looking at them with him. They went on and on. Gabe knew Henry better than anybody else in the world, but now suddenly he wondered whether he really knew him at all. The bug zoo had been Gabe's and Henry's special project until now. Watching them together made Gabe sad, he didn't entirely understand why. He told himself he was just being dumb.

Gabe shuffled over to Girls House.

"Elkie, are you in there?"

"What do you want?"

He didn't actually know what he wanted, but remembered she said she was staying with Ari because her mom was sick. "How's your mom?"

"You can come in."

Gabe crawled inside. It felt very cozy, but uncomfortable. There were books and silver jacks and girl stuff lying around.

"Why did you ask me about my mom?"

"I just wondered."

Elkie said, "I wish I could see her. They never let me. I miss her."

"Who won't let you?" Gabe asked.

"None of them. Ari's auntie took me to visit her in the hospital once but that was a long time ago. You got to wear a mask."

"Why won't they let you visit her?"

"I think because once I went and I didn't want to go back to the foster lady, so I held onto my mom's bed and kept yelling. I was littler then."

"You really did that?"

"Do you think I'm lying?"

"No."

"Do you like riddles?" Elkie asked.

"Sure. Everybody likes riddles."

"What goes up and down but doesn't move?"

"I heard that one. It's a staircase. What doesn't get any wetter no matter how much it rains?"

"What?"

"The river"

Elkie said, "That's a good one. What can you break without touching it?

"I don't know."

"A promise."

Gabe picked up the little red ball and fiddled with a few of the metal jacks. "How do you like living with Ari's aunt?"

"She's usually nice, but she mostly just cares about Ari's uncle and her cousins. She just doesn't know what to do. She just keeps pretending. She doesn't even protect us."

"From what?"

"They pester us."

Gabe thought a moment, then asked, "When were you living with that foster lady?"

"First when my mom got sick, that's when they made me live with her. She couldn't even remember my name, and I had to go to this school where everybody was really mean. Finally they let me stay with Ari. Now they won't let me see my mom. She's going to die in this hospital and I'll never see her again."

"How can you just say that? Doesn't it make you cry?"

"I already cried so much, I don't feel like crying any more. One of these days I'm just going to go visit her by myself, I don't need them to take me. I just want to see her and tell her don't worry, I love you. And as soon as she dies, the foster lady's going to come for me. But I'm not going to go with her."

"What will you do?"

"Can I trust you?"

"You can trust me, Elkie."

"Do you lie?"

"Just once in a while."

"I hate liars."

"So you never lie?"

"Only to people who lie to me. Do you lie to me?"

"No."

"Then if you don't lie to me, I won't lie to you either, Gabe. When they come to get me, I'm going to escape. Ari's going to help me. She's going to come with me. We've got it planned."

"Both of you are going to escape together?"

"Ari's not going to stay there alone without me. When her auntie's not there, her weird uncle and her stupid cousins do anything they want. They're both in high school, and they just copy everything her weird uncle does, he's their hero."

126

"What do they do?"

"They're always bothering us."

"Like, they hurt you?" Gabe asked.

"They don't hurt us, they just bother us. I can't explain."

"Do you tell Ari's aunt on them?"

"She doesn't do anything. If they ever try to touch us again, we're going to run away."

That took Gabe's breath away. "What hospital is your mom in?"

"That one down there on the other side of the bridge."

"I know where that is."

"Want to go there with me?"

"Okay."

"Don't say that if you don't mean it."

"I mean it. If you want to go, I'll go with you."

"When?"

"Whenever you want."

Elkie said to Gabe, "Let's go now."

Outside, they ran through the tall weeds, along the deer trails, ducked under the fence out of the Little Woods into Fort Tryon Park, around the winding paths, between the beds of bright flowers.

At the park entrance, an old woman in a long purple dress was feeding bread crumbs and peanuts to squirrels and pigeons, while other old people watched or talked or read newspapers. A man in a white hat was selling pops from an ice box on a bicycle.

A bus appeared, headed for the traffic circle. A few people stood and moved toward the bus stop.

"Come on," Elkie said.

Several people stepped out of the back door of the bus. Before the doors swung shut, Elkie and Gabe slipped in, up the stairs, and found a seat all the way in back. The bus started down Fort Washington Avenue, past row upon row of apartments.

As they passed the church yard, Elkie said, "Did you ever see Mother Cabrini in there?"

"Who?"

"She's right in there, in a glass box, in the church. Mother Cabrini. She died a long time ago. She's a real person. She was a nun. She's like stuffed or something."

"You mean, like a mummy?"

Elkie nodded. "Except her face is sticking out. She looks like a doll. She's kind of eerie. She looks just like she's alive, only she's dead."

"I don't think I ever saw her," Gabe replied.

"You'd remember if you did."

"Is she really dead?"

"I think so," Elkie said.

"It sounds scary."

"It's not so scary like it sounds. My mom used to take me there. She always lit a candle."

Past the school, past Bennett Park playground, past Henry's house, past the bridge.

"This is where we get off."

It was confusing. People were rushing all over the place. They walked through the hospital lobby, up to a booth where two women in nurse uniforms were sitting.

"We're looking for my mom," Elkie said. "We went to the bathroom and we got lost."

The woman looked up her name and said, "Oh dear, you did get lost. She's in the other building. How did you get all the way over here?"

"I don't know," Elkie replied.

The other woman said, "They can't get back there all by themselves. I'll walk them over."

Gabe and Elkie left with her. They crossed the street and walked up a block, into another building, to the elevator, up to the twelfth floor, and down a hall.

The nurse lady said, "Here's your mom's room. Wait here, I'll peek in, just to make sure." She stepped inside.

Gabe and Elkie stood waiting in the hall. Elkie took his hand.

The woman held the door open. "You can go in now."

Gabe could feel Elkie's fingers shaking as they stepped inside.

"Hi Pumpkin," the woman said, in a shaky voice. "They didn't tell me you were coming." She had a bandage around her head. Tubes and wires were hooked up to contraptions all around.

Elkie let go of Gabe's hand, rushed over and hugged her. "I love you, Mommy."

"I love you too, Pumpkin." She stroked Elkie's hair. "Who's your friend?"

"That's Gabe, from my class."

"It's nice to meet you, Gabe."

Gabe couldn't find any words, so just stood there awkwardly.

"How is school?"

Elkie said, "School is fine."

"What are you studying?"

"Lots of things."

"Like what?"

"When are we going home?"

"I wish it was today, but I don't think so. Is everything all right where you're staying, at Ari's house?"

"Everything's fine."

"Are you sure? If there's any problem I want to know."

"There isn't any problem, Mom. I just want you to get better, so we can move back to our house and things will be just like before."

"I wish I could make everything better, Pumpkin, I would if I could, but things just are what they are, so we've got to make the best of it."

"What do you mean?"

"I just mean I love you more than the world."

A nurse poked her head in the door. "What are you two doing in here?"

"This is my daughter," Elkie's mom said. "They can stay."

"No, they can't. We're getting you ready for procedures. And they need to be wearing masks. Who's accompanying them? They can't be up here alone. They have to leave, immediately. How did you get in here?"

Elkie's mom was mad. "Let me say one more thing to my daughter. I've got to say one more thing to her."

"Okay, but then they have to leave."

"Pumpkin," she said, "live every day like it's your last."

Back outside they walked silently along the block. Elkie took Gabe's hand again. Shafts of sunlight broke through the clouds between buildings. All the trees wore long shadows.

Suddenly Elkie burst out sobbing.

•

The next day in the hideout, Elkie said, "Thanks for coming with me yesterday."

"I hope your mom is okay."

"It meant a lot to me."

"Sure," Gabe replied.

"I got something for you."

"What?"

She handed him a Brooklyn Dodgers cap.

"I don't want to take your cap," he said.

"I've got another one. I thought you like the Dodgers."

"I do, kind of. But I can't wear this around the neighborhood. The kids would give me a hard time."

Elkie said, "Try it on."

"Okay." Gabe put it on.

"It looks cool on you."

"You think?"

"You can wear it down here."

•

"What's that racket?" Roco yelled.

Jack, who was up in the lookout tower by the front slits, shouted back, "There's some kind of machine out there, but I can't see it."

The lookout stations were now elaborate constructions, made from ladders, boards, and wooden vegetable crates. From that vantage point looking north, you could see where the highway snaked around a bend near the meadow, and that's where the noise was coming from.

Outside, they crept through the tall grass and trees, up to Bear Rock, and gazed down at the meadow.

A tractor.

Ari said, "They're mowing it all down."

Men in hard hats and orange vests. The tractor was hitched to a mowing machine. The driver drove it through the grass, weeds flying in every direction. Two other men, standing at a distance from each other, were doing something with telescopelike contraptions on tripods. A panel truck was parked on the highway shoulder.

Henry said, "I'm going down and check it out."

"I'll go with you," Gabe said.

"I'll go too," Roco said.

"Three's too many." Henry said.

Gabe and Henry circled around, so it looked like they were coming from the opposite direction, and approached one of the men with the tripods.

"What are you doing?" Henry asked.

He looked surprised. "You kids aren't supposed to be down here. It's dangerous."

"They said it's okay."

"Who did?"

"The parkmen. What are you doing?"

"Surveying."

"What's that mean?"

"We're measuring the lot. Making a map." He was fiddling with the telescopelike thing.

"Why are you doing that?"

"They're going to put up apartments here."

"Apartments? Here?"

"That's what they tell us."

132

"Why do they want to do that?"

"'Cause people need a place to live, I guess."

"But animals already live here," Henry said. "What about them?"

The man shrugged. "You can't stop progress."

"And what about the trees?" Gabe added.

"They're going to cut them all down, I guess."

"Who is?"

"The people who are going to build the apartments here."

"Who are they?"

"They own those big fancy buildings down there. Some corporation. Monarch Towers." He motioned.

Henry said, "They can't just cut everything down."

"I'll tell them you said so. I'm sure they'll be glad to hear that. Don't worry, we're not cutting it all down today, just these weeds so we can finish surveying. They won't start construction till next fall. This lot is still zoned open space. Before they can do anything, they've got to rezone it for residential or get what they call a variance. And it's right up against the park, so the parks people have to sign off on the deal, and that's not easy to get them to do, unless you know the mayor. It's also close to a school, and I think the school people have to sign off on it too."

"That's our school," Gabe said.

"Then if you're concerned, tell your principal not to sign off on it. Anyway, you guys aren't even supposed to be down here."

Gabe and Henry ducked back into the high weeds.

As soon as they were alone, Henry blurted, "Have you got your mirror with you?"

"In my pocket."

A little while later, bursts of light from the grove of pines up on the hill flashed in the mower's and surveyors' faces, distracting them. The mower stopped and wiped his eyes. The flashes kept coming, shining in his eyes, blinding him. Finally he turned off the engine, jumped down off the tractor, and conferred with the two surveyors. The three men stomped through the tall grass, following the flashes up into the woods, but as they approached, the flashes stopped, and they found nothing.

They returned to the meadow, where one of the transits had vanished. At the tractor, the mower reached for the ignition key, felt his pockets, stepped off again, and searched everywhere on the ground.

Roco and Jack crawled into the hideout through the secret entrance, carrying the tripod.

Henry threw the tractor key on the ground. "What should we do?"

Elkie said, "Tell Mrs Hopper, like they said."

"She's not going to do anything,"

Ari said, "Maybe she will. Tell her. You're in the office all the time, it'll be easy for you to do."

"She's never there."

Elkie said, "Then what about Miss C.? Tell Miss C."

"You're such a simp, Elkie," Henry replied.

They set up the transit in the middle of the hideout, and took turns sighting around the walls. They moved it up to the lookout tower, and sighted through the slits at the highway and the river.

"They'll be back, you know," Henry said. "What do we do then?"

"We'll bomb them," Roco said.

Kelly punched his palm. "Yeah, let's bomb them."

"With what?" Jack said.

134

"Cherry bombs." Roco replied.

"You know where to get them?" Jack exclaimed.

"Bennett Playground. They're peddling them."

"Who is?"

"Some kids."

"How much?" Jack said.

"Quarter each."

"They got sparklers too?"

"I don't know."

"Nobody's going to bomb nobody," Henry said.

"Why not?" Roco said.

"Throwing cherry bombs at them isn't going to save the Little Woods from Monarch Towers."

"What you got against cherry bombs, Henry?" Roco said. "They're fun."

Elkie said, "I still think we should tell Mrs Hopper."

"I got a better idea," Ari said. "Let's tell everybody."

"What do you mean?" Henry said.

"Nobody except us knows about it now. If we tell everybody that that Monarch Towers wants to cut down the Little Woods, maybe somebody will know how to stop them."

Gabe said, "How are we going to even tell everybody?"

Ari stepped over to the concrete wall and wrote in big letters in red chalk:

SAVE THE LITTLE WOODS
FROM MONARCH TOWERS

"We come to school real early," Ari continued, "before anybody else gets there, and we write that all over the sidewalk, and when they all ask what it means, we tell them."

Kelly said, "That's won't work."

"Why not?"

"Because we're the only ones who call it the Little Woods. They all think it's part of Fort Tryon Park."

"Then let's tell them to save the park from Monarch Towers. It even almost rhymes."

Ari wrote in big red chalk letters:

SAVE THE PARK

FROM MONARCH TOWERS

The next morning when everybody gathered in front of the school gate, the sidewalk was covered with words printed in chalk. Everybody was talking about it.

The seven were spread out in the crowd, talking in different clusters of kids. Gabe and Elkie and Ari stood with one group.

Ari said to a girl, "What I heard is that Monarch Towers is going to build apartment buildings there."

"I heard that too," Elkie said.

"Me too," Gabe said.

Rumors spread quickly. Some kids said it was really true that Monarch Towers was going to cut down Fort Tryon Park, and some said it wasn't. The teachers were talking about it in the break room.

•

That night at home, Gabe was at the kitchen table with Benjo. Mom was standing by the stove.

"Grampa, you know Mrs Hopper from outside of school?"

"I used to."

"Can you ask her something for me?"

"What?"

"Ask her if she's going to let Monarch Towers cut down the park."

"What park?"

"Fort Tryon Park."

"Where did you hear that?"

"From some kids."

Benjo looked at Mom. "Do you know about this?"

Mom shook her head. "This is the first I've heard. I can't believe it's true. It must just be a silly rumor somebody made up. Don't pay any attention to it. Why would Monarch Towers cut down Fort Tryon Park?"

"They don't want to cut down the whole park. They just want to cut down part of it," Gabe explained. "To build some more apartment buildings there."

Mom said, "Everybody loves Fort Tryon Park, nobody would let Monarch Towers cut it down and put up more apartments there."

"Grampa, just ask Mrs Hopper for me. Please."

•

The next day in class, Miss Odelia said, "Did everybody remember to bring your V-Pad? As we all know, today is collection day. Everyone place your V-Pad on your desk. Rory and Jim will go around and collect them."

Rory grabbed Gabe's V-Pad and dumped it with the others in a box in the front of the room.

When the second bell rang, Miss Odelia said, "Assembly time. Everyone straighten your shirts and ties."

They lined up in size place and took partners. This time Gabe and Henry were dressed properly. As they filed down the stairs to the auditorium, Rory poked Gabe in the back.

Gabe turned. "Stop that."

Miss Odelia said, "Is something wrong, Gabriel?"

"No."

The principal was out sick again. Miss M. Drannily announced, "We all pray for her speedy recovery." After the singing, she put her finger to her lips to shush the murmurs. "We have a surprise announcement, a reward for all of you who have made Columbus School tops in the city. The VIP Program has been extended. This afternoon, teachers will hand out a new V-Pad to each pupil, as well as collect last week's V-Pads. We will be continuing this special initiative through the end of the school year. Go ahead, applaud yourselves." She clapped.

Later in the day, when Gabe and Henry dragged themselves to Drannily's office, Mr Blinka was there with her again.

"Are those the seats I assigned you?"

"Yes, Miss Drannily."

"You didn't change seats, did you?

"No, Miss Drannily."

She smoothed her dress and sighed. "Inside those boxes are more V-Pads. Today you will collect the completed pads from in front of each class, and also deliver new ones. Grades five and six on the third floor, and three and four on this floor. You may use the elevator. Leave two bundles of new pads with each class. Then return here, and for the rest of the remaining time, continue your erasure duties. Understood?"

"Yes, Miss Drannily."

They rolled the carts to the elevator, up to the third floor, down the corridor, picking up boxes of V-Pads.

On the elevator going down Henry started reading one.

"Wow, this is some crazy stuff," Henry said.

"What does it say?"

138

"Man sleep on newspapers. Next door lady yells bad words. A dead rat. George stomped my foot. Sister pinches and kicks. Somebody peed in the lobby. Dog in a hat. People running backwards on 181st Street. Miss Larrosun said McCarthy is the one who's not American."

"What does that mean?" Gabe said. "The last part, about Larrosun."

"It means some kid in her class wrote her up. It's one of the V-Pads from her class." Henry leafed through the pad. "Whoever it was, he didn't put his name on it."

"Read it again."

"*Miss Larrosun said McCarthy is the one who's not American.*"

"Who's this McCarthy?" Gabe bit his lip. "My family keeps talking about him."

"I think he's some government guy," Henry replied.

"I think so too."

"Either that or a baseball guy."

"Baseball?"

"Jack and Roco talk about him too. They got two leagues, right? The Yankees are in the American League, right? That's probably why Larrosun said he's not American, because he's in the National League now. That explains it. I think this McCarthy guy used to be a Yankee, the manager or something, but he's on a different team now."

Gabe racked his brain. "Oh, yeah, I heard something about that. But how come you know so much? I thought you hate baseball."

"It's the most boring thing in the world, but this just stuck in my head."

"But why would some kid write her up for saying that?"

Henry rolled his eyes and made a funny face. "Maybe we should ask Blinka."

The elevator doors opened back on the second floor. They wheeled the carts past the secretary. Drannily wasn't in her office, and the door to Hopper's office was shut tight.

Gabe put his ear to the wall but didn't hear anything.

Henry whispered, "Keep chickie."

Henry explored the room, jiggled Drannily's desk drawers but they were locked, rummaged through some files and papers.

Gabe eyed the secretary through the clouded glass door. He heard a sound, gave a little whistle.

Henry scurried back to his seat.

Through the wall Gabe could hear people entering into Hopper's office. The voices were muffled. It was Drannily and Blinka. He didn't understand everything they were saying. He didn't hear Hopper's voice.

Henry tiptoed over, crouched beside Gabe, and put his ear to the wall too.

Drannily said, "And you were able to capture it all on one of those Dictaphone cartridges."

"You take the cartridge right out and insert a new one. We collect everything, and keep it in our back pocket for when we need it. That's how we always stay a few jumps ahead of them."

"Amazing. This is what my dear daddy, rest his soul, back in Iowa, used to call Yankee know-how. And he didn't even like Yankees."

"Even when we don't get a smoking gun, we usually pick up dirt. Then with their guilty minds, they fill in the blanks themselves."

"Hypocrites, every one of them. They'll do anything to keep from being exposed."

"This cartridge here is the one we caught them on in the teachers' lounge," Blinka went on. "We need you to identify the voices."

Static. A woman's voice, scratchy and metallic: *"Are you okay?"*

"That's Batra," Drannily interjected. "Social studies."

*"I must be showing it."*

"That's Odelia."

*"You look a little tired."*

*"I'm about to cry. My kids are driving me up the wall. This is insane."*

A man's voice: *"Relax, Selene. The semester's almost over."*

"That's Daumer," Drannily said. "Science."

*"I don't know how much more of this I can take. I've got to get out of here before I wind up in a strait jacket."*

"That's Odelia again."

*"Just last week you said you enjoy your class."*

*"It's not the class. The kids are great. Challenging and stressful, but I can deal with that. First it was this strict curriculum. And now this junior spy business."*

*"We're all in the same boat."*

*"I'm worried about saying something wrong in class, that could be construed in some way. I've even started talking like them."*

*"We've filed a grievance."*

"That's Batra again," Drannily interjected.

*"For all the good it'll do."*

*"Why bother? Most of those stupid V-Pads are probably lost or in the garbage. They're not even serious about all this subversives stuff. It's just a shell game."*

*"To what end?"*

141

*"To bust the union."*

*"Why would Mrs Hopper want to bust the union? She was president of her local when she was teaching."*

*"People change."*

*"Mrs Hopper doesn't understand what's been happening. She's been out sick so much this year, she barely knows what's going on. It's hard to get past Drannily to even talk to her."*

*"You've got that Golman kid in your class, don't you Selene?"*

*"One of the Stoloff kids too. And I'm very careful about what I say around them."*

*"Selene, we're having a special caucus meeting on Saturday. We're going to try to talk with Hopper away from Drannily, outside of school. We want to hear what she says when Drannily's not around."*

"That was Daumer again," Drannily said.

*"I think I'll just hunker down and finish out this year if I can. Drannily makes it pretty clear she doesn't like me. Don't expect me back next fall."*

*"Selene, please come back in the fall, if they let you. We need you."*

*"Well, maybe things will look different to me after I get away for a while this summer."*

*"Where are you going?"*

*"As far away as I can. Mexico. Oaxaca."*

Batra said, *"Well, time for me to scoot back to class."*

The sound of chairs shuffling. A door shut.

Miss Odelia said, *"Jeff, come see me tonight."*

*"I can't, sugar."*

*"I'm feeling so bad."*

*"It's impossible. My mother is coming for dinner."*

142

*"How about tomorrow night?"*

*"Saturday's the caucus meeting."*

*"Don't put me in this position. It's not fair. I'm not putting up with this."*

*"I'm doing the best I can."*

*"Come with me to Oaxaca this summer."*

*"I'm walking on eggshells. Come to the caucus meeting on Saturday. I know you agree with what we're trying to do. We can slip away early and spend some time together, just the two of us."*

Blinka stopped the recording. "That's all the voices we need identified."

"I thought I had Odelia pegged," Drannily exclaimed. "I'm mortified. There is even more improper behavior going on than I ever suspected. Oh, naive me!"

"Nothing out of the ordinary, really. And take it from me, I've seen it all. They're like this all over. Their propaganda is infectious, and they use that union to spread it. It's just the usual few rotten apples. Once you weed them out, the others toe the line."

"I hope you're going to send one of your people to that caucus meeting of theirs."

•

# CHAPTER NINE

At home later that night, Gabe was at his desk when Benjo came up behind him.

"Grampa, did you ever ask Mrs Hopper about Fort Tryon Park, like you said you would?"

"I haven't seen her yet." Benjo picked up a V-Pad that Gabe had left sitting on the dresser. "What's this?"

"Just something they give to all the kids at school."

"What's V mean?"

"It's for Vigilance. V-i-g-i-l... Vigilance."

Benjo opened it. "They give these to all the kids at school?" He leafed through it.

We're supposed to go around the neighborhood and look for suspicious people and write stuff about them. Do you know anybody I can write up? Me and Henry are the monitors."

"Monitors?"

"We go around collecting them from all the classes for Miss Drannily and we give them their new ones. It's our job."

"What do they do with these things?"

"She gives them to Mr Blinka."

"Who's Mr Blinka?"

"He's just this man."

"Is he a teacher?"

"No, he's a P-man. He takes all the V-Pads and drives them away in his car."

"Can I borrow this? There's somebody I'd like to show it to."

"I'm supposed to hand that one in."

Benjo set the pad down on Gabe's desk.

Gabe reached into his bookbag. "Here's another one you can have."

Benjo perused it. "How's about you and me taking in a movie tomorrow night, Saturday, just the two of us."

"What movie?"

"Any one you want."

It wasn't often that Benjo took Gabe to the movies, and he was pleased.

•

When Gabe got home from the Little Woods late the next afternoon, Benjo reminded him about the movie. Although he was kind of bushed, Gabe immediately got his second wind and geared himself up.

Mom said, "But don't come back late. What movie are you going to see?"

Benjo answered, "We haven't decided yet."

As they walked briskly to the bus stop, Gabe asked, "Where are we really going?"

"There's a couple of friends of mine I want you to meet."

They got off the bus at a downtown street.

"There's a theater," Gabe said. "It's a cowboy movie."

"Later."

They walked a few blocks to a big brick building.

"This is my old union hall," Benjo said as they approached the door. "I used to come here all the time when I was shop steward."

"You were what?"

"Shop steward. That meant I had to make sure that everything was in compliance with the contract. I was shop steward for many many years. Whenever the guys had a gripe they'd come to me. A lot of the old farts still hang around the union hall. That's what we're doing tonight. You're going to meet an old fart friend of mine. He belonged to a different union, but we used to work together. His name is Foxx."

"You mean like the animal?"

"That's what they used to call him, the fox."

"Are any other kids going to be there?"

"We'll see."

"Why don't we just go to a movie?"

Upstairs was a big room with tables and chairs and a few bunches of people in little groups. To one side some musicians were tuning up.

"This is where everybody gets together and talks about stuff and have some fun too."

Benjo led Gabe to a table on the far side, where a big bald man and two ladies were sitting.

"This is my grandson, Gabe. These are my friends, Foxx and Daisy. And this must be...?"

"Marianna," the other lady said. "I work with Daisy."

The man stuck out his thick hand. Gabe's disappeared inside it. "Pleased to meet you, Gabe. Your grampa has told me a lot about you."

They sat down.

"Why do they call you fox?" Gabe asked. "Are you really like a fox?"

"I'm just an old lap dog." He guffawed.

"Foxx was one of the best picket captains in his day."

"Me? Your grampa was legendary. He probably never told you this, but he could tell you stories."

"Don't get started, Foxx."

"Now they're all too scared to even utter the word strike."

Benjo said to the second woman, "Sorry, but what's your name again?"

"Marianna."

"She's in the Alliance," Foxx put in.

Benjo leaned toward Gabe. "These ladies work at your school, you might have seen them around. I don't think I ever mentioned my friend Daisy to you."

"They mostly don't see us. We usually come in after they leave."

"These ladies know a lot about your school, probably more than some of your teachers do."

"Daisy is the crew leader," Foxx said.

Benjo said, "That means she's the boss."

"The crew leader isn't the boss," Daisy said.

Benjo pulled out the V-Pad and set it on the table.

"Gabe, can you explain to Foxx what this thing is and how you got it?"

Foxx picked up the pad, leafed through it, pushed his horn rimmed glasses back up over the bump on his nose. "I already heard some from Daisy about these things, but this is the first one I seen. I sure would appreciate hearing the whole story from you, Gabe."

Gabe said, "Me and my friend Henry are the V-Pad monitors."

When Gabe finished telling his story, Foxx said to Benjo, "I can't believe Helen's going along with this."

Daisy said, "Mrs Hopper has been sick, and the vice principal has been running the school."

"Is Grayley still working there?"

"He's still there," Daisy said. "But he's thick with them."

"That's not the Grayley I knew."

"He just don't want to lose his job."

Gabe noticed a group at a table on the other side of the dance floor. He pulled Benjo's sleeve. "That's Miss Odelia, and some other teachers from our school."

Daisy said, "Odelia is the one in blue. The hair is Batra, the scarf is Larrosun, the lipstick is Grainger, and the man is Daumer."

"They're all teachers?"

She nodded. "Batra is the union rep. Grainger and Daumer are the PTA liaisons."

Foxx said to Benjo, "Let's go talk to them."

Benjo put his hand on Gabe's shoulder. "Would you mind staying here for a short while with these lovely ladies, while me and Foxx go talk with those other folks?"

"I want to stay with you," Gabe replied.

"But we might be talking about some really boring stuff."

"I'll be okay."

As Benjo, Gabe, and Foxx approached the table, their conversation stopped.

"Sorry to interrupt you," Foxx said. "But if you have a few minutes, we'd like to talk to you about something."

Most of them knew Laurrinto Foxx, and he introduced Benjo and Gabe.

"Sit down," Batra said. "Pull over some chairs."

These, Gabe thought, are the teachers he heard talking on Mr Blinka's Dictaphone recording.

"Very nice to see you here, Gabriel," Miss Odelia said. "I don't get the chance to see many of my pupils outside of class." She added to Benjo, "I hope Gabriel hasn't been giving our class a bad report card."

"The truth is, he doesn't talk about school much to me at all, except when it's something that he doesn't want to tell his mom and dad. Isn't that right. Gabe?"

"No."

Gabe was seated next to Benjo, right across from Miss Odelia. He couldn't stop looking at her. She looked so different here, like a different person, and it felt so strange to be here talking to her.

"This is what we want to talk to you about." Foxx placed the V-Pad on the table. "How in the world did you let these things into your school?"

"They sprung it us. We didn't see it coming," Batra replied.

Miss Odelia kept glancing at Gabe, with a funny expression on her face. He was making her uncomfortable.

The adjoining table was empty. Gabe pulled Benjo's cuff. "I'm bored. I'm going to go sit over there, okay?"

"Okay," Benjo said, "but don't go too far."

He ensconced himself in a chair at the other table, pulled out another V-Pad from his pocket, and started drawing a picture of a blue jay. He could hear most of what they were saying at Benjo's table.

"Golman and Stoloff are behind it. They're running the PTA. And Miss M. of course."

"This whole 'subversives' thing is just a scare tactic."

"To what end?"

"It's really weird how Stoloff and Golman took over the PTA. As first year parents, technically they weren't even eligible to run."

"What happened?"

"The former PTA officers resigned suddenly last fall. We had to hold a special election. But all the most active parents, the ones you'd expect to run, all stepped back. Even though nobody really knew them, Golman and Stoloff were the only ones running, so they took over."

"It almost felt like a coup."

"They both live in Monarch Towers, they both moved in last fall. And the Drannilys live there too. Maybe it's just a weird coincidence."

"They all live in the same building?"

"Don't the Drannilys live on Pinehurst?"

"They moved over to Monarch Towers less than a year ago."

"How can they afford to live in Monarch Towers, on teachers' salaries?"

"They obviously don't eat much."

Foxx said, "Let me get this straight. This Golman and Stoloff run the PTA. But what do they do for a living?"

"Mrs Golman runs an art gallery."

"That's her hobby. Her husband is some kind of corporate tax attorney."

"Stoloff calls himself a financial advisor, whatever that means. He's got an office downtown."

"The Drannilys are sisters?" Benjo asked.

"Fifty years ago, you'd call them spinsters."

"Some of us think that the vice principal is behind all this, and some of us think it's coming from Golman and Stoloff."

"The three of them brought this government guy Blinka and his V-Pads into the school. Now he comes in at least three time a week, and hangs around her office."

"They all work closely together."

Foxx said, "What about the principal? How is Helen involved with this? You know, Me and Ben knew Helen and her husband Duncan from the old days."

"Wasn't he in the trades?"

Benjo said, "Electrical, Foxx's union. Helen we mostly just knew socially, and from marches and actions. She was teaching then. She always seemed solid. They were leaders. She was president of her local."

"Poor Mrs Hopper. Miss M's got her coming and going."

"And the other Drannily sister, what's her name? How does she fit in?"

"Miss C. She's just a mouse. She looks really dismayed these days. She just does what M. tells her to."

"I've got to defend the principal," Batra said. "Until she took ill, she worked very constructively with the union."

"Just what is her illness?"

"They keep doing tests, but I hear they're always inconclusive."

Batra said, "Promise me this won't leave this table, but I got to say this. This is the story I heard, that the former PTA president and vice president were visited by IPA agents and told to not run again, and all the other candidates were told to withdraw too."

Gasps. "I knew it!"

151

"With all the rumors that keep flying around school, it's getting scary."

"Like what rumors?"

"Whatever anybody's paranoid imagination can dream up. Like the school is bugged and they're listening to everything."

"I believe it."

"I do too. Don't you?"

"Most of the time, no."

Foxx said, "Have you tried asking Grayley?"

"The maintenance man?"

"The maintenance man would probably know if they bugged the school. Whether he'd tell you is another story."

"It could be dangerous to ask."

"How do you know Grayley?"

Foxx said, "Me and Ben knew him in the old days."

Benjo said, "He used to be okay, I think."

"He was an electrician then," Foxx continued. "I remember some kind of accident. Lost track of him until now."

"You know who else might know something?" Batra said. "The cleaning crew, and two of them are right over there at that table."

Daumer leaped in. "Whoa. We've got to be very careful talking about this. Our jobs are on the line."

"Maybe we should go to the newspapers."

"They're too cowed to touch it."

When Gabe finally said goodbye to Miss Odelia, she replied, "Gabriel, I would appreciate it if you don't mention to the other pupils that you saw me outside of class."

"I won't," he answered without thinking. Then he wondered if she meant to include Henry, and what about the

152

others? She looked at him in a funny way and he looked back. He understood that they were both seeing each other differently. There was a secret between them.

A while later, Benjo and Gabe were back outside, and a few blocks further on, they were buying popcorn at the movie theater.

•

# CHAPTER TEN

After a long boring time in class, the bell finally rang for lunch.

Gabe stopped off in the boys' room. At the urinal, a low voice beside him said, "Tell Henry we want to talk."

It was Jim Stoloff.

"Tell him yourself."

"Just do it."

"Why do you want *me* to tell him?"

"Just tell him we got some stuff we need to talk about. Meet us in Bennett Park after school, near the drinking fountain." Jim sauntered away.

Down in the lunchroom, the walls echoed with voices and laughter. Across the room, Gabe saw Henry, Roco, Kelly, and Jack already ensconced at their usual table in the far corner. As usual, Elkie and Ari were at another table nearby with a few girls they hung out with sometimes. The girls and boys mostly seated themselves separately. Everyone would have talked if the two girls started joining the guys' table.

Gabe made his way over and joined the other boys. They talked in low tones, although it was always hard to hear what anybody was saying over the din.

A half hour after school let out, Gabe and Henry were nervously mulling about near the drinking fountain in

Bennett Park. It was alive with kids, parents, old people, dogs, squirrels, butterflies, sparrows, pigeons. Gabe took a mouthful of cool water from the fountain, while Henry shifted his weight from foot to foot. A ways away, Elkie and Ari were playing hopscotch. Out on the lawn, Kelly and Roco were throwing around a pink Spaldeen. Next to the monkey bars, Jack was pumping on a swing.

Gabe scanned the park apprehensively, from face to face, wondering if any of them were in the Stoloff gang.

Henry muttered, "Here they come."

The Stoloff brothers and Rory Golman ambled slowly toward them from the far entrance to the park, beyond the swings. They stopped about six feet away.

Preston spit into the bushes. "Too much traffic here. Let's move."

Keeping some distance, Gabe and Henry stepped cautiously toward the tall hedge, where sparrows were flitting.

Henry said, "Okay, here we are. What do you want to talk about?"

"No hard feelings." Preston held out his left palm to Henry.

Henry ignored the gesture.

Preston continued, "How many guys in your gang? How many you got?"

"How many *you* got?" Henry threw back at him.

"How about those jerks you're always sitting with in the lunchroom, who just happen to be hanging out over there today, they in your gang?"

Henry replied, "You got a good imagination."

"Okay. Let's get down to it." Preston said.

Henry said, "Why are you guys such bullies?"

"Bullies? I think we got a misunderstanding."

"Till now all you ever wanted was to bully us."

Preston leaned toward Henry. "We were just testing you, to see if you were punks."

"Why were you doing that?"

"Columbus School sucks, right?"

"Maybe."

"We know you hate them. We been watching you. We hate them too. That's why we sprung you out of kindergarten, so you can work for us. We can work together. You took our jobs, our V-Pad monitor jobs. Just to prove we don't hold grudges, we'll put it behind us. But you owe us. Now you're in the office and we're not. There's something we need you to do there for us."

"You want us to do something in the office?"

"You and us, we're going to prank them."

Gabe said, "Prank them? Why do you want us to prank them?"

Preston replied, "They got it coming, don't they? Just to mess with their heads some. Nothing hard. It'll be a lark."

"Why do you want to mess with them? I thought your dad's such a big shot in the school."

"All the more reason."

Henry said, "Do it yourself."

Preston held up two five dollar bills. "We don't expect you to work for nothing."

Henry said, "I don't want your money."

"I don't either," said Gabe.

"Maybe we got something else you want."

"Like what?"

"Maybe you want to see your files."

"What files?"

"Our dad's got files on you. Both of you. On you and your families."

"Why does he got files on us?" Henry asked.

"He keeps files on everybody. He knows everything. He's got files on everybody in the neighborhood."

"What do I care?" Henry said. "Your dad can keep me in whatever files he wants."

"Whatever. It's your funeral. And your names are on the list too. Your families are on the list. Both of you."

"What list?" Gabe asked.

"The list is more important. When you're on the list, that means you're flagged. Work for us. We'll show you the list."

"Why are we flagged?" Gabe asked.

"Who knows? It could be anything. Maybe you said something to somebody. Or your dad said something, or your mom. What do you think those V-Pads are for? Rory and Jim write down everything you say in class, and they put it all in your files. Right, guys?"

Jim and Rory, who were standing nearby watching, both smiled.

"That's why you and your families wind up the list," Preston went on, "because you don't watch out what you say. They're going to come get you and put you away. They're going to put your whole family away."

"Who is?" Gabe said.

"Want to see your files?" he continued. "Want to see the list? We do neat things for our friends. We let them know when they're on the list. We keep an eye on their files. We know how to make things appear and disappear in those files."

Henry said, "What makes you think we believe you?"

157

"Come on over to our house. Right now. Nobody's home. Work with us. We'll show you your files. We'll show you the list. Want to see them?"

"So you got files on everybody in the neighborhood?" Henry said.

"Right."

"How about Fort Tryon Park? Do you got a file on them?"

Preston looked at him curiously. "On Fort Tryon Park?"

"Yeah."

"What about them?"

"On those buildings they want to build in the park. Does your dad got a file on them?"

"You mean that new Monarch Towers project?"

"Yeah."

"I don't know. I haven't seen that file, but that doesn't mean anything. He's got files on everything that goes on in this neighborhood, so he's probably got a file on it."

Jim jumped in, "I know where it is. It's in with Drannily."

Preston pursed his lip. "With Drannily? Why's it in there?"

"How should I know? It just is."

Preston said, "Wherever it is, we'll find it. Just stay put here till we're across the street. Wait till we're halfway down the block, then follow us. Act like we're not together till we get inside."

"Inside where?" Henry asked.

"You know, where we live. Monarch Towers. We'll meet you next to the doorman."

Preston, Jim, and Rory sauntered away, crossed Pinehurst and disappeared into the alley.

As soon as they were out of earshot, Henry said, "Let's play with them."

Gabe said, "What if it's a trap?"

"Are you scared of them?"

"No."

"I'm not either."

Henry and Gabe flashed hand signals to the rest of the gang. Then without another word, as if pulled by some force, they followed Preston's steps across Pinehurst, through the alley, down the stairs to Cabrini, where they saw the Stoloff gang across the street, headed toward Monarch Towers.

They crossed Cabrini, followed along the curving cement paths, through the carefully mown lawns and clipped hedges, the pretty colored flowers in neat rows, toward the main entrance.

Preston, Jim, and Rory were waiting for them in the entryway. The doorman held the towering glass door open, his white gloved fingers wrapped around the glass handle, in his black coat with two rows of white buttons, his black flat-top cap with a little brim in front, with MT embroidered on it in gold thread, and gold stripes around his cuffs and down the side of his pants. He was exactly as Gabe remembered him, from the time they tried to sneak into the lobby behind some moving men who were carrying in furniture.

The doorman showed no sign of recognizing them, and instead held the glass door wide open and said, "Good afternoon, gentlemen."

The lobby was enormous, mirrors soaring up every wall, all the way up to the huge sparkly chandelier hanging from the towering vaulted ceiling.

As they approached the elevator, Preston said, "We live on the top floor. Corner suite. Rory's right next door. Now, don't go ape shit when you see the view out our window.

The Drannily lovelies are fifth floor front. They hate us. That's why they made you the V-Pad monitors."

Gabe asked, "Why do they hate you?"

Jim said, "'Cause we know their apartment smells like pee."

Preston added, "And we know what's in their files." He pressed a button.

Henry said, "You really got Drannily's file?"

Preston smiled. "And Hopper's."

Rory said, "And Odelia's."

To Gabe's surprise, the elevator started down instead of up. The door slid open on a concrete corridor in the basement.

"Why are we down here?" Gabe asked warily.

"Party favors."

Preston stepped out. The others followed him onto the painted cement floor. He pushed on a metal door with DANGER painted on it.

A huge furnace and boiler. A coal pile and shovels. A coal chute leading up to the metal doors where they slid the coal down into the basement from the trucks. Embedded into the concrete floor was an iron grate.

They must have been right on top of the hideout.

"Why'd you bring us here?" Henry asked.

Preston grinned. "We're going to dig up buried treasure."

Jim and Rory picked up shovels, dug into the coal pile, and uncovered a big burlap sack.

Jim dusted it off, untied the drawstring around its neck, and pulled out a red sphere the size of a walnut. He held it out, cupped in his palm. "Want a gumball?"

"That's not a gumball," Henry said. "It's a cherry bomb."

Jim handed it to him.

Henry turned it over in his palm.

Gabe had never seen a cherry bomb up close before. He felt a rush of excitement. The danger made him recoil. He reached out and touched it with a finger. He wanted to hold it in his hand, if only for a minute.

Henry said, "We heard somebody's been peddling them in the playground."

Preston replied, "Some punks from Broadway. We told them, no way, not in Bennett Playground you don't."

Henry replied, "Are those the same punks you said are going to rub our noses in the dirt?"

"Did I say that? They're out of the picture now." Preston said. "Here's the deal: on the street they're a quarter a pop. Seller keeps a nickel. Sell two, you got enough for a comic book. We got stuff to move. With you guys, we'll have the neighborhood covered. You don't have to decide now. Think about it. Take a few. We got plenty. Fill your pocket. Our treat. We treat our people right." He held the bag open.

Henry handed Jim back the cherry. "I'll think about it."

Preston went on, "We don't need the money. We just peddle them for fun. But some easy bucks always sweeten the pot."

"Don't hide them in the coal pile," Henry said.

"Why not?" Preston replied.

"Find some other place," Henry said. "Coal piles heat up. They heat up just sitting there. It might explode."

Preston perked up. "Really? How come you know so much?"

"I'm studying to be a super when I grow up," Henry responded.

"Well, you're ambitious." Preston grinned. "Oh, that's right, you live in a cellar. I read that in your file. Anyway, the cleaning ladies are all over our apartment, so we have to stash the cherries down here. Safest place in Monarch Towers, this time of year."

Henry said, "You're going to burn your own house down."

Preston cracked a smile. "Then we'll have to live somewhere else. I can't stand the excitement. Maybe we should bring some to school, and warm up their coal pile too."

Preston tied up the neck of the burlap sack, and motioned to Jim and Rory, who buried it back in the coal pile and shoveled nuggets and dust over it.

In the elevator again, they started up. The car stopped at the lobby, the door opened, an elderly couple flashed them a suspicious look, got on, then exited on the third floor.

They continued to the top floor, off onto a long red carpeted hallway with many doors.

Preston said, "Before we go inside, we're going to take a little detour up to the crow's nest."

He led them all up a stair case, opened the door at the top. They stepped out onto the tar and gravel roof. The view took Gabe's breath away. They were as high as the top of the bridge, even higher. It felt like the top of the world. Gabe and Henry peered over the dizzying side. Gabe could see the roof of his building. It looked so little alongside the bridge.

Preston said, "It's a long ways down without a parachute."

Jim said, "How about a round of dive bombers?"

Rory said, "Yeah, let's do dive bombers."

Preston said, "Roger, and out. Everybody set your hardware at ready alert."

Jim held out a handful of cherry bombs to Gabe.

Almost as if Gabe wasn't controlling his own hand, it shot out. Jim dropped three cherries into his palm. It felt so strangely thrilling holding them.

Jim held out another handful to Henry.

Henry just stood there.

"Catch." He tossed one toward Henry.

Henry grabbed it out of the air. "Are you crazy? Don't throw those around."

Rory chuckled, "Yeah, these guys are crazy!"

Preston, Jim, and Rory each held a handful of cherry bombs.

Gabe nervously moved the cherries around in his palm with his thumb.

Preston said, "Ready for dive bombers? It takes four and a half seconds for these babies to bounce."

Gabe's hand was shaking.

"Three-two-one! Scramble! Alagaroo! Geronimo!" Preston tossed his cherries up into the air and over the side of the building.

Jim and Rory threw theirs. "Alagaroo!"

Gabe shouted "Geronimo!" in a small voice, threw his cherries up and over the side of the roof, then wondered if he'd done the right thing.

Explosions.

Preston, Jim, and Rory dashed madly toward the roof door. Gabe and Henry ran after them as fast as they could, and caught the door just before it closed. They followed the others down the stairs into the hall, around a corner, to the last apartment on the corridor. Everyone burst into laughter.

Preston turned the key.

A huge room with windows stretching the full length, looking out over the river and the Palisades. It was filled with the most gorgeous stuff Gabe had ever seen, like a palace. He walked around, dazzled. On one wall was a big painting of a beautiful woman in a bright red dress, who looked like a queen.

"That's our gramma. She's dead," Preston said.

"Was she nice?" Gabe asked.

"Nice? She wasn't nice. She wasn't mean. She wasn't anything. I don't think she ever even touched me."

"Not even once?"

"Maybe once. C'mon let's go to our dad's office."

A desk, with file cabinets all around.

"Don't move anything. He knows exactly where everything is." Preston held up a brown paper bag. "Here's the deal. There are three envelopes in here. One for Drannily, one for Hopper, and one for McKlosky. There are gloves in the bag. Wear them before you touch the envelopes. Put the envelopes in their middle desk drawers. If they're locked, slide them in through the little space on top. They'll fit. Piece of cake. Just a prank. If you get caught, you eat it. That's prank buddies code. That's it. Agreed? Deal?"

Henry said, "Let's see those files."

Gabe said, "And the list. The one with us on it."

"After we seal the deal."

"After you show us the stuff."

Preston shrugged. "You drive a hard bargain." He pulled out one of the file drawers, pushed it back in, pulled out another drawer, rummaged through some folders.

"I don't see the list. He must have put it somewhere else."

"So now maybe it don't even exist?" Henry said.

"It exists, all right. He must have moved it." Preston lifted a folder from one of the drawers. "I'll show you something even better. Here's your file, Gabe. Want to see it?"

"Sure," Gabe replied uncertainly.

He set it on the desktop. Gabe gazed curiously at the label on the front with his family's name on it.

Rory set another file in front of Henry. "Here's yours."

Preston placed one hand over each file. "First we seal the deal. You do the job, we'll get you off the list. Then when they come rounding up people to put in jail, you won't have to worry about your family."

Henry said, "What about the park?"

"You mean the new apartments?"

"Let's see their file."

"Don't worry about that. They're not cutting down the park. Just that empty lot on the other side of the wall."

"I still want to see the file."

"Here it is," Jim said. "Here's some of it." He set two folders on the table.

Preston held up the brown paper bag again. "Ready to deal now? One envelope in each desk drawer. That's all you got to do. Drannily, Hopper, and McKlosky. Wear the gloves, don't forget. If you get caught, you don't know us. Agreed? Deal?" He set the bag on the table between Gabe and Henry.

Henry nodded at Gabe, grasped the paper bag, and stuck it under his shirt.

Preston said, "Go ahead now, open up your folders, look them over. But leave them just like they are, they're all in some kind of order. And nothing leaves this room."

Gabe and Henry leafed through the papers.

Gabe muttered, "I don't understand most of this stuff."

Preston replied, "That's just the way lawyers write. They make it all into babel, that's their job, that's what my dad says, and he ought to know."

Henry pulled out some architectural drawings, unfolded them, spread them out, gazed intently at them. "Who is Monarch Towers anyway?"

"Who?"

"Yeah, who?"

"Just some corporation guys. They come in here all the time, talking to our dad, in their smelly gray suits."

"What's a corporation guy?" Henry asked. "What does that mean?"

"It means they pretend they're not people. But they're people all right. They're crooks. My dad's got the goods on all of them. And they know it. That's why they give us the best apartments."

Jim said, "We get the best of everything."

Henry said, "If your dad gets you the best of everything, then why are you trying to screw him around?"

Preston said, "Why? Why? Why do you think? Because he's got it coming. He deserves it."

"Does he hit you?" Gabe asked.

"Hit us?" Preston responded. "Most of the time he's too busy to hit us."

"Then what does he do?" Henry asked.

"For one, he lies. About everything. Everything he does is a lie."

"Do you hate him?"

"Don't you hate yours?"

"I don't even know him," Henry replied.

"Well, you're lucky. If you knew him you'd probably hate him."

166

"I hate my grandma's husband," Henry said.

"Where we come from, everybody hates their dad, or almost everybody."

"Where do you come from?" Gabe asked.

Jim said, "You guys don't even know the half of it."

Rory said, "Tell them, Preston. They're working for us now. We're prank buddies."

Preston looked Henry in the eye. "Now that we're prank buds, I want the truth from you. Who else is in your gang?"

Henry said, "There is no gang. I was just bluffing. It's just us two."

Preston said, "That's what I thought. Well here's the truth about us. The truth is, we really don't even live here. Our real houses are in Westchester."

"If you live in Westchester, what are you doing here?"

Preston said, "Okay. Last year we were all in boarding school in Connecticut."

Jim said, "That's where they really know how to prank."

"Why did your parents send you to boarding school?" Gabe asked.

"Why do you think?" Preston replied. "They don't like having us around."

Gabe said, "Did you like it there in boarding school?"

"Of course not. Everybody hates it. But you know what? This is even worse, just being around them all the time. They should never have had kids. The only reason we're even here at all is because they need us in your stupid school so they can be on the stupid PTA for their stupid job."

"What's their job?" Henry asked.

"What do you think? Why do they have all these files on everybody? What are the V-Pads for?"

It suddenly dawned on Gabe. "They're helping Mr Blinka."

"Blinka's a real piece of work. He comes here all the time. Drannily comes too sometimes. They all get together right here."

"For what?"

"To plot and bicker."

"About what?"

"About subversives of course. About who to put on the list. We just think it's funny. Like they're in a cartoon."

"How about Hopper?" Henry asked. "Does she come here and plot with them too?"

"If you really want to know, Hopper's the main one they talk about. She's on the list, right at the top of the list. She's going to jail."

"Mrs Hopper?" Gabe gasped.

"Half the teachers in the school are going to jail. Or at least five or six. The ones on the list."

"Which ones are on the list?" Henry asked. "Is Odelia on the list?"

"Sometimes she's on, sometimes she's off. They can't make up their mind. It keeps changing."

"Why do they want to put everybody in jail anyway?" Gabe asked.

"That's just what they do. They catch subversives. This neighborhood is full of them. They don't even care who they put in jail. They just round up enough people to look good."

"So you're helping the subversives?"

"No, no." Preston waved his hands. "Why should we care about them?"

"Then what do you want?"

"They promised us, our dad promised us, he swore up and down, we only had to be here in your stupid school for a few months, while he worked on this case. Now he keep dragging his heels. He keeps lying to us about it. He's the world's biggest liar. I'm not kidding. That's his job. He lies to everybody. But he's not going to get away with lying to us this time. We're going to make him blink, ready or not. We're getting this over with, so we can go back home and be with our friends. There's no way we're coming back to this dump next fall. Case closed."

"How is your prank going to do that?"

Voices in the other room.

"That's them. We're screwed," Preston exclaimed breathily. We got to get out of here." He gathered up the folders.

"I'm not finished looking at it," Gabe said.

"You can come back and look at it again after you do the job. If you do it right, we'll have more work for you. Give Jim or Rory a heads up when you got the job done."

Preston opened a door, they all ducked in, he shut it behind them. They were in a bathroom.

Gabe heard people coming into the office where they had just been. At the other end of the bathroom was another door. Preston led them out into what looked like their parents' bedroom, through the kitchen, around and out the front door into the hall.

Gabe and Henry ran to the elevator. Gabe caught his breath as they descended rapidly.

At the entry, the doorman said, "Careful out in the street there boys. Some of those hooligans are starting up with fireworks early this year."

Gabe and Henry hurried silently up Cabrini Boulevard.

As soon as they were out of sight of Monarch Towers, Gabe blurted, "Why did you take that paper bag with the envelopes from him?"

"I thought that's what you wanted to do. You didn't?"

"I don't know, I'm not sure, maybe."

"Well, it's done now," Henry said.

"Do you think they're really going to arrest everybody?"

"Maybe. Those guys are really crazy."

"I wonder what's inside those envelopes."

"I got something else, too." Henry lifted his shirt. Besides the brown paper bag, he had a file folder stuck into his pants.

"What's that?"

"Monarch Towers."

•

# CHAPTER ELEVEN

When they arrived at the hideout, the others were anxiously waiting for them.

Elkie burst out, "What did they say? Tell us everything."

Gabe began, "They said they're going to round up a lot of people in the neighborhood and put everybody in jail. Not everybody, but a lot of people, the ones who are on the list."

"Why?"

"That's just what they do," Gabe replied. "That's what they said."

"Drannily's a P-Man," Henry said. "Their dad's a P-Man too. They're running the school. They got files on everybody. They decided the school and the whole neighborhood's full of all these subversives and they're going to put them all in jail. That's what they said. Me and Gabe, we saw our files and they said we're on the list."

Gabe said, "They're going to arrest Mrs Hopper and some of the teachers."

Kelly said, "Which ones?"

Henry said, "He said they keep changing their minds."

Gabe said, "We're not making this up. We heard them talking about some of this stuff in Drannily's office too, and we wrote it up on our V-Pads."

Jack said, "They can put my family in jail any time they want, it's okay with me."

"They won't get me," Roco said. "No jail can hold me, I'll break out."

"Are they really going to put kids in jail?" Kelly asked.

Gabe nodded. "That's what they said."

"They won't put kids in jail," Elkie said.

"Yes they will," Henry said. "This is serious. They're coming for us."

"How about Odelia, are they going to arrest her?"

Gabe said, "Maybe. They weren't sure if she was on or off the list. They're going to arrest all the teachers on the list. They said it keeps changing."

"Maybe we should tell Miss Odelia," Elkie said.

"Are you crazy?" Roco said.

"Who's on the list? Are we on the list?" Kelly asked agitatedly.

Gabe replied, "We don't know about you or anybody else, but me and Henry are on it for sure. Our whole families are on it. That's what he said. We didn't see the list. He said he couldn't find it. But we saw our files."

"We got to warn everybody," Ari said. "We got to warn our families."

"I don't get it," Jack said. "This don't make any sense. Why did they tell you all this stuff?"

Henry said, "He was trying to scare us."

"They want us to do something for them in the office," Gabe replied.

"What?"

Henry pulled out the brown paper bag.

"What's in there?" Roco asked.

Henry turned it over. "Don't nobody touch anything." Out tumbled a pair of thin leather gloves, three birthday-card envelopes, and two five dollar bills.

"Look, there's money." Jack picked up one of the five dollar bills.

"I just told you not to touch it."

"Well, it's too late now." He held the bill up to the light.

"Don't touch anything else."

Gabe said, "I didn't see Preston put that money in that bag. Did you?"

Henry shook his head. "He's slippery." He reached in his pocket, rolled a cherry bomb onto the rug. "He's peddling these. He's got a whole big sack full of them."

"You still got one?" Gabe said, "I threw mine off the roof."

"I didn't throw mine."

"I hope mine didn't hit a bird."

"Anyway, he wants us to sell these for him," Henry continued.

Jack picked it up. "What's our cut?"

"Seller keeps a nickel apiece."

Jack said, "That's a good deal. We can sell tons of them."

"No way. We don't need his money," Henry said.

"We need money," Jack said.

"It's a trick," Roco said. "He's got something up his sleeve. It's a set up."

Henry said, "Let's see what's in those envelopes." He slipped on the gloves, lifted the envelope marked McKlosky in letters cut from newspapers:

Inside was a note:

WE kNOw

ALL

AbOUT YoU

He set it on the rug, then opened the envelope to Drannily, and placed it on the rug next to the other.

BeWARE

the SecreTARy

IS NOT yOUR FrieND

WaTcH YouR  StEP

And the note to Hopper:

YouR DOCtOR

is  POISoNinG

YOU

"What do they want you to do with those?" Kelly asked.

"Stick them in their desk drawers," Henry replied.

"Do you remember which one goes in which?"

"I think so. I don't know if it matters."

Roco said, "Are you going to do it?"

Henry said, "We can stall them for a while."

"If we do it," Gabe said, "they're going to take our families off the list. At least that's what he said."

Elkie said, "They're just trying to get you in trouble."

"Why don't they do it themselves?" Jack asked. "Why do they want *you* to do it?"

"Cause we're in the office," Henry replied, "and they're not. That's what he said. He also said this isn't the end, he's got other stuff he wants us to do. He thinks he's got us hooked. He's just playing with us."

"If you take his money," Ari said, "he's your boss."

Gabe said, "Let's not do it. Let's give him back his money,"

"That's bunk. You should do it," Roco said.

"Why?" Henry said.

174

"For fun," Roco said. "If you don't want to do it, I'll do it. Just to see the look on their faces."

Jack said, "I'll do it too. I'll do it with you, Roco. We get to keep the ten bucks, right?"

Gabe said to Henry, "What do you say?"

Henry said, "Okay. It'll be easy to do. Hopper's a cinch. She's never there. Drannily and McKlosky are trickier."

Gabe said, "We can figure something out."

Henry opened the file folder. "Look at this. We stole their plans." Henry pulled out the architectural drawings, unfolded them, and spread them out on the rug.

Everybody gazed at the drawings.

Ari said, "You got this from Preston?"

"He don't know we have it," Gabe replied.

Roco said, "Do you understand this stuff?"

Henry pointed, "This is before and after. There's Cabrini. There's the wall. There's the Little Woods. And there's Monarch Towers' new apartments right on top of the Little Woods."

Page by page they went through the file. There were lots of pages, some of them with no drawings, just full of legal stuff. Gabe didn't understand a lot of it, but some of it he did, or thought he did.

"Look, this one says something about Drannily."

"What does it say?"

"I read it over a couple of times. It don't make sense."

•

When Gabe and Henry arrived at the office the next day, Drannily was preoccupied at her desk for a long time. They worked quietly on their erasure project until she finally went out into the hall. Gabe kept chickie while Henry slipped the note into her desk.

The door between offices was ajar; no one was in Hopper's office. Henry scurried in and slid the envelope through the narrow space above Hopper's center desk drawer.

He hurried back, took off the gloves and slipped them to Gabe.

From inside the clouded glass door of Drannily's office, Gabe watched the moving shadows of foot traffic filing back and forth past the secretary. McKlosky's desk was right out there in the outer office where everybody came and went, and she was almost always sitting at it.

When things looked momentarily quiet out there, Gabe stuck his head out of the door. "There's a big bug on Miss Drannily's desk."

The secretary made a face, stood and hurried inside. "Where is it?"

Henry said, "It just flew into Mrs. Hopper's office." He led her through the open door, into the adjoining room.

In the secretary's alcove, Gabe pulled the envelope out of his pocket.

McKlosky perused the principal's office. "I don't see it. Do you?"

"I saw it a minute ago," Henry said, "but I don't see it now."

McKlosky shook her head. "I'll notify Mr Grayley. He'll take care of it."

She returned to her desk.

A short while later the school bell rang, ending recess. As Henry and Gabe passed her on their way out, they mumbled, "Good afternoon, Miss McKlosky."

"Good afternoon, boys. Have a wonderful afternoon. See you tomorrow."

•

That very same afternoon, Grampa Benjo entered Mrs Hopper's living room, overlooking West 166th Street.

"This is a cozy little pad."

"I moved here after Duncan passed. To be closer to the school."

"How's the grandchildren? How many do you have?"

"Five. Six. I keep losing count. You just have that one, Gabriel. Right?"

"Sorry he's giving you a rough time"

"It was serendipitous. Without him, you and I might not have connected again. He hasn't given Miss Drannily any more trouble, at least nothing I've heard about. Although I haven't been around the school a lot lately. Doctor's orders."

"You looked a little under the weather when I saw you in the office. You're looking a lot better today."

"Oh it's these stupid meds I've been taking. All these side effects. Don't tell my doctor, but I got fed up and stopped taking them two days ago, and now I feel much better. They make my tongue numb. When I take them, I have to struggle just to talk. I get that lisp, that infernal whistle, you must have noticed it. I can't control it, and that makes me so anxious."

"You're not whistling now. Aren't there any other meds they could give you?"

"Those seem to be the only remedy they have for my blood pressure and cardiac condition, according to them."

"Your heart?"

"It's not life threatening, I just need to keep it under control."

"Well if it was me, and if I was feeling better without my meds, I'd probably just try it for a while without them and see what happens."

"I don't know what to say to my doctor. He's so solicitous. He's always calling me in for more tests, and he never fails to ask me if I've been taking them. And Maude, the vice principal, she's been such a life saver, asks me almost every day if I've taken my pills."

"If it was me, I'd get another opinion."

"I probably should. Duncan always said his meds were killing him, and maybe they were."

"He was a good guy," Benjo muttered.

"He lived a full life. Those were good times."

"They certainly were. Before the war."

"My granddaughter—she's twelve—her class was studying the Great Depression, anyway she asked me about the nineteen thirties, and I said something like, those were good times, and she just thought I was crazy. How I could say that? How could it have been a good time, with all that suffering? Even now it sounds a little crazy when I say it, but I know you understand."

"I understand exactly."

"None of us had much, but everybody was helping each other, everybody believed better times were coming, we were all working together for a better world. It was an exciting time. A time of hope. Almost anything seemed possible. We really believed that." Helen shook her head. "I could never have predicted the world we're in today."

"Who could?"

"Sometimes I look around and wonder, is this is what all those people died in the war for? But we're not allowed to wonder about things like that these days, are we? Maybe

I shouldn't have said that. Can I still trust you? Can I can still confide in you?"

"Helen!"

"They're investigating me. They've interviewed me twice. They keep asking me about Duncan and the Alliance, all those things he was doing—we were doing—with the Alliance in the thirties."

"None of it was illegal then," Benjo said.

"Duncan wasn't involved with anything I don't know about, was he? If he was, don't tell me, I don't want to know. They've sent an agent into the school to try to turn all the pupils into spies."

"I know. Gabriel brought home one of those Vigilante Pads. Actually, that's the immediate reason I'm here, besides wanting to get to know you again, of course."

"I take full responsibility. I apologize. I never should have let them bring those disgraceful things into the school. But I've been gone so much, I've missed a lot of what's been going on, and Maude has been running everything. Thank goodness for her."

"How did it happen?

"It started with the PTA. I guess all this stuff coming out of Washington about subversives lurking in every shadow scared some parents, so they called the IPA and convinced Maude. I just didn't have the grit to fight them all. Fortunately, the V-Pad program is over and done now, and we can move on."

"Those spy pads are over? That's not what Gabe says. He says they're going to be doing them for the rest of the year."

"He's mistaken. The program is terminated."

"Are you sure?"

"Of course. I haven't been into the office since last week, but Maude keeps me fully informed, and I've heard nothing to the contrary. It was just a one week program, and it's over and done. Oh dear, it's getting late. A few teachers from the school are coming over to discuss an upcoming PTA meeting, and I need to make some preparations. I expect there'll be a big uproar about those V-Pads. A lot of parents are upset about it. But in this political climate I don't know what to expect. It's the annual meeting next week. Are you planning on attending?"

"I can't say I've ever gone to one of those things."

"They're usually pretty routine. Ordinarily you might not find them very interesting. But I expect some people will be harsh on me for letting the program into the school, and it would help to have friends there." She stood.

"I'll try to make it."

She stepped into the small kitchen, opened the refrigerator, took out a tray, set it on the table, and removed the wax paper covering. "Would you like a canapé? Chicken salad."

"Looks good. But, you know, I'm a vegetable now."

"I'm sorry, I forgot. I have another plate with celery and cheese. I'll go get it. Didn't you once have a chicken farm in New Jersey? Or am I remembering that wrong?"

"No, that really happened."

"It's so different from your old union job. How did you become a chicken farmer?"

"See, when I came here from the old country, I saved my pennies. I was never planning on working in a sweatshop my whole life. A lot of the guys were all talking about, you know, five acres and independence. The union was even behind it. Well I got a deal on seven acres, so I thought I was on easy street, but unfortunately it turned out that all the chicken farmers were going bottoms up."

"How could you be both a chicken farmer and a vegetarian?"

"That chicken farm is what made me into a vegetarian."

They both laughed.

"Do you still have the land?"

"I still got it, but I'm just hanging on by a thread. After the farm failed and I came back to my old job here in the city, for a long time the land taxes were almost nothing. I still stay out there part of the year. Gabe's spent summers there ever since he was little, and it means a lot to him. He has a harder time here in the city. Now the land's all at risk, they're trying to take it away."

"What's the problem?"

"I don't really understand all this legal stuff. The words they use, it's like a secret language, nothing ever means what it usually means. I think they're just coming after me."

"Why would they do that?"

"Maybe for the same reason they brought those V-Pads into the school. Anyway, I really still love that land, and I don't want to let it go, I want to pass it on to Gabe someday. Oh, by the way, Gabe wanted me to ask you about Fort Tryon Park and Monarch Towers."

"What about them?"

"Somehow he thinks you can tell them to not build more apartments there."

"It's not Fort Tryon Park where they want to build, but on that empty lot on the block before. The school actually does have some influence over its land use. You can tell Gabriel that I have no intention of signing off on its change of use. It's wonderful to have such a beautiful wild place so close to the school, just to walk along, even if we can't go down into it."

"Well, thanks for your hospitality, Helen. I'm on my way right now for a walk in the park myself. If you weren't busy, I'd ask you to join me."

"Another time, hopefully soon."

# CHAPTER TWELVE

The next morning at the gate, Jim slipped up to Gabe and Henry.

"Preston wants to talk to you." He motioned down the block.

They moseyed over.

The first bell rang, the kids pressed toward the door.

Preston was slouching in the shadows of an alley.

"You should have heard them squawking at our house last night. Well done. They're all at each other's throats. From now on you're our eyes and ears in the office. Tell Jim and Rory everything you see and hear. Act like you don't know me. We don't want anybody seeing us talking."

"Whatever you say, Preston," Henry said.

"Did you take our families off the list?" Gabe asked.

"Don't worry, they're off, at least for now. You don't got to thank us."

The second bell rang, the doors opened, the kids funneled inside.

•

Later, as they approached the office, Miss McKlosky the secretary had a crazy look on her face, and was whispering intensely into her headset.

Inside Drannily was wringing her hands, her eyes darting around the room. "I have a special job for you boys today. Mrs Hopper is on her way over, after being out ill, and I need a festive treat to welcome her back. I want you to go down the block to Griswald's and pick it up. I already called them. You know where the bakery is, don't you? Just tell them I sent you. Here's your pass, and don't lose it."

She gave them each a pass, a special piece of paper that said they were on a school errand. Griswald's was a couple of blocks away.

The streets were empty, except for a few old people. It was exciting being out there when all the other kids were in school.

Over at the bakery, instead of getting right in line, they took their time examining the amazing treats in the glass cases, so many different shapes and colors, each pastry tempting in different ways, with little icing swirls teasing Gabe's desires. Finally they got in line, and when it was their turn they told the lady in the pink apron and hairnet that Miss Drannily had sent them. She said, "Here is what she ordered: two Napoleons," and handed Gabe a small pink cardboard box.

They strolled back along the street. They were in no hurry. Gabe set the box on the fender of a parked car, lifted the tape and opened the top. Lots of flaky layers and yellowish creamy stuff. A little of the cream was bulged out on one side. Gabe scooped off some with a finger. Vanilla custard. Henry scooped some off too. Now it looked like somebody had messed with it. So, to even it up and make it look better, Gabe smeared the side of the pastry with his finger. He retaped the box closed again, and licked his finger again.

Back inside the school, they approached the office. Miss McKlosky was still at her desk with her headphones on. Her eyes were shut, she looked like she was listening to something.

They walked past her, into Drannily's office. No one was there.

Voices from Mrs Hopper's inner office. The door was ajar. Hopper was standing at her desk. Drannily was on the other side, arms folded. They were preoccupied with each other, and didn't notice Gabe and Henry come in. Gabe was holding the bakery box.

Hopper was mad. "Why did I have to hear about this from the teachers?"

Drannily leaned toward her, looking grim. "I assumed you would approve."

"Well, I don't, and don't tell me you didn't know that. You can't just sign off and extend a program like that without my approval. We had that discussion many times."

"I've done my best to fill your shoes while you've been ill."

"The V-Pads were not your decision to make."

"I apologize for my enthusiasm."

"And why in the world are you helping those real estate people? Why do you care about that empty lot?"

"It may have been hasty but it's done now."

"I'm informing the superintendent that both of those were approved in error."

"If you understood the situation, you wouldn't do that. You're not thinking clearly. Helen dear, calm down. Have you been taking your pills?"

"Why are you always telling me to take those pills? I've stopped taking them. Someone just warned me I'm being poisoned by my doctor. Maybe they're right. Strange things are happening in this school."

"Oh dear, perhaps you should sit down. Do you want me to call your doctor?"

The secretary poked her head in. "Excuse me. Mrs Golman, Mr Stoloff, and Mr Blinka are here."

They all entered.

Hopper set her arms akimbo. "If you're here to gang up on me, it won't work. Miss McKlosky, show them out."

The secretary didn't respond.

Drannily said, "Mrs Hopper and I were just discussing why the VIP Program had to be extended through the end of the school year."

Stoloff muttered quickly, "It was necessary and inevitable."

"Let's just accept it," Golman added.

Blinka stroked his mustache. "I'll lay it to you straight, Principal Hopper: The VIP Program is part of an open investigation, and hindering an investigation is obstruction of justice."

"Whatever do you mean?"

"I think we understand each other. You're getting near the end of your game."

"Sherrie, Maud, what is he talking about?"

Drannily pounced. "You filled this school with radicals and subversives. You brought them in. That's how the troubles here began."

"Whatever are you talking about?"

"You know exactly what we're talking about," Blinka said. "Just can the act and come clean. We got more than enough evidence. We all know what you're hiding."

"I'm not hiding anything."

"We fully understand why you did it. You were vulnerable," Blinka continued. "Cooperate with us and we'll go easy on you. Just give us names. We'll put them away for a long time. They had you over a barrel, didn't they? They threatened to expose you. That's blackmail."

"You think I'm being blackmailed for something? How could I be blackmailed? I have nothing to hide."

"Your husband's radical associations."

"My husband has been dead for over ten years."

"You still have close personal associations to them to this day."

"If you mean the Alliance, yes, my husband worked with that organization. It was part of his work with his union. I was there too. Those were the nineteen thirties. Nobody was hiding anything, we were proud of it."

"So you admit he was a member."

"Don't play that game with me. That's absurd. Even if he was a member, so what? What if he was?"

"So you're finally admitting what you denied twice to federal investigators. That's perjury."

"What am I guilty of? Associating with my husband? Associating with my own teachers? I'm a public school principal, not a spy."

Mrs Golman, who had stood there quietly, intoned, "As PTA president, it makes me sad to do my duty, Principal Hopper. You've broken the public trust. I call on you to resign."

Hooper shook her head in disbelief. "I never expected this from you, Irene."

Mrs Golman looked away.

Stoloff said, "You can't continue in your position now. You need to resign."

Hopper turned to Drannily. "Maude, aren't you going to say anything?"

"What can I say, Helen? You're ill. You've brought this on yourself. You're under so much stress. Perhaps it's best if you don't attempt to finish the semester." She turned to the others. "Please excuse her. She hasn't been taking her pills. That's probably why she's been so uncooperative. She's not thinking clearly. Before you arrived, poor dear Mrs Hopper even claimed that her own doctor is poisoning her."

They all smiled.

Stoloff held out a piece of paper. "It will be better for everyone, including yourself, if you sign this."

Hopper said, "Get out of my office. All of you."

None of them moved.

Hopper continued, "I'll never resign. I'll fight you every inch of the way." She stormed out of the room.

Drannily, Blinka, Golman, Stoloff, and the secretary all stood there for a few moments, looking at each other.

Blinka bared his teeth. "They always hang themselves."

Drannily scrunched her nose. "Perhaps this could have been accomplished some other way. I only hope those pills you told the doctor to prescribe haven't done any permanent damage to her brain."

The secretary jumped in. "Whatever are you talking about, Miss Drannily?"

"No one was speaking to you, Miss McKlosky," Drannily intoned. "You may return to your desk now. I need to speak with Mr Blinka, Mr. Stoloff, and Mrs. Golman alone."

"She stays," Stoloff interjected. "We need her here. There are matters we need to get moving now. That PTA meeting is Thursday."

"On the contrary," Drannily insisted. "Certain items need to discussed only in a confidential setting."

Blinka said, "McKlosky has clearance."

"What does that mean?" Drannily said.

"You can speak freely in her presence."

"Frankly, Miss McKlosky has lost my confidence."

"You don't understand." the secretary said.

"No, you're the one who doesn't understand. You don't need to pretend. Do not play dumb with me, do not trifle with me. I know you're not my friend. Leave the room, now. This is not your affair."

The secretary exclaimed, "The Dictaphone is still on."

Everyone stopped short.

"Oh yes," Drannily muttered. "The Dictaphone. Of course."

Golman said, "For goodness sake, turn it off!"

The secretary scurried out of the office and returned a few moments later with a funny-shaped thing with little spools of wire. "It's all here."

"I'll take that." Drannily grabbed the cartridge from the secretary's hand. "I need to review it."

Blinka reached toward her. "That cartridge is evidence."

Drannily clutched it to her chest. "I'm the one who'll have to answer to the school board for Helen's dismissal. I need to review what was said. It all happened so fast. I need to clarify my memory."

Stoloff said, "Then let's play it now. Let's all listen to it."

"I need to do it alone, so I can focus. Just give me an hour."

Blinka said, "I'm afraid, Miss Drannily, that's not possible."

The secretary gasped loudly.

The others turned toward her, then all saw what McKlosky was staring at.

Gabe held up the pink cardboard box. "We brought you your stuff from the bakery."

"How long have you two been in here?" Drannily enunciated, her expression changed to horror.

"We just walked in," Henry replied.

Nobody said anything.

Finally Blinka muttered, "We'll be back in an hour."

As they exited, Drannily followed them to the door, shut it behind them, and let out a deep sigh.

Gabe handed her the pastry box. She set it down and laid the cartridge next to it. She opened the pink box top. With a long thin fingernail, she scooped a little custard off of the side of the many-layered flaky pastry, then licked it off with satisfaction. "Didn't they give you napkins?"

"No, Miss Drannily."

A rapping on the door. Stoloff stepped back in.

"What do you want?"

"We need to talk." He waved a finger at Gabe and Henry. "You two, out."

"Don't you boys dare move," Drannily commanded. She riveted her gaze on Stoloff. "These boys are under my supervision, not yours."

The secretary reentered. "Sorry to bother you again, Miss Drannily, but the school board attorney is on the line."

Drannily quickly picked up the phone, began talking tensely, in a hushed shrill tone, swiveling back and forth in Mrs Hopper's big chair. She waved her hand dismissively at Stoloff and McKlosky, then pivoted away from them to face the window overlooking the yard.

Stoloff looked around nervously, then left; the secretary followed him out.

Drannily glanced back over her shoulder at Gabe and Henry, who were still standing beside her desk. She held her hand over the mouthpiece. "Back to your erasures." Then she turned to the window and started whispering intensely again.

Henry nudged Gabe.

Gabe hesitated, then grasped the cartridge, stuck it under his shirt, and followed Henry out.

In the adjoining office, they quickly slipped the cartridge under a book pile.

A short while later, the door burst open.

Drannily looked frantic. "Did you take something out of the other office?"

"No, Miss Drannily."

"Did you see Mr Stoloff or Miss McKlosky pick up something and carry it out?"

"No, Miss Drannily," they both replied.

•

# CHAPTER THIRTEEN

Evening in their apartment was usually so pleasant. Miss Chloe Drannily prided herself in always doing what it took to keep everything nice. She received that gift from her mother, while her big sister, whom she otherwise admired to death, inherited a different set of qualities from their stern father.

Chloe usually tiptoed around when Maude was out of sorts, but today she couldn't avoid the unpleasantness. Miss C. set a cup of steaming spearmint tea on the small table at her sister's end of the couch, and a cup of chamomile at her own end.

"Maude, tell me what happened."

"I already told you, Chloe."

"Oh, Maude."

"Put on some Chopin. Please."

Miss C. chose a piano Nocturne. She lay her head back on the dusty sofa and let the familiar passages flow in. As the passion of the music intensified and climaxed, Chloe felt increasingly brave.

"For goodness sake, Maude. What's going on? The whole school is shaken."

"I wish I could tell you."

"You know you can tell me anything. I forgive you in advance."

Miss M. spoke like a bursting dam. "They are removing her of course. I love her dearly, but she brought this on herself. She filled the school with them. All her protestations won't wriggle her out of this. Her involvement with those radicals is a matter of public record. She even admitted it, right in the office. We recorded it secretly on the Dictaphone. Got her dead to rights. Mr Stoloff and Mrs Golman and Miss McKlosky witnessed it."

"They recorded Helen? On the Dictaphone? Is that legal?"

"Of course it's legal. Mr Blinka arranged it. It's one of their latest advances for collecting evidence. It's called an operation. They set her up. It was very exciting. Mr Stoloff and Mrs Golman and Miss McKlosky and I were what they call players."

"They did that right in the office?"

"They've been recording in the school for months."

"Then those rumors are true. I never believed them. Why didn't you tell me?"

"To protect you. I've wanted to tell you, but they made me promise not to. I'm sorry. I thought you wouldn't approve."

"Of course I don't. Have they been recording the teachers too?"

Maude clenched her jaw. "They've done only what was needed."

"So they're going after the teachers too?"

"At least five will be removed with her. You can guess the ones."

"That's excessive, to say the least. They're all good teachers."

"Oh, Chloe, you're such an innocent. It's both your strength and your albatross."

"Maude, stop talking to me like this is your grammar class. Talk to me like a regular person." Chloe was starting to get mad. "This is serious."

"Good teachers do not bring subversive ideas into the classroom."

"What in the world do you mean? From all I've ever seen, every one of these teachers and that group of theirs, they all actually hold very traditional values. Even Daddy would not disagree with most of the things they say."

Maude stomped her foot. "Chloe, that is unworthy of you! We live in a bleak, difficult time. Those people are trampling every ideal, every value that Daddy held dear, that you and I grew up with, every code of character, of conscience, of conduct, of morals, as... as so much garbage. Maybe you've given up hope, but I cling to those ideals. I cling to those values."

"Oh Maude, get off your high horse. For once, open your mind. It was a grave mistake to bring that government man into the school."

"It was unavoidable. Helen was dragging the entire school down. I refused to let her."

"Helen has been principal for over six years now, and never once did you ever say any of these things about her until Mr Stoloff and Mrs Golman came into the school last fall. Listen to me for once, Maude, for God's sake. You've let them cloud your thinking on this entire situation. They've distorted your perspective."

"On the contrary," Maude snapped. "Everyone thinks that Mr Stoloff and Mrs Golman brought in Mr Blinka, but in reality, Mr Blinka brought in Mr Stoloff and Mrs Golman. And I brought in Mr Blinka."

"Whatever do you mean?"

"They're all government agents. Even Sherrie, I think."

"Miss McKlosky?"

"I think she is at least. The others I know for sure. I'm almost certain Mr Blinka arranged for Mrs Golman and Mr Stoloff to take over the PTA. Remember when the last secretary suddenly quit last fall? McKlosky was here the very next day. I think Mr Blinka arranged it. He got rid of her and sent in McKlosky. I don't trust her. She knows everything that goes on in the school. She's a hawk. She's up to no good. She's got an agenda. I wish I could just dismiss her."

"You're letting your imagination run away with you."

"Not at all." She reached into her purse. "I found this in my desk drawer." She handed Chloe an envelope.

Chloe's eyes narrowed as she read the words. "This is ridiculous. *Beware. Watch your step.* Why would Sherrie want to harm you? Who could it be from? Did you inform the police?"

"No."

"Why not?"

"I told you, I think she's a government agent, she's one of them. I've been very trusting toward her. I haven't been watching my words around her at all, have you? I don't know whom to trust now. I'm sure my desk drawer was locked. Someone must have the key."

"Let me get this straight. You were upset with Helen because you disagreed with the way some teachers were conducting their classes, so you reported her to the federal government, and they sent in Mr Blinka, and he brought in Mrs Golman and Mr Stoloff, who are really government agents, along with Miss McKlosky."

"That's more or less it."

"Why didn't you just bring your concerns to the superintendent?"

"They don't listen."

194

Chloe took a sip of tea. "I'm speechless, to say the least. Why would the federal government go to all this trouble over Columbus School?"

"I'm afraid we may be caught up in something bigger."

"What?"

"Something in Washington connected with those Senate hearings. I don't know. I don't understand everything that's going on. It may be spinning out of my control. Oh, it's a slippery slope."

"What in the world were you trying to accomplish?"

"I just wanted to push her into early retirement. I thought it would be best for her. I never dreamed it would come to this."

"Don't tell me now that you want to be principal in Helen's place."

"No, no, nothing like that."

"Then why push her out? I thought she was doing an excellent job before she took ill."

"I suppose I have to tell you. Remember last year before we moved in here, the property manager was telling us about the new development? Well I promised him that the school would not oppose it. I had to say that. He was going to give our apartment to somebody else. How do you think we got such a deal?"

"We never should have moved in here."

"You were right, I should have listened, we should have stayed on Pinehurst and moved into one of those rent-controlled units. I yielded to temptation. I should have told you about this, but I was just trying to shield you, Chloe dear. What do I know about these things? It seemed just like ordinarily standard procedures. The property manager kept pressuring me about it. God knows I tried to talk reason into Helen, but she was never willing to listen."

"So you told them she's a subversive because she wouldn't approve some real estate deal?"

"She is a subversive. Her husband was at least. I did not make that up. This all didn't have to happen. No one had to lose. Helen can be so hard headed. She gets such fixed ideas into her head. Foolish. She almost dares you to break her will. It would have cost her nothing. Everyone would have won. She simply refused. And now look where we are. If she would have simply agreed last fall, everything would have been fine, and none of this would have happened. This was the only way left to me. The development will improve the neighborhood. That stretch of sidewalk is isolated and dangerous."

"So you signed off on the construction project in her absence, and Helen found out about it. Was that what she was so nettled about today?"

"That and the V-Pad program. She started arguing with me about it. I should have said nothing, In the heat of the moment I forgot that the Dictaphone was on. I forgot to be careful about what I was saying, she drew me into it. And now I might have put us in jeopardy."

"How?"

"By some things I said that they recorded."

"What did you say?"

"I'm not sure. I wanted to play it back and listen to it afterwards, to know for sure what I said, but they wouldn't let me. It makes me nervous. I had the cartridge in my hand. Then there was some kind of confusion, and they took it. Which they deny. McKlosky or Stoloff, one of them took it. I think it was McKlosky. I could kill her. Now they're saying I took it. I don't know what they want. They're playing with me."

"Playing with you?"

"That's what they do. They go around collecting information, and then they play with people. I've seen Mr Blinka do it. Help me with this, Chloe, don't blame me. We can't let the building manager think that I've reneged on his deal, or that I've talked to any of the government agents about what Monarch Towers has been up to. The last thing they want is for the government to put them under a microscope. I think they've got many ghosts in their closet. We've got to stay on good terms with them all, if we want to get through this. We've got to stay on their good side. They've got a lot on money at stake, Monarch Towers does. According to the building manager, that land is worth almost nothing as an empty lot, but for apartments it's worth a fortune. I promised him I'd keep this quiet."

"What could they do to us?"

"What do you think? They could put us out in the street."

•

James J. Blinka, Community Operations Specialist at the Manhattan district office of the Internal Protection Agency, was on his way to meet with his immediate supervisor, Miss Rebecca Unter-Tractole. He arrived in the building a few minutes early. He had to decide whether to dawdle in the downstairs lobby or wait in the reception area outside her office on the thirty-sixth floor. He knew that Senior Analyst Unter-Tractole would keep him waiting for at least ten minutes no matter what.

Why should he care? He was being paid for it. Still, she only kept him waiting to remind him of his position in the pecking order. He decided to arrive exactly one minute late.

He made sure that his watch was in sync with the big clock above the bank of elevators. He sat uncomfortably on the hideous lobby sofa, opened his briefcase, and pretended to peruse some papers. A number of people gathered at the elevator. At the right instant, he stood and joined the group.

"Thirty-six please," he said to the woman standing closest to the buttons.

Then wouldn't you know it, the elevator went down to the basement, then to the sub-sub-basement, and in both stops several people got on. The ride back up was excruciatingly slow, and by the time it got to Blinka's floor, he was alone in the car and over five minutes late.

He scurried down the hall and gingerly turned the handle.

Unter-Tractole's receptionist, a young man of unusual facial proportions, pretended not to notice him.

Blinka cleared his throat. "I believe I have a one o'clock with Miss Unter-Tractole."

"Be seated," the receptionist replied without looking up.

The minutes ticked slowly by. Thank god, he only had to endure fifteen more months to early retirement. He knew how to control himself. Finally the receptionist uttered, "Miss Unter-Tractole will see you now."

The window was behind her, the backlight casting her face in shadow.

"Hello, Blinka."

"Hello, U-T. How's it going?" Despite her austere exterior, and even though he hated her, he did not find her unattractive.

"What the hell happened?"

"Everything's fine. We're fortunate it was Friday. We've got the weekend to sort it out."

"McKlosky's cover is blown. Stoloff's and Golman's probably are too."

"We don't know that."

"Assume. Who slipped that note in McKlosky's desk?"

"Probably one of the union perps."

"And who mishandled the evidence?"

"The Dictaphone cartridge? Ask Stoloff. Or Golman or McKlosky."

"You're the project manager."

"I wasn't there."

"What's your best guess?"

"There were four people in the room besides the subject, and three of them were us. Drannily has to have it."

"So get it from her. You're her handler, for God's sake."

"Then let me handle her. I've got her under control."

"Did you get the cleaning lady in there?"

"She didn't find it."

"Did you search her apartment?"

"We did a visual. We're not ready to tear it up. At this point we don't want to lose her. She's already thinking of jumping ship. Anyway we don't think the wire's in her house."

"That lady's got you waltzing in the dark."

Blinka restrained himself. "We have limited leverage with her. We need her." He wrung his hands. He wanted to stick a finger in her eye.

"How, limited? We got a hook on her. Use it. Play her."

"I'm doing my best. She's slippery."

"The PTA meeting."

"Just unlucky timing. They schedule those things eight months in advance. Better not to shut them down. We can handle it. A few malcontents want to blow off steam. Let them. Hopper's not going to be there. As soon as she's suspended, the judge will give us a T.R.O. That'll keep her away from the school. If she shows up, she'll face time."

"She's not suspended yet?"

"I'm not a magician."

"When are they going to do it?"

"On Monday."

"Why don't they suspend her today?"

"The school superintendent is in Cape Cod. Don't worry."

The intercom light flashed. U-T flicked a switch.

A voice sputtered, "Mr Stoloff, Mrs Golman, and Miss McKlosky are here."

"Have them wait." She flipped the switch again and said to Blinka, "If all their covers are blown, then what?"

"Maybe we should send in replacements."

"Just listen to yourself, Blinka, sometimes you sound like the stupidest person in the world, or is that just an act? Do you really think we can just send in a new PTA president and vice president? And we need McKlosky sitting in the receptionist chair now more than ever. Otherwise it will be chaos."

Blinka clenched his teeth. "You're the boss."

U-T flicked the switch again. "Send them in."

Irma Golman entered, tense and stiff, followed by Sherrie McKlosky and Warren Stoloff.

U-T said, "Now that we're all here. You're better off falling on your swords than pointing fingers. Who didn't do their job?"

"I had nothing to do with it," Golman said quickly.

U-T held up the McKlosky note with a pincer. "This came back clean from the lab, except for Sherrie of course. *WE KNOW ALL ABOUT YOU.* So what does that mean?"

"It could mean anything, it could mean nothing."

U-T flared her nostrils. "It means they know you're Agency. How'd it get in your desk?"

McKlosky replied, "At least thirty people passed by. Any of them could have done it when I was away for a minute or I was distracted."

Stoloff said, "Whoever it was, they did it at this particular moment for a reason. It means they're running scared."

"Who's on your short list?"

"Batra, Grainger, Daumer, Larrosun, Odelia. You know the ones."

"Odelia has been pricing airfare to Mexico. She's a flight risk."

"What about Grayley?" U-T snapped.

"He couldn't have left the note. He wasn't around my desk."

"If they know you're Agency, it means there's a leak. How about Grayley for the leak? Grayley could be the leak."

"Maybe. He's spineless and he drinks."

Stoloff said, "How about Drannily's sister?"

"She's a mouse."

"She's a manipulator."

"Blinka, did you interview her sister?" U-T adjusted her small round glasses.

"Not yet. We're monitoring her."

"And?"

"Borderline."

"How about Drannily herself? Could she have left the note?"

McKlosky's eyes widened. "It's possible. She was acting strange all day."

"How, strange?"

"You should have seen the way she was looking at me. Suspicious. She never looked at me like that before. Then during the Hopper operation, she said something like, 'I know you're not my friend.' She said other things too. I don't remember exactly. It's all on the wire."

U-T said, "Not her friend? She must have heard some gossip around the school. Did you badmouth her behind her back?"

"Of course not."

"*Of course not,*" she mocked. "If I had a nickel for every time you badmouthed somebody around here, I'd be in Honolulu. Let's get back to the missing evidence. Blinka, you told Drannily that destroying evidence is a felony, didn't you?"

"Of course, but that didn't faze her. She's still claiming one of us took it."

"Well that Dictaphone cartridge didn't just vanish into thin air. Why in hell's name would she take it?"

"I think maybe she's worried about something she said on it."

"Like what?"

"I don't know," Stoloff replied. "Maybe something about Hopper's pills. She said something about the pills that I know is on that wire, something she shouldn't have said. Or maybe she's worried about something else. Drannily and Hopper were already arguing before Irma and I got there. We didn't hear the whole thing."

U-T said, "You were listening from your desk, weren't you, McKlosky?"

"Nothing stands out that I remember from before we entered the room. I've got to get a better headset. I need to listen to the wire again. She did say something about the pills. That raised red flags after we were all already in the room."

"What pills?" U-T threw out. "What did she say about pills?"

McKlosky glanced at Blinka.

Blinka said, "Don't look at me. You're the one who was there."

McKlosky said, "Somehow Hopper became suspicious about the pills. She said somebody warned her that her doctor is poisoning her. She didn't say who. Then after Hopper left, Drannily said she hoped they didn't cause any permanent damage to her brain. Drannily said something like that, and it was caught on the wire. She implied we knew the pills were fake and were causing the symptoms."

U-T scrunched her lips. "What pills? What symptoms?"

Blinka jumped in, " I didn't tell you about this, U-T, I didn't think it was necessary. Maybe it wasn't needed, but we wanted to get Hopper away from the school while we went after the teachers. Hopper kept throwing up obstacles. We got her doctor to put her on these pills. They just incapacitated her. They didn't do any permanent damage."

"Let me get this straight. You got Hopper's doctor to give her pills that made her sick."

"Right."

"Hopper found out about it. Drannily knew about it, and they both said something about it on the wire."

"Right, U-T."

"We can't play that for a grand jury," she enunciated. "That's tainted evidence. Any judge will throw us right out and hang us by our toes."

"It's only a few seconds in an otherwise great wire."

U-T bristled. "As soon as it's secured, send it to the garage. Get that part off, quick!"

"If we had the cartridge in hand," Blinka replied, "we'd wipe the slip and everything would be fine. But somebody let Drannily walk away with it and now she's got it hidden somewhere."

"Why's she playing it like this?" U-T asked.

"I don't know. She's probably trying to use it as leverage," Blinka replied.

"Leverage for what?"

"We haven't figured that out yet. There's probably some quid pro quo she wants that we don't know about yet. In the end she's got to produce it."

"Blinka, I want that cartridge in this office today. This is crunch time. If Drannily and her sister are implicated too, take them out with the rest."

Blinka stroked his pencil mustache. "We're better off not hammering Drannily too hard just yet. It could be counterproductive. We don't need that cartridge to indict Hopper. We've got plenty of other evidence against her. But we do need Drannily on board for the PTA meeting. With Hopper out, Drannily is acting principal. All the teachers are afraid to cross her. Get rid of Drannily, and we're hanging out there alone."

"If I may," Stoloff jumped in. "Drannily wants us to keep the lid on, take out Hopper now and wait till summer to go after the teachers. Other than the project manager..." He glanced at Blinka, "...the rest of us aren't buying that scenario for a minute. It just stalls out the whole operation. Unnecessarily. Otherwise, we're good to go. We can't wait for summer. We need to finish what we started. We've got the evidence. We've got them all dead to rights."

Blinka braced, expecting U-T to take Stoloff's side once again. For an instant the rumors about her and Stoloff crossed his mind, and he wondered if he could gain anything by making an oblique reference to them, but thought better of it. "Though you may find it hard to believe," Blinka responded, "I've actually grown fond of that school. Taking out those five teachers now will be a major disruption, and that will make us look bad. If we just take out Hopper now

204

and wait on the others, it'll be smooth, and we'll get all the perps in the end."

Stoloff was visibly fuming. "Wait till summer if you want, but don't expect me to be around. I'm out of here at the end of the school year. That was our agreement. When I took this assignment, U-T, you promised it would end with the school year. This has involved our whole families, and has placed a lot of stress on my marriage. On Irma's marriage too, but she can speak for herself."

Unter-Tractole held up her palms. "Slow down, Stoloff." She shifted her gaze to Blinka. "What is the reason for this investigation? In a nutshell."

Blinka replied, "We all know, so why ask?"

"Maybe some of us are thick. Assume I'm stupid. Spell it out for me. What is the reason for this investigation?"

"To expose subversion in the school system."

"Specifically?"

"To root it out in Columbus School."

"Do you agree with that assessment, Stoloff?"

"More or less."

"Golman?"

"Yes."

"McKlosky?"

"Of course."

"And who is behind this subversion, Blinka?"

"Hopper."

"Be specific."

"Columbus School is deeply infiltrated by the Social Action Alliance, by radicals, facilitated by Hopper. We've proven that beyond any shadow of a doubt."

U-T flared her nostrils and emitted a deep sigh. "Give me a break, Blinka. The Social Action Alliance couldn't infiltrate their own toilet. Just labor flunkies and armchair revolutionaries, who go around spouting harmless garbage, organize an occasional futile march or rally, a stupid panel discussion on some topic that nobody cares about or goes to. Nobody takes them seriously."

"If I may disagree with you, U-T. Many of their events are actually very well attended," Blinka rejoined defensively. "They're on every subversive list. And it's not just the school. The entire neighborhood is riddled with their cadre. They've got the tenants up in arms. We hear it from all the supers. They're organizing rent strikes. This is real."

U-T took off her glasses and sighed. "Do you seriously think Washington has gone to all this expense just to see a few union simps quietly removed during the summer? Let's cut the crap. The reason for this investigation, in a nutshell, is to satisfy some politicians. And what they want is to see the papers full of pictures of subversive teachers marched out of their classrooms by men in blue uniforms, with their desk drawers seized as evidence."

•

# CHAPTER FOURTEEN

Foxx hobbled slowly along the sidewalk, a cane in one hand. Miss Daisy walked beside him, their arms linked. Mom and Benjo followed behind, and Gabe hopped along at the rear.

"Oh fudge," Mom exclaimed. "I think I might have left the kettle on."

"You worry too much," Benjo replied.

"I always make a final check, but I skipped it, we were in such a rush. Now I'm not sure. I have to go back and check. I'll catch up with you."

Benjo stopped. "You go on. I'll go back."

Mom said, "No, I'll go back. I'm kind of tired anyway. I think I feel a cold coming on. I might just lie down. Do you want to come back with me, Gabe?"

"I'll stay with Grampa."

Foxx and Daisy were stopped a ways ahead. Gabe and Benjo caught up with them.

Foxx said. "Sorry I'm such dead weight. Making you late."

"We're not late."

"Damn sciatica. Just lean my corpse up against a wall. I'm not going to be much help."

"Nobody's going to abandon you," Daisy said.

On the street in front of Columbus School sat several police cars. The school doors were wide open, a crowd arriving from all directions. People were handing out flyers to the grownups.

It was packed. They edged their way into the auditorium. Men with cameras on tripods blocked the aisles, policemen lined the back of the room, and more cops stood in a line down front.

Gabe said to Benjo, "I'm going to go say hello to my friends."

"Don't go out of sight."

"I'll be right over there."

A few other kids from his class. Kelly was across the way, trapped with his family. Finally Gabe saw Henry with his gramma, and caught his eye.

Miss C. hit a chord on the piano, played 'Glory, Glory, Hallelujah', took an appreciative bow. Onto the stage strode Miss M. Drannily, followed by Golman and Stoloff. She stepped to the podium, blew into the mic, and started talking.

Henry met Gabe in the aisle.

"Kelly's over there, stuck with his folks."

"See anybody else?"

"Ari's aunt, I think. But Ari and Elkie aren't with her."

Drannily finished thanking outgoing PTA president Golman and vice president Stoloff for their numerous incredible contributions to Columbus School under such difficult conditions, then she yielded the podium to Golman.

Golman began, "First on the agenda are several reports on our accomplishments this year, before we get to what most of you have come for, nominations and the election of next year's officers."

Someone shouted, "We're here about the spy pads. When are we going to talk about that?"

"If you mean the VIP program, it will be covered in one of the reports, and after the election, time is allotted for discussion."

"Some of us can't wait around all night to talk about it. Tomorrow's a work day. Why can't we talk about it now?"

A person shouted out, "What happened to Mrs Hopper, where is she?"

Another voice, "Where is Mrs Hopper? We want to hear from Mrs Hopper."

Golman replied, "The agenda has been posted. That is standard procedure."

Someone shouted out, "Reorder the agenda."

"I'm afraid we can't do that. We have too much to cover."

"You've put those spy pads at the end because you don't want us to talk about them."

"Nothing could be farther from the truth."

"Then reorder the agenda. Let's talk about it now."

Golman said, "That's not possible. We will proceed with the meeting."

People from the audience kept shouting out, while Mrs Golman tried to maintain order.

Stoloff and Golman exchanged words to one side, then Drannily joined them and the three huddled.

Golman stepped back to the mic. "I'm afraid I must officially deliver the sad news. As many of you have apparently heard rumored about, Mrs Hopper has been suspended from her duties, and Miss Drannily is now acting principal."

Gasps and cries went up around the room.

Drannily took the podium. "We will weather this crisis. None of this will affect any of the pupils. No one need worry. The school is in strong hands now."

"What happened to Mrs Hopper?"

"Where is she?"

"Why was she suspended?"

"We can say no more about this, it involves confidential personnel matters."

A woman stood. "That is utter nonsense. There's been all kinds of crazy things going on in this school, and we here have a right to know what's been going on."

"We want to hear from Mrs Hopper. Why isn't she here speaking for herself?"

Drannily snapped, "We can't interfere with an ongoing investigation."

Many people started talking at once.

"Come to order. We can't proceed unless you come to order." Mrs Golman banged a hammer on the podium.

"We want Hopper. Where is Hopper?"

"Why isn't Mrs Hopper here?"

Stoloff said, "She's not here because there is a court order against her coming within a hundred yards of the school!"

"Why?"

"Why was she suspended?"

"Who suspended her?"

"The school district suspended Mrs Hopper because—and you must know the unvarnished truth—because she has been implicated in subversive activities."

Grainger and Daumer, the two teachers' reps, who had been standing silently to one side until then, rushed the podium. "That is not what happened! Those accusations are false, and you know it."

Everybody started talking and yelling at the same time.

"Let's get out of here," Henry said to Gabe.

"Some of this is interesting," Gabe replied.

"It's just grownups yelling at each other. Let them kill each other. I got a Spaldeen. Want to go into the hall?"

A gasp went up. The room was suddenly silent. Mrs Hopper stood near the back of the stage.

Hopper enunciated in a loud clear voice, "I intend to answer you all personally, tonight, about what's been going on, whatever the consequences."

Gabe and Henry left the auditorium. In the corridor near the main entrance, they began playing box ball using the cracks in the concrete floor for the lines, while people were still pouring into the building, trying to squeeze through the doors into the packed auditorium.

"There you are." All of a sudden Jim was beside them. "Preston's been looking for you," he said in a low voice. "We've got an action planned."

"An action?"

"Just stay right here. Don't go anywhere. I'll be back. We'll let you know what to do." Jim disappeared into the auditorium.

Gabe said, "Let's go."

"Where?"

"Anywhere he won't find us."

They ducked into the stairs alcove, down the flight to the basement.

At the bottom landing they heard voices. The basement door was open a crack.

It was Mr Grayley and Mr Blinka. They could see them through the crack.

Grayley said, "I don't know why it didn't buzz."

They were both holding walkie-talkies.

"You don't have it turned on."

211

"Yes I do."

Blinka pushed a button on his handset, and Grayley's buzzed.

Blinka said, "That means it's working now. Make sure you keep it on. We've got a very volatile situation up there, and we need to keep all our options open. Stay on ready alert. No more guzzling. Understood?"

"I haven't touched a drop."

"You smell like a brewery."

"I don't feel real good about this," Grayley said. "Why don't you just do it yourself, from up there? You'll have more control that way. You don't need me to do it down here. You can kill the lights from that bank of switches right up there. And there's a fire alarm up there too."

"Where?"

"In the back of the auditorium, just to the left as you go in. Do you want me to show you?"

"Make it quick."

They disappeared out of the line of sight.

Gabe could hear the elevator door open and close, and the gears grinding.

Henry pushed the door open some more, peeked into the basement. "They're gone." He opened the door wide.

"I don't like this. Let's go back upstairs," Gabe breathed.

"In a minute. Keep chickie." Henry started poking around the room.

"C'mon, let's go. What are you doing?"

A sound behind him. Gabe wheeled.

Preston stood at the foot of the stairs, with Jim and Rory. "Now, isn't this perfect? The fun continues." He snorted.

212

Gabe said, "They'll be back any minute. They just went up in the elevator."

"Who?"

"Mr Grayley and Mr Blinka. We got to get out of here before they get back."

Preston muttered to Jim and Rory behind him, "Shut the door."

Rory closed the door to the stairs.

Preston stepped over to the electrical bank on the wall near the coal pile, and put his hand on the largest switch. "When I flip this baby, it'll be the end of their little party upstairs."

"Do it, Preston," Rory said.

"First we're playing gumballs. Jim, give our friend Gabe some ammo."

"We're not working for you," Gabe said.

"Leave us out," Henry said.

Jim held out a handful of cherries. Gabe didn't move.

"Rory, show our friend Henry a shovel."

Rory picked up a shovel that had been leaning against the wall, and held it out to Henry.

Henry didn't take it. "What are you going to do with those cherry bombs?"

Preston grinned. "Don't play dumb. You taught us this little trick. We're going to bury the treasure in the coal pile."

Gabe exclaimed, "Do you want to blow up the school?"

Preston replied, "You *are* clever. We don't have such ambitious dreams. When these blow, it's just going to be a lot of noise, pop their ears out, big bangs, let them know we're out here watching, let them know we got their number, remind them of what they deserve, give them a little taste of

213

justice. What are you worried about? You'll be far away when they blow."

Henry said, "Why don't you just do it yourself?"

Preston replied, "We can't leave you out now, even if we wanted to. You know that. You're in this up to your necks. You know too much. Once you're in, you're in. Besides, this game is so much more fun this way. Let's get pranking."

Henry said, "We're not playing your game."

"You're playing all right," Preston said. "Want your families back on the list?"

Gabe said, "But what about Mr Grayley?"

"What about him?"

"What if he shovels some into the furnace?"

Preston pondered an instant. "Well, if he's stupid enough to do that, maybe that poor fool shouldn't have been working here."

"Why are you even doing this?" Henry said. "Why don't you just go back to where you really live and leave us alone?"

"Don't worry, we'll be gone, we're out of here. They're playing their last cards in that disaster upstairs. It's all over for them. This is just a victory celebration, a little kicker, a goodbye present from us, to show our appreciation."

Jim said, "Stop fooling with them, Preston. We got no more time for cat-and-mouse. We got to get this done."

"Okay, time to play gumballs," Preston said. "This is it. Let's get to work and have some fun."

Gabe heard the elevator gears starting to grind.

Preston continued, "Don't just stand there. Take those cherries. Bury them in the coal pile. Grab that shovel. Jim and Rory, help them out. Let's get going."

To Gabe's surprise, Henry replied, "Okay, Preston, you're right." He grasped the shovel, then looked at Gabe. "Don't just stand there. Take those cherries. Let's get going. This is going to be fun."

Gabe was stunned. Jim dropped a handful of cherries into his palm.

Henry stepped to the coal pile, slid the flat shovel blade along the floor into the coal, scooped up nuggets and dust. "Right, Preston, just like you said, we'll give them what they deserve, a little taste of justice."

The elevator door opened. Mr Grayley stepped out, looking down at his walkie-talkie, and did not notice them. Grayley muttered into the receiver. "Yes, I can hear you, Blinka."

Henry heaved the shovelful of coal and dust into Preston's face, lunged at the electrical bank, threw the light switch. Blackout.

Gabe hesitated a second, then hurled the cherries against the wall. Explosions rocked the room.

They broke toward the exit door, through it, into the schoolyard. The fire alarm went off.

In the dark, Gabe felt someone grab him by the neck. They were punching him.

Preston spat, "You're dead." Shadows ran across the yard, out the gate, and disappeared.

Henry came up to Gabe. "You okay?"

"Kind of. I think so. You?"

They circled around to the front. People were pouring out of the darkened building in panic, into the street.

"I better find my gramma," Henry said.

"Wait. You got coal dust all over you." Gabe dusted him off some.

Gabe looked around for Benjo, but didn't see him anywhere.

The crowd opened for an instant, and Gabe caught a glimpse of two small girls in pajamas.

The wall of bodies closed back around the girls. It happened so fast that a minute later, Gabe wasn't sure of what he'd seen. He could have sworn he'd seen Elkie and Ari.

Benjo appeared, with Henry and his gramma.

"There you are," Benjo said. "I was starting to worry about you."

"I'm okay."

"How would you feel about going home with Henry and his gramma for a little while? And I'll pick you up at his house later. I got to go somewhere now."

"Where are you going?" Gabe asked.

"I'm going to be hung up with stuff about Mrs Hopper for a while. I got to help her. She's got a problem. I can bring you home first, if you want."

"I'll just stay with Henry."

Henry's gramma said, "We go to sleep early. Better he spend the night."

"Sure it's okay? I bet they'll cancel school tomorrow anyway. I'll tell his mom and dad what's happening."

Benjo disappeared into the crowd again.

Gabe walked down the block with Henry and his gramma.

When they got to Henry's basement, his gramma said to Pimple Simon, "Heaven knows what's been going on in that school."

Pimple Simon said, "What about those two little girls?"

"What girls?"

"It's all over the radio. They took 'em. Right out of their room, right here up on Fort Washington Ave. Stabbed the uncle with an ice pick and took the girls. Got something to do with that principal who was causing all the trouble. Radio said it was whatever they call them, those subversives. They're holding them for ransom."

Gabe ducked with Henry into his room.

Henry said, "My gramma always goes to sleep around now. Pimple Simon's probably going to watch wrestling. My mom's out working, and when she works nights, she's usually gone all night."

A short while later they were out the window, hurrying along the block, trying to keep in the shadows. The school was still surrounded by police cars with lights flashing, people mulling in the street.

·

# CHAPTER FIFTEEN

In the dark the Little Woods felt very different, invisible creatures prowling the bushes, sounds they never heard in the day. They stepped cautiously along the obscure trails. Gabe kept telling himself not to be scared. They knew the terrain so well, they could navigate it.

They finally got to the hideout. The small lamp was on, casting long shadows. Ari and Elkie, in their pajamas, were huddling inside Girls House.

"Did he hurt you?" Henry asked.

"He didn't get a chance to. I stuck him with my pencil," Ari said. "It went right in. I killed him."

"Don't say that." Elkie hugged her rag doll.

"I thought I'd be glad when he's dead, but I'm not."

Henry said, "He's probably not dead."

"Then he's going to try to find us."

"We won't let him come near you," Gabe said.

Elkie said, "He thought we were asleep, but we never sleep when Ari's auntie's not there. We were ready for him. We always keep sharp pencils next to our bed. We heard him come in."

"How'd you get out?" Gabe asked.

Ari said, "We climbed down the fire escape. First we went looking for my auntie at the school, but everything was crazy there, so we came here."

Elkie stroked Ari's arm. "We'll take care of each other."

"They're all out there looking for you," Henry said. "It's on the radio."

Ari said, "They're not going to catch us, we're not going back."

"I'm cold," Elkie said.

Ari wrapped her in a blanket, and crawled in with her.

"Try to get some sleep," Henry said.

"Can you bring us a cookie?" Elkie asked.

After a while, Gabe and Henry laid out some blankets and stretched out on the rug. The ground was hard and lumpy. The rug wasn't much of a cushion.

Many hours later, Gabe woke with Henry shaking him.

Henry said, "We got to get back to my house before my gramma's up."

Gabe felt groggy, stiff, achy. He hadn't slept much. Light filtered in through the slits.

They peeked into Girls House, where Ari and Elkie lay sleeping, enfolded in each other's arms.

"We'll be back later," Gabe said in a low voice.

Elkie stirred, made a small groan, eyes still shut.

Gabe and Henry stole though the streets, as police cars cruised by.

Finally in Henry's room, they kicked off their shoes and climbed into bed.

The next thing Gabe knew, Henry's gramma was saying, "Gabriel, your grampa's here."

As he'd predicted, Benjo said that school was cancelled.

Gabe and Benjo walked down 181st Street.

Benjo said, "That was pretty nuts last night."

"I guess."

"I haven't had a wink, how about you?"

"I slept a little."

"I had to go downtown with Foxx and some other folks, helping out Mrs Hopper, and it took pretty much all night."

"Is she in jail?"

"She's back home now. They're charging her for disobeying some court order to stay away from the school. But I don't know what's really going on. A lot of people are trying to figure that out."

"Is she still our principal?"

"She's what they call suspended. I guess you must have heard about those girls in your class."

"What about them?"

"What they must be going through." Benjo shook his head. "And their families. And now they're trying to blame the Alliance. There's no connection, they're just making it all up, to muddy up the water. What an insane world."

As soon as Gabe walked in the door at home, he started working on his mom.

"Please, Mom. I've got to go. I promised Henry."

"I don't want you out on the street alone. It's dangerous out there. Those girls from your class are still missing."

"We won't go out in the street. We'll just stay in Henry's house and play in his room."

He kept hammering at her, and finally wore her down.

Mom went next door, where they had a phone, called Henry's neighbor, who went and got Henry's gramma.

Then Mom said to Gabe, "I'll walk you there."

"I can get there by myself."

"You are not going into the street alone."

Dad yelled from the other room, "He's ten years old, for Christ's sake. Let him grow up."

Mom insisted on walking him to 181st Street, then let him go the rest of the way by himself.

A short time later, Gabe and Henry were slipping out of Henry's room through the back way.

They scuttled cautiously along Fort Washington Avenue, and in no time they were crawling through the secret entrance into the hideout.

All the others were already there.

"Everybody quiet down," Henry said. "This is an assembly. What are we going to do?"

Roco said, "We don't got to do nothing. They'll never find them here in the hideout."

"Yes, they will," Jack said. "They'll break down the door and drag us all out."

Kelly said, "Maybe it might be better if you just went back now."

Ari said, "I'm not going back."

Elkie said, "Neither am I."

Kelly said, "You know they're going to find us. What do we do then, when they're banging on the door? We can't fight them."

"Why not?" Jack said.

Henry said, "The hideout's too close to the school. We got to get you further away."

Roco said, "I got a cousin down on 157th Street, where I hide out sometimes. They'll probably let you stay there for a few days."

"That's not far enough." Jack said. "You got to get out of the city, into some other state. The police can't follow you there."

"Why can't they follow you?"

"That's just how it works. Those are the rules for when you're making a getaway. If you can get across some line in the road, into a different state, like Connecticut or Long Island, then the police can't follow you any more and they got to stop and turn around, and you've made your getaway. That's just how it works."

Henry said, "I know somewhere you can go."

"Where?" Ari said.

"To Gabe's grampa's old place."

Gabe exclaimed, "To Maroon?" He wasn't ready for this, even though he realized he should have been.

Henry continued, "Gabe's grampa used to be a farmer. It's out in the country, across the bridge, in Jersey. It's a different state, it's across the line. Nobody lives there now. You can hide there. We can hide you there. They'll never find you in Maroon. Me and Gabe were going to go there anyway this summer. We'll just go a little sooner than we planned. Gabe's been out there lots of times, haven't you, Gabe?"

"Yeah," Gabe said. "Lots of times."

"What's it like?" Ari asked.

"It's really nice," Gabe replied cautiously. "There's a little yellow house with a red roof, and fields all the way to the crossroads. It's full of forests all around there. The big pines are right behind the old chicken coop, and they go on and on, it's a whole pine forest, and there's a stream, you can really hear it babble, and a pond with frogs and skeeters and little sunfish and white water lilies, and stuff. But I don't really know if the house is still even there, or what's still there and what isn't there, because my grampa says, and my mom says it too, some guys are knocking it down."

Henry said, "That don't matter. If the house isn't there, we can hide in the chicken coop, and if the chicken coop's not there, we'll go into the forest and build us a tree house where nobody can find us. Me and Gabe already been talking about this for a long time, right, Gabe?"

"Yeah. Maybe we'll build a tree house," Gabe said.

"What did you call this place?" Ari asked.

"Maroon."

"What a funny name."

Elkie said, "That's my favorite color."

"It's not maroon the color," Gabe explained. "It's maroon like on an island. Like when your ship hits a rock, you swim to an island, and you're marooned. But marooned in a good way, because you never want to be found or come back."

"That's not marooned," Elkie responded. "That's the opposite of marooned."

"No it's not."

"Yes it is," Elkie said. "If you don't want to be found, it's the opposite of marooned."

Gabe said, "Then it's the same opposite thing."

"What does that even mean?"

Ari said, "How will we get there?"

"We got a map," Henry replied. "Gabe got it from his grampa. Where'd we put it?"

Gabe ran over to a box of stuff near the bug zoo, rummaged through it, returned with the map and spread it out.

Henry pointed. "Here's the school. Here's the bridge. We go across and turn here, and go down this road, and then go this way, and then that way, and that way and then there we are, in Maroon."

"It looks far," Elkie said.

"It looks further than it really is," Henry said. "That's just the way maps are."

223

Gabe said, "It's not that far. My uncle always drives us there in his car."

"Your uncle's not going to drive us," Ari said. "How will we get there?"

"We'll walk," Henry responded. "We'll leave early. We'll have all day to get there."

Gabe said, "Maybe somebody in a car will see us and stop and give us a ride. Out in Maroon all the kids just stick out their thumbs and people give them rides. They call it hitching."

Ari said, "I'm not getting in a car with somebody I don't know."

Henry said, "Once we're out of the city, you don't got to worry about that. Everything's different out there, right Gabe?"

"Right. It's not like here in the city. Everybody knows everybody else out there. Everybody helps each other out there. The country kids will help us."

"You're sure we can trust them?" Elkie asked.

"They won't snitch on us. They're not snitchers."

"We'll need money," Ari said. "We've got to bring some money."

"We won't need money there," Henry said.

"How will we even eat?" Ari said.

Henry said, "They got farms all around, right, Gabe? Everywhere it's not forest, it's farms, so there's plenty of food around, you can just go into the fields and take it, nobody cares. And the stores don't make you pay."

Gabe said, "Well, there's a store up on a hill a ways away down the road, and the store lady lets you take things and pay some other time."

"It's almost the same thing," Henry said.

Elkie said, "What if on the way there we get hungry, we'll need to buy lunch."

Jack said, "We got two five dollar bills right here."

Gabe said, "That's Preston's money. We're giving it back. We can't just keep it."

"Why not?" Roco said.

Elkie said, "How are we even going to get to the bridge from here if all those policemen are all over, looking for us."

Henry said, "We got to take our chances. We'll go in disguise."

"We don't have any clothes here," Elkie said, "except dress-up clothes."

"We'll get you clothes," Gabe said.

"Get food, too," Ari said.

Henry said, "Our worst chance of getting caught is in the neighborhood streets on the way to the bridge. But we don't even got to go through the streets. There's another way to the bridge. Along the highway. There's lots of brush and weeds on the sides, to hide us. That's our best chance."

Ari took both of Elkie's hands in hers. "What do you want to do?"

Elkie said, "I don't know. How about you?"

They were nose to nose.

Ari said, "I didn't think we'd ever escape him, but we did. We can do it again."

"Do you think we really can?"

"We have to."

Elkie nodded. "Okay, let's do it."

Ari said, "Let's take our chance."

Elkie said, "Let's go to Maroon."

Henry said, "So who's all going? Who's in? If you're in, say so now."

225

"Wait a minute," Jack said. "Everybody's got to be in. We all got to go."

"Why?"

"I don't like the idea of somebody not coming."

"I don't either," Roco said. "Everybody knows where we're going. We can't leave nobody behind."

Henry said, "We got to trust each other. We're all in this together."

Gabe said, "I'm in."

"You know I'm in," Roco exclaimed.

"Don't worry about me," Jack said. "I'm in."

"So am I," Ari said.

"I'm in too, Elkie said.

"I'm in," Kelly said.

A silence fell over them.

Roco said. "What are we waiting for? Let's get our stuff together, and get out of here. I'm not wasting another minute in that stupid school."

"Slow down," Henry said. "We got to do this right. We got to get everything ready. We got to lie low here till things cool down in the street. It's going to take us a few days to get ready."

Jack said, "So what's the plan?"

Everyone looked at Henry, but he said nothing and looked at Ari.

Ari finally said, "Everybody gather up everything you need, and bring it all here. We've got to be organized. We need a list of stuff to get and who's going to get it. Everybody's got to take a job."

"I'll make a list," Elkie said.

"We need more money," Jack said.

Ari said, "Everybody get all the money you can find and we'll pool it all together, so we have it when we need it."

"We're going to need it," Jack said.

"I know where to get some money," Roco said.

Jack said, "Where?"

"From my uncle's wallet."

Elkie said, "Don't steal from your family."

Roco said, "Why not? He's the worst person in the world."

Elkie replied, "It's not right. If you steal from him, maybe you'll steal from us too."

"Don't say that," Kelly said. "That's bad luck."

Ari said, "Everybody just scrape together as much money as you can. We'll pool it all, and however much it is, it will be enough."

Henry said, "Bring it all here, whatever you want to bring to Maroon, bring it to the hideout. When everything's here and we're ready, we'll all leave the house in the morning just like we're going to school. By the time they figure out we're gone, we'll be in Maroon. We'll have the whole day to get there. What do you think?"

Jack said, "It's a plan."

Roco said, "That's cool."

Ari blurted, "But I love my little auntie. She already hurts so much, I don't want to hurt her any more. She's probably going crazy worrying. She probably thinks we're dead. I've got to let her know we're okay. I can't just disappear forever."

Elkie said, "You're right. We can't just run away and disappear."

Ari said, "I've got to send her a note."

Elkie said, "We've all got to tell our families something. And what about the other kids, and the neighborhood people? It's not right for us just to escape to Maroon by ourselves. A lot of them never even heard about those files or that list, or Preston's dad coming to get them. We've got to warn them all. They don't understand what's going on."

Henry said, "We'll tell them. We'll warn them."

"How?"

"Me and Gabe collected a ton of evidence from the office. We got it all in a box. We just got to figure out what to do with it."

"And what about the Little Woods?" Elkie exclaimed. "Who's going to take care of the Little Woods, who's going to save it from Monarch Towers when we're gone?"

"We'll do it. Somehow we'll do it all," Henry responded. "We don't got to figure it all out now. Once we're in Maroon, we'll figure it all out."

•

Columbus School was almost empty on Monday. A lot of kids didn't show up, and neither did some teachers. Miss Odelia seemed all freaked out. They didn't do much all morning.

When the recess bell rang, Odelia said to Gabe and Henry, "Miss Drannily is not going to need you two today. You can go to recess with the rest of the class."

They joined the others in the yard, playing dodge ball.

Both were hit and taken out pretty quickly, and wound up standing to one side watching.

Henry said, "Do you want my fish? Pimple Simon will dump them in the toilet as soon as I'm gone. Maybe your mom will feed them."

Gabe thought a minute. "Are you sure?"

"Of course I'm sure. Otherwise, I wouldn't ask."

"All of them? Even the angel fish and neon tetras?"

"Otherwise, I'll bring them back to the pet shop."

"Okay, I'll take them. What about the strays? Who's going to feed them? How about the cat lady in your building?"

"She's too old. She never goes out any more. They'll just have to fend for themselves."

"What if nobody feeds them and they die?"

"They know how to take care of themselves, probably more than we do."

Gabe said, "How about we let all the bugs loose from the zoo today?"

Later in the hideout, Elkie said to Gabe, "How long does it take for the postman to deliver a letter, from when you put it in the box?"

Gabe shrugged, "A couple of days, I think. You're mailing it to your mom in the hospital?"

She nodded. "That nurse is mean. Do you think she'll throw it away?"

"I don't know."

"I bet she'll just throw it away. Are you going to write something?"

Gabe said, "Maybe."

"What are you going to write?"

"I don't know yet. Maybe nothing."

Jack said, "I'm not writing nothing. They won't even notice I'm gone."

"Mine won't miss me," Kelly said. "That's for sure."

Gabe struggled with his note. He started three times, writing as neatly as he could manage, then tore them all up. He thought he knew what he wanted to say, but when he read

229

it over, it didn't sound very good, it wasn't what he really meant, so he kept writing it over, trying to say it in a better way.

He wrote, *I am running away for a while. They have got a big file on us. I saw it. Our family is on the list, but I did not see the list. I did not repeat anything I heard anybody say at home. Please do not let them put you in jail. I will find you and come and visit you.*

He added a reminder about feeding the tropical fish, and corrected the spelling of a couple of words. Then he read it over again, decided that it wasn't what he wanted to say, made a big X across it, wrinkled up the page and tossed it.

Kelly said, "Anybody want to play pick-up-sticks?"

Gabe and Elkie joined him, but they were abstracted, and played listlessly.

Kelly said, "Do you think we're going to make it there?"

"Where?"

"To Maroon."

"We'll get there," Gabe said.

"What do you really think?"

"I don't know."

"Something keeps telling me I'm not going to get there," Kelly said. "Something keeps telling me I'm never going to get across that bridge."

"Don't say that," Elkie said. "Nobody wants to hear to that."

Kelly said, "Do you ever get a feeling like you're not going to live a long time?"

"No. How can you even talk like that?" Elkie replied.

"I do, sometimes."

Elkie said. "You're weird."

"I know. I guess I'm just weird. Sometimes I wish I was somebody else, but I'm not, I'm just me."

"We like you just like you are," Elkie said.

"I keep having this dream," Kelly said.

"What dream?" Gabe asked.

"A bad dream. I had it twice last night."

"I have bad dreams sometimes too," Elkie said.

"I don't even like going to sleep now, 'cause I know it's out there. I don't like thinking about it either. Everybody's in it. I don't remember everything about it. We're on our way, we're half way there, we're up on the bridge, and then they catch us."

Elkie said, "Is that how your dream ends, when they catch us?"

"They don't catch me. I jump into the river."

"That's a stupid dream," Elkie said.

"I know."

"Do you drown?" Gabe asked.

"No, I wake up. But, you know, if we do get up on that bridge in real life, and they do catch up to us, I just might do that, I might just jump off into the river."

"Don't you like being alive?" Elkie said.

Kelly shrugged. "Don't you ever wish you were dead?"

"No," Elkie replied.

"You would if you lived in my house, with my family, you'd wish you were dead."

"This is your house now," Elkie said. "You don't live there any more. You live with us. We're your family."

Henry and Roco brought over the cardboard grocery box where they kept the Dictaphone wire cartridge, the file folder on Monarch Towers, and all the V-Pads where they wrote them up.

231

Henry said., "What should we do with the evidence?"

"I don't know," Gabe replied. "What do you think?"

Henry said, "I don't know."

Roco said, "I don't know."

Nobody else said anything.

Finally Gabe said, "My grampa's got a friend they call Mr Fox, and I think he knows a lot about what to do with stuff like this. I can leave it for him in my grampa's room."

Gabe and Henry packed the bug zoo into cardboard boxes, carried it all outside. They headed toward the meadow.

At the foot of the elm, Gabe said, "Remember that big white pelican? I wonder where he is now."

They opened the jars one by one, let all the bugs go free.

On the way back, they passed a familiar spot.

Henry said, "Isn't this where we buried that little garter snake?"

"Yeah, under that rock. I wonder if he's still there."

"Probably just his skeleton by now."

"Do you want to turn it over and see?"

"No."

"Remember how those chickadees attacked that hawk?"

•

The streets were more dangerous to navigate now. Alarm was everywhere. Grownups eyed them suspiciously. Everyone was on the lookout. They had to be extra cautious in the Little Woods, not to be seen by people looking down over the wall or driving on the highway.

They brought in food and clothes, stocked up on everything they could think of, all they might need, packed their bookbags and backpacks for the escape.

They took shifts climbing up to the lookout stations, where they could see through the ventilation slits facing west toward the highway, south toward the bridge, north toward the Little Woods. Police cars cruised slowly by on the highway. Helicopters circled the area.

Ari's uncle came on the radio with the mayor, pleading with the kidnappers to let the girls go, and the mayor called him a hero. The radio stations kept bringing on different people to talk about the kidnapping and their theories of what happened or didn't happen and they made a big deal about it.

Ari started crying. "I got to tell my auntie soon."

Elkie rubbed her back and comforted her. "Did you finish your note?"

"No."

"Well, finish it. I'll finish mine too, and we'll put them in the mailbox on the way to the bridge. Then they'll know we're okay."

Nobody felt much like playing. Everybody was just mulling around. Tension hung thick in the air.

Jack and Kelly slipped in through the secret entrance.

"There's a reward out for you," Jack spurted.

"A reward?" Elkie said.

"There are kids from school all over the neighborhood out looking for you right now."

"It's true," Kelly said. "I was in the candy store, and they had the radio on, and I heard it on the radio. They're all talking about it."

Jack said, "They're paying twenty-five dollars to any kid who brings them a clue."

"They said a thousand dollars on the radio."

"Twenty five is the word on the street. We sure could use that money," Jack said. "How about we give them an old shoe or something, tell them it's a clue."

"Are you out of your mind?" Henry said.

Roco said, "That is really stupid."

"Not as stupid as seven of us running away on twelve dollars."

"We got more than that now," Ari said.

"About seventeen dollars, I think," Gabe said.

"How much we got, exactly?" Jack said. "How much is in the kitty?"

"It's over seventeen," Ari corrected. "We just counted it an hour ago."

"So how much do we got?"

"Seventeen eighty-three," Ari said.

Jack said, "Well, where is it? Bring it over here. Let's count it again, where everybody can see it."

"Don't you trust me, Jack?" Ari opened her backpack, pulled out an old half-pint milk carton, and dumped the money out onto the rug. "Count it, Jack. It's all there."

Jack counted the money. "This isn't enough for all of us to run away on. We're going to spend it all in no time."

Henry said, "We just need enough for the road, just to get us there."

"Don't you like to eat?"

"If you're hungry," Roco said, "eat a cookie."

Jack said, "Hey, this is no joke. This is risky. I'm putting myself on the line with you guys."

"We're doing it too," Roco rejoined.

Jack said, "Kelly, what's seventeen eighty-three divided by seven?"

Kelly scribbled on the back of a comic book. "It doesn't come out even."

"Approximately."

"Two-fifty, plus a little more."

Jack said, "That's all we got, two-fifty each."

"We're not going to divvy it up," Ari said.

Jack said, "Do you just want to just carry it all yourself?"

"It's not a lot of money, and it all belongs to all of us," Ari replied. "We've got to keep it all together. We all need to decide how to spend it."

Jack came back, "What if we don't agree?"

"You're always making things hard, Jack," Elkie said.

Henry said. "Let's cut it in half, let's cut the money in half, and two people can carry it. Then if somebody loses it, we'll still have half."

"Okay," Jack said. He picked up the money and started counting it into two piles. "Me and Ari will carry it."

Roco said, "You can't carry the money, Jack. You're always losing things."

"No more than you."

"And you can't add," Roco said. "What did you get on the last arithmetic test?"

"You can't even do batting averages."

Henry said, "It don't matter who carries the money."

"Yes, it does," Elkie said.

Gabe said "Let's just leave it all in one place for now."

"That's a problem," Jack said.

"Everything's a problem with you, Jack," Roco said. "You're always making problems, you're always making trouble out of nothing."

Henry said, "Cool down, Roco."

Jack almost yelled, "Do you want to be out there starving to death?"

Henry said, "What are you so hot about, Jack?"

"Why are you taking sides?"

"I'm not taking sides."

Roco said to Jack, "If you're too scared to go, just say so."

Jack replied, "Don't mess with me, Roco."

"If you're looking for excuses, if you don't really want to come with us, get out now."

Jack said, "Maybe you're the one who better get out."

"Nobody's getting out," Henry said.

"I didn't join the gang to have Roco lording it all over me."

Roco said, "Sorry you joined, Jack?"

"I'm not playing around with you."

"I'm not playing with you either."

"Don't get me started," Jack shouted.

"You started it."

Jack lunged at Roco, and suddenly they were rolling around on the ground fighting. Jack was on top, the money scattered in the dirt.

Gabe and Henry pulled him off.

Henry said, "Why are you guys fighting? You can't act like that."

"Now you're telling us how to act!" Jack shouted. "Who made you the boss?"

"I'm not the boss. But we all got to act right," Henry said.

Roco, still lying on the ground, said, "Yeah, you got to act right, Jack."

"You're the one who got to act right, Roco," Jack spat.

"Maybe you should be the boss, Jack."

"Maybe you should be the boss, Roco."

"Well, it's sure not going to be you."

"Cut it out, you guys," Ari interjected.

Henry said, "Nobody's boss. We don't have a boss. We don't want a boss."

Roco stood. "Maybe you shouldn't come with us, Jack."

"You want to kick me out, Roco? Is that what you're saying?"

Henry said, "Nobody wants to kick anybody out. We're in this together."

"Right," Roco said. "Nobody can get out now."

"Now nobody can get out?" Jack said. "Who decided that?"

"That's just the way it is," Roco said. "We don't want somebody out there squealing on us."

Jack shook a fist. "Don't mess with me. I'm going to kill you."

Henry said, "Don't talk crazy."

Jack wheeled to face Henry. "I thought we were friends, Henry, I thought you and me were friends!"

Jack lunged, knocking Henry down, jumped on top of him and held Henry's wrists.

Henry said, "I'm not fighting you, Jack."

"How do you like it now?"

Gabe yelled, "Everybody, calm down."

"Get off him," Ari shouted. She picked up the cookie jar and held it in front of Jack's face. "Let him go or I'll break this on your head."

Jack loosened his grip and stood.

Everybody was quiet for a few moments.

Jack said, "Why is everybody so serious all of a sudden? We were only kidding around. Right, Henry? Right, Roco? We're pals."

•

Preston Stoloff leaned against the fence near the swings in Bennett Park playground. From his vantage point, he could see everyone entering and leaving. Jim and Rory slowly circulated around the paths. Jim flipped Preston a hand signal, and Preston replied in kind.

Jack appeared at the east entrance by the stairs and continued around the path to the swings.

Preston said, "You hang with Henry."

"I used to, sometimes," Jack replied.

"Are you in his gang? Who's in his gang? How many in his gang?"

"He don't got a gang. That's just dumb talk. He just wants everybody to think he's got a gang. It's a big bluff."

"What do you want?"

"I heard somebody's looking for kids to sell cherries."

"I heard that too. Probably those kids from Broadway. I don't see them around here today."

"That's too bad."

"How many cherries you want?"

"I don't know. A bunch."

"On the street, they're a quarter a pop. The deal is, you buy ten for two bucks, that's what I heard, then you sell half and get your money back. It's a good deal."

"If you see them, tell them I'm interested, but I don't have the two bucks right now. Do you think they'd give somebody the cherries, then when somebody sold them, he'd pay?"

"I'll ask around."

"Another thing, how about that reward?"

"What reward?"

"You know, for the girls. Are they still giving that out?"

"For a clue. You got a clue?"

"What if somebody had a clue but he didn't want anybody to know it was him, could he get the reward?"

"I think that could be arranged."

"How much is it again?"

"Twenty green."

"I heard twenty-five."

"We're not going to quibble."

"How would somebody know he wasn't going to be cheated?"

"Somebody might get a down payment." Preston tucked a couple of cherries and a dollar bill into Jack's tee shirt pocket.

"You sure?"

"Don't worry about it. Just tell somebody to bring us the clue, and he'll get the rest."

"Maybe I'll tell somebody."

"Somebody knows where to find me."

As Jack left the playground, Preston signaled to Jim and Rory.

"Shadow him."

An hour later, Jim and Rory were back.

"We lost him in Fort Tryon Park. He disappeared into the bushes, down where the path curves around toward the highway."

"Do you know where he lives?"

"I think so."

"Get me a piece of his clothing, his cap, a handkerchief, anything. In a paper bag. Don't touch it with your hands."

•

# CHAPTER SIXTEEN

Warren Stoloff handed the wine glass to Irma Golman. They sat on the couch in his long, high-ceilinged living room, overlooking the majestic Palisades.

She swirled it, admired the liquid legs on the inside of the long-stemmed glass, brought it to her nose, took in the subtle aromas. "Nice. What is it?"

"Chateau Lafleur."

"Reminds me of St. Emilian."

"A close cousin. *Á votre santé!*"

They clinked glasses.

The wine circulated smoothly around Golman's palate. "Excellent." She sighed. "I needed that. Has U-T ever been up here before?"

"No. Why?"

"She's going to be jealous as hell of the view."

"You think?"

"Maybe you should pull the drapes shut."

Stoloff stepped to the window and pulled the cords. The drapes slid from both ends to the center, closing off the large panes of glass.

"How about we exchange drafts of our reports for comments before we turn them in? Just to make sure we're in sync."

"Absolutely. You never know who's going to read them. How are you concluding?"

"In my report or just between us?"

"The report."

Stoloff smiled tensely. "Of course I've been telling U-T the facts, but in my written report—it gnaws at me to give Blinka any credit—in my written report I had to conclude that the program was a limited success. I'm recommending improvements to roll it out better in other schools."

"Maybe I should tone mine down too, in line with yours. I mostly blame Blinka too. If he had rolled it out with any finesse, we wouldn't have generated any serious opposition. He made it seem like we were shoving those V-Pads down everybody's throat."

"Agreed. Those are the facts on the ground. Blinka was the root of the problem. We all know that. But we have to present it in a way to give U-T flexibility."

"You mean deniability."

Stoloff tapped his toe. "They'll be here any minute. Let's get to the PTA meeting. We need to be on the same page. It wouldn't have been such an unmitigated disaster, if only you'd have followed my instructions."

"I chaired it just like you told me to."

"No, you didn't. What did you expect, an after party like at your Madison Avenue art gallery? When we make a game plan we have to stick to it."

"I told you last year before we even started, I'm not good at these things. They kept yelling at me," Golman protested. "No matter what I did, they kept yelling that I'm not following the right procedures."

"The rule of thumb in parliamentary procedures is just to make something up. It's all smoke and mirrors. Bang your gavel and move on."

"You're the one who insisted that I be president. You should have been president and I should have been vice president. I'm not a professional. I'm just the wife of one. I don't know what I'm doing."

"Then follow instructions."

She shut her eyes and shook her head. "God knows why I ever let you and Claude talk me into doing this."

"You've done great until now. Have you ever met Commander Galush?"

"Claude's met him. I don't recall if it was business or party or golf. Claude says he's not the sharpest pencil in the box, but he gets to cocktails on time."

"I hear he steers a tight ship. That's his profile anyway, for all that's worth. How about the chief detective? What's her name, Rendorf."

"I know nothing about her. Why should I?"

The front door slammed. Stoloff cringed.

"I'm home!" A young voice from the hall.

"Come in here, please," Stoloff yelled.

Preston peeked in. "What?"

"Is Jim with you?"

"No."

"Where is he?"

"I think he went with Rory."

"Where?"

"How should I know?"

"You're supposed to keep an eye on him, on them both."

"I'm tired of them always hanging onto me. I want to go back to Hilldale, so I can be with my friends. It's not fair."

"Come here."

Preston approached reluctantly. "What?"

243

Stoloff said, "Life is not fair. Now go out and find Jim and Rory, and bring them back here. And do not slam the door."

"I think they went out looking for those girls."

"What?"

"That's what everybody in the neighborhood is doing."

"That's dangerous."

"What do you expect when you put out a reward?" Preston spun, disappeared into the hall. The door slammed behind him.

Irma Golman pursed her lips. "I get the same kind of sass from Rory. All the time. They're just not happy here. They don't fit in. After this, never again. These are our kids' lives. Our lives too."

Stoloff bit his lip. "They'll thank us for this some day. Let's just move ahead. Finish your wine. The wrecking crew will be here any time."

They both drained their glasses. Stoloff cleared everything away.

A few minutes later, the others arrived.

Senior Analyst Rebecca Unter-Tractole began the intros: "Commander Ron Galush of Special Operations, NYPD, and Chief Detective Marcia Rendorf. These are Special Agents Warren Stoloff and Irma Golman. You all know Community Operations Specialist Blinka, of course. And Technician Garson is Blinka's assistant for communications."

Golman took Commander Galush's hand in both of hers. "It is quite an honor to finally meet you. My husband is Claude Golman. You might also know him as Junior Golman."

"Oh yes, Junior Golman. I didn't make the connection. If I don't get to see him soon, give him my regards."

Blinka stepped to the window and pulled the drapes wide open. "This is what I told you about, U-T, a view to kill for!"

U-T said, "How did you manage to weasel this flat, Stoloff?"

"It was just a routine assignment."

Detective Rendorf said, "What do you think, Commander?"

Galush surveyed the room. "Not bad at all."

"What's going on?" Stoloff asked U-T.

"If this location is suitable for communications control," Unter-Tractole replied, "we're going to move the joint command center here."

"Here? You want to set it up here? This is where my family lives."

"Just cowboy up for once, Stoloff."

"I wasn't complaining, U-T. There's no problem."

Technician Garson, carrying equipment and wearing earphones, said, "Technically it's perfect. Top floor of the tallest building in the neighborhood."

Stoloff muttered to Irma Golman, "Anita's going to kill me when she gets home."

"This won't last long," Golman replied under her breath. "But if it gets impossible here, you can camp out in my place for a few days, the boys can share Rory's room, and you and Anita can sleep on our couch."

"Well, thanks. If we have to, but just as a last resort."

U-T said, "Stoloff, show us the rest of the flat. The grand tour."

"Certainly. Everyone, follow me." Stoloff opened a door. "This is my home office and library."

All except Blinka and the technician stepped past Stoloff into the large room lined with banks of file drawers.

Detective Rendorf said to Stoloff, "This is quite a library. What do you keep in all these files?"

"They're mostly related to my work as a financial advisor."

Commander Galush said to Analyst Unter-Tractole, "I still don't understand the connection you IPA people are making between that Social Action Alliance group and the missing girls. Detail it for me."

U-T replied, "Trust us, the connections are there. We have overwhelming evidence."

Galush replied, "Everything I've seen is circumstantial. Our department would never have released a press statement like that without a smoking gun. If you've got a smoking gun, share it with us. As far as the NYPD knows, there's no connection beyond that so-called radical literature on the floor and the aunt going to the PTA meeting. Using the media to promote unsubstantiated allegations just muddies the waters, creates a very volatile atmosphere, and makes serious investigation even more difficult."

"That will all come out during the investigation."

"What's their motive?"

"We're dealing with people whose way of thinking is very different from ours, so we don't need to understand their every motive at this point. They're not always predictable."

"You can say that because you don't face what we face every day," the Commander said. "The press is breathing down our necks. Haven't you seen the papers? Don't you listen to the radio? Watch TV? If you've got the goods on this Alliance group, like you keep saying, just round them all up."

"We'll make our move when we're ready. At the proper time," U-T replied. "We're not going after just a few fellow travelers. We going to nail their entire leadership cadre."

"This is not up to NYPD standards," Galush grunted.

"We're all well aware," U-T replied through her teeth, "that NYPD and IPA operational standards don't always mesh. But we are the lead agency here."

Commander Galush stopped short. "IPA is the lead agency in interstate subversive activities. NYPD Special Operations is the lead agency in municipal child abductions."

U-T said, "In the interests of getting something done, we've got to accommodate each other and work together."

Galush said. "First we've got to straighten out the chain of command. We've got overlapping authority. We're risking confusion. It doesn't make sense to have two separate teams working at the same time, particularly in rescue operations with dogs and helicopters."

U-T said, "Why does the confusion level always seem to rise when we're working with you guys? Don't have a stroke, Commander. They'll be coordinated. Our elite counter-subversion tactical unit and commando hostage rescue team is the best in the world."

Galush enunciated slowly. "Our dogs are out at this very moment. Are yours?"

U-T took a deep breath and straightened her back. "We've dragnetted the entire neighborhood twice. Send your dogs home. We'll find 'em."

Irma Golman jumped in, "That's a big park. Sometimes I jog there, or at least I used to. There's room for both dog teams."

In the living room, Blinka said to Technician Garson, "Where do you want to set up the equipment?"

247

"Right there by the window. The signal's best there, and we can do visuals on the air and the highway. We'll have to move the furniture around."

"Good. So it's decided."

"Then I'll have them bring the rest of the equipment up right now," The technician continued. "They're in the lobby." He got on his receiver and gave instructions. "While we're waiting, help me move the couch."

A few minutes later, men in blue workmen uniforms appeared at the door. They wheeled in carts of electrical equipment, and set it all in the room.

U-T returned to the living room from the office, followed by Galush and the others.

Stoloff was startled by the way they'd rearranged the room, but said nothing.

U-T said to Blinka, "Well, everything's under control here now, right?"

"I got it," he replied.

She extended her hand to Galush. "I've got to move on, Commander. Detective Rendorf, it's been a pleasure. Agent Blinka will be coordinating our end of the operation here on the ground from now on. I'll be in and out. I'm always available when something breaks, any hour."

On her way out, Unter-Tractole pulled Blinka into the hall. She tapped her fists together. "Until this is over, you're living here. I'll be blunt. You're responsible for this mess. You better get it right."

"Don't worry, U-T. I'm on top of it."

"This is your last chance, Blinka. You better produce."

"Everything's going fine. Just give me a chance, U-T, I'll pull it out of the fire. We'll come out smelling like roses. Guarantee. Just one last chance."

"You've got forty-eight hours to produce. Has Drannily's been searched?"

"I'm expecting the warrant later today."

"All it takes to get a warrant is a phone call."

"It's not always so simple."

U-T just gave him a disgusted look, turned and strutted toward the elevator.

Blinka shrugged it off, sauntered back inside.

Technician Garson was now set up on the couch, the walnut coffee table piled with equipment.

Commander Galush was pacing back and forth in front of the long window, barking orders to teams in the field through a handset.

A voice came over the line, "We've searched every corner of the park. Nothing."

Galush said, "Where did the dogs lose the trace?"

"Just north of the schoolyard, before the park entrance. They could have gone anywhere from there."

"Search the river," Galush snapped.

Blinka realized he was already a few steps behind. He hurried over and sat next to Technician Garson. "Which is my handset?"

"Here you go." The technician handed Blinka one. "Everything's working. I just checked in with all the field sets."

Blinka pushed a button; it started to hiss. One by one the others in the circuit checked in with him.

Galush sat down at the opposite end of the sofa from Blinka, with the technician in the middle. Both started talking on their walkie-talkies at the same time. The replies came through the speakers. Both sets hissed with static when someone wasn't speaking.

In the other room, leaning against the library wall, Golman asked Stoloff, "What should I be doing?"

"I don't have the slightest idea," he replied. "I plan to mainly just stay out of Blinka's way. I always expect chaos with him in charge."

"Did the boys get home yet?"

"I didn't hear them come in," Stoloff said. "Maybe they're next door, over at your apartment."

Golman said, "I feel pretty useless here. I'm going to go to my place and see if they're there."

Stoloff picked up his crossword puzzle and filled in some boxes.

In the living room, Commander Galush waved a hand at Blinka. "Keep it down. You're making too much noise. I can't hear."

"Don't tell me to keep it down. You keep it down."

Chief Detective Rendorf said, "This isn't working out. It's way too noisy with both of us using walkie-talkies here in the same room. It's interfering with communications."

"We could put one of you in the bedroom," the technician said. "But of course that could make coordination difficult."

Blinka said, "If you want to move somebody, move them. It's all right with me. I'm not going anywhere."

"Don't look at us. We're not going anywhere."

The technician said, "This is a long room. Let's try it with you two at opposite ends."

Galush and Rendorf moved to one end of the room and Blinka and Stoloff to the other. The technician was sprawled on the elegant sofa in the center, his equipment spread over the coffee table.

A key turned in the lock, and Mrs Anita Stoloff entered the apartment, thinking only of putting her feet up. She could barely believe what she was seeing. She caught her breath, stormed over to her husband and whispered, "Get those people out of my living room."

"I can't, sweets." His voice cracked. "It's just for a day or two."

"You promised me this kind of thing would never happen again."

"Just calm down. It's going to be okay."

"It's not okay"

"Go watch TV over at Irma's. I think the boys are already over there."

"Move this circus to her apartment. You have seniority."

"Keep your voice down. I tried. I got overruled. Please just don't humiliate me like this in front of them."

"You'll pay for this, I swear you will." She stomped out of the room.

He followed and caught her in the foyer just before she reached the front door. "I'm sorry, I'm sorry."

"You better be." She opened the door and gasped at the sight of four large men in the hallway striding toward her.

"We're here with the warrant," one of them uttered gruffly.

Over her shoulder, Anita gave her husband a look to kill. She pushed past the men and headed down the hall toward Golman's apartment.

Stoloff flashed the men a sheepish grin. "Agent Blinka's in charge. I'll tell him you're here. The target's down on floor five."

Back inside, Stoloff tried to catch Blinka's attention, but Blinka continued chatting into his handset. Finally Blinka covered the mouthpiece and said, with annoyance, "What?"

"The search team is here."

"Send them down to Drannily's."

"One of us has got to go with them. If she's home, she'll need some talking to."

"So go."

"You're her handler."

"I can't leave here," Blinka said. "You go. Have you got the master key?"

Reluctantly Stoloff took the search team down to apartment 514 and rang the bell. No one answered, so he slid the key into the lock, warily opened the door, and led the team inside. It smelled musty and somewhat like urine. They spread out and began to search. Stoloff positioned himself in the hall near the kitchen door, where he could keep one eye on the team's activity, and his other on the entry.

Something caught his eye on the counter near the sink. A cockroach. It upset him to see it here in Monarch Towers. He'd only had a few upstairs in his own apartment, which he made sure was kept scrupulously clean. He watched it dart and stop, moving its antennas back and forth. He felt a deep instinctive repulsion. Despite his better judgement, he stepped into the kitchen and glanced around for something to hit it with.

A scream pierced the air.

Stoloff hurried back out to the hall. The Drannily sisters now stood near the umbrella rack just inside the front door, expressions of horror on their faces.

He hurried over. "Sorry, Maude, Chloe. This wasn't my idea. They've got a search warrant. It's for the missing Dictaphone cartridge."

"Get them out of here, or I'll call the police. I told you, I don't have it. If you don't have it, McKlosky took it. She's not trustworthy. Get these men out of my home."

"I tried to convince them not to do this. Blinka's in charge, not me. He's upstairs in my apartment. Go yell at him, not me."

"I intend to do just that. Chloe, stay here and guard our things."

Miss M. Drannily stormed down the hall to the elevators, Stoloff not far behind. Half way there, he stopped short, fearing a nasty confrontation in the car on the way up. He watched the elevator door close behind her, then waited impatiently for the car to return.

When Stoloff finally arrived back in his own apartment, Drannily was yelling at Blinka, who was concurrently talking on his hand set.

"Keep it down, please keep it down," Stoloff implored. "The neighbors."

Commander Galush blurted, "I give up!" He threw his walkie-talkie at the couch, stomped out of the room.

Chief Detective Rendorf followed him into the office, and shut the door behind them.

"This is getting ugly," Galush spat.

Rendorf shook her head. "Why don't they just get the hell out of the way, so people who know what they're doing can get some real police work done."

"That's not their M.O.," Galush replied. "They don't even belong on this case."

"Do you think they just invented that link between the subversives and the girls?"

Galush responded, "I sure wouldn't put it past them."

"They're under a lot of pressure from those Senate hearings."

"All they care about is how it looks on TV. Un-American, my big toe, if you'll excuse the expression. This whole thing smells more and more like a red herring."

"To what end?" Rendorf asked.

"To cover up that train wreck PTA meeting. Connecting the subversives to those girls was shrewd. That knocked their own incompetence right out of the headlines. By the time the smoke clears, they figure, they'll be back in their hole in Washington."

"So where do we go from here?"

"Bring the uncle in for questioning again. His story just doesn't add up. The aunt goes to the school meeting. The girls are in bed. The perps get into the room. Either they had the key or the front door was left open or they climbed in through the fire escape. The uncle hears the noise. They're wearing ski masks. They struggle. They stab him, grab the girls, drop some radical literature, and run. It doesn't make sense."

Rendorf said, "And those two teenagers were right in the apartment, and didn't see or hear anything. As to that radical literature, all they've produced are teachers' union flyers to the PTA meeting."

"Bring those teenagers, the cousins, back in for questioning again too."

"And what about those boiler room explosions at the school? And the maintenance man's story? And the blackout? And the fire alarm?"

"That Grayley character doesn't know what he saw. He's a tippler. As to the explosions and the blackout and the alarm, it could be a coincidence, but they got IPA thumb prints all over them. They were awfully conveniently timed. The meeting wasn't going their way, so they decided to dissolve it into chaos."

"They certainly succeeded."

•

# CHAPTER SEVENTEEN

Columbus School was still barely functioning, but most of the kids and teachers were back.

Everything was almost ready for the getaway. It would just look like a regular day, like they were leaving home in the morning for school, then meet at the hideout. They decided that the safest and quickest route to the bridge was to skirt the city streets entirely, to follow the highway, slip through the bushes and tall weeds along the shoulder, past Gabe's house, up the ramp and onto the span.

On their last school day, all five showed up for Miss Odelia's class. Everybody was quiet, and not fooling around like usual. Gabe found himself looking around the room and at Miss Odelia. He wanted to make sure he remembered what they looked like.

After school they hung out all afternoon in the hideout, not saying or doing much, the air bristling with tension. They gathered up everything they were going to bring into a pile.

At twilight the boys sadly, reluctantly, and awkwardly left the girls and made their way out of the park.

On Cabrini, Henry said to Gabe, "I'm going to feed the strays one last time, tomorrow morning, real early. Want to do it with me?"

"What time?"

"Like, seven."

"I'll meet you at the garbage cans."

When Gabe got home, Mom said, "Is that a new cap?" "I've had it for a while," he replied. Until now, Gabe had only worn his Dodgers cap in the hideout, but he'd forgotten to take it off. "I got to leave early tomorrow morning for school."

This was his last night at home, and he felt sad. He moped quietly in the living room with his family.

Gabe sat next to Mom and Dad on the couch. Benjo was across the room on the green stuffed chair. Dad was reading his sports section. A comedy show was on the radio.

Gabe said, "Mom."

"What?"

"What was your school like when you were in fourth grade?"

Mom said, "Well, you know, that was back in Maroon. It was very different in those days. The school was up on that hill a ways down the road. They didn't really have classes like you have here. They just had all the grades in two rooms."

"Did you like it?"

"It was all right."

"I bet you and Aunt Julia were sad when Grampa and Gramma decided to move to New York."

"We were sad to leave Maroon, of course. But we were excited to come and live here. The city looked very glamorous to country kids. Me and Aunt Julia, we thought Manhattan was the center of the world, and we were just missing out on everything."

"I think it's better out there," Gabe said.

"Like Gramma used to say, *Familiarity breeds contempt*."

"What does that mean?"

"I can't explain. Ask Dad."

Dad was busy with his sports page. Gabe knew not to bother him when he had that look on his face.

Gabe crossed the room, and sat on the hassock next to his grampa.

"What was it like when you were my age, Benjo?"

Benjo shut his eyes. "I don't remember. That was too long ago."

"Where did you live?"

"In this little village. That was back in the old country."

"Did you like it there?"

"It was okay."

"Why'd you leave?"

"I just wanted to try my luck someplace else. There, you could work your whole life and never have enough to get some land."

"How old were you?"

"When I came here to America? A little older than you."

"Did you come with your parents?"

"I came by myself." Benjo hesitated. "I ran away."

"You ran away?"

"Well, I wasn't all by myself. I had some friends. I was lucky I didn't get killed."

"Didn't you miss your parents?"

"Sure. Sometimes. But they had already passed. My sister was here in New York. I stayed with her for a while. I got a job."

"Are you ever sorry you left?"

"How could I be sorry? If I didn't come here, I wouldn't be here with you today, would I?"

In his room later, Gabe stuffed some tee shirts, underwear, and socks into his backpack.

On his desk he set the V-Pads with all the stuff they wrote up, the Dictaphone cartridge, and the file folder on Monarch Towers and the Little Woods.

He carefully printed, "Grampa, This is evidence is for Mr Fox" on a sheet of paper.

Then he noticed his mistake. He had written *is* twice. He erased the second *is,* then wrote it back again and erased the first *is*. He placed the paper on top of the pile of stuff, then covered it all over with a tee shirt.

He pulled out the last version of the note he'd been working on in the hideout. He still wasn't very happy with it. He read it over and changed a few things.

He couldn't sleep all night.

In the morning, he made his bed and placed the envelope on top of his pillow. He tiptoed past Benjo snoring in bed.

His parents' bedroom door was open, and he could see nobody in there.

A light was on in the kitchen. He heard some sounds coming from there.

He poked his head around the door jamb.

"Why, you're up early," Mom said.

"Me and Henry are going to feed the cats. I told you last night. Where's Dad?"

"He had to work night shift."

Gabe sat down at the little table. She placed a steaming bowl of oatmeal with milk and melting butter and honey in front of him. "I don't know what those stray cats would do without you two."

"They'd be okay, I think."

He took a spoonful in his mouth. "Mom, what would you and Dad and Grampa do if I wasn't here?"

"Why, you know, we'd be very sad."

"But you'd be okay, wouldn't you?"

"Don't say such silly things."

He kissed her goodbye and took off.

Henry was waiting for him by the garbage cans outside his building, carrying the cat food bag.

Gabe said, "I can't do it."

"You're saying this now?"

"I'm sorry."

"Then go back home."

"Don't be mad at me."

Henry said, "We just don't got time for this."

"I don't know what to do."

"Let's go feed the strays."

They walked silently to the first alley, a ways up Fort Washington Avenue. Near the garbage cans, Henry poured a small mound of kibble. A silverfish scurried along a crack in the sidewalk. They retreated to the curb and watched. A skittish orange tabby poked her head out, glanced suspiciously about, looked straight at Gabe and Henry, then dashed to the kibble, followed by three kittens. They scarfed it down.

Preston Stoloff stepped out onto the sidewalk.

"And what have we here?" Preston said. "What are our mischievous little friends up to today?"

"What do *you* want?" Henry said.

Gabe glanced over his shoulder. Jim and Rory were behind them.

"You still got dues to pay."

Henry said, "And just what are our dues?"

"Those caps on your heads."

"Why do you want our caps?"

"C'mon, give them here."

"You want my cap? Take it."

Henry flung it.

Preston grabbed at him. Henry dropped the cat food bag; it splattered on the sidewalk.

Gabe felt a tremendous blow on the back of his neck.

The next thing Gabe knew he was lying on the ground, covering his face and head with his arms, while they kicked him.

Preston said, "Where's your gang now?"

He heard footsteps fading away, and wondered if they were gone. He lay there for what felt like a long time.

Gabe pushed himself up, aching all over. He got to his knees, wondered if he could stand. He was shaky on his feet. His shoulder hurt. His backpack was by the garbage cans. He didn't see his cap. He felt sharp, piercing twinges when he moved his arm. He felt nauseous. He took a couple of steps.

Henry was writhing on the ground nearby. Gabe had thought that he had gotten away, but they must have caught up with him, or else Henry came back to try to help.

Gabe helped him to his feet. Henry was limping.

An elderly woman with a cane said, "Are you all right?"

"We're fine. Thanks," Gabe said.

Somehow they made it to the hideout. The others were already there, ready to go. Except Jack.

Gabe and Henry lay down on the rug, hurting.

"We can't go like this," Ari said. "We got to put it off. We've got no choice. Henry can't walk."

Henry said, "I just need a day to get my leg back. We'll be all right. We'll just lay low here today and leave tomorrow morning as soon as it gets light."

"This is a mess," Roco said. "You guys made a mess of this."

"I'm sorry," Henry said.

Ari said, "Don't say that, Roco, it's not their fault."

Kelly said, "I knew we shouldn't have mailed those notes yesterday. I kept saying that, but nobody listened."

"You never said that," Roco scolded.

"I heard him," Elkie said.

Kelly went on, "Once they get those notes, they're going to be out looking for us all, and we're not even gone."

Gabe said, "Where's Jack?"

"He's always late," Roco replied.

Gabe said to Elkie, "They took my Dodgers cap."

Roco climbed up to the lookout platform, stationed himself at the surveyor's transit, watched the patrols cruising past on the highway and the helicopters flying back and forth.

Elkie said, "Maybe something happened to Jack."

Roco said, "Maybe he's not coming."

After that, nobody talked much, nobody felt like playing, time went very slowly, tension grew. Every once in a while the radio issued statements and gave updates. Henry and Gabe were still both lying down, Henry with his shoe off and his foot propped up on a pillow, Gabe feeling half in a daze, his shoulder still hurting whenever he moved.

Time passed lethargically.

Elkie said, "He's here."

Jack crawled through the secret entrance.

"Where you been?" Roco shouted from the lookout station.

"I was followed. I had to circle all around the park to ditch them."

261

Roco jumped down from the perch. "Kelly, take my place." He approached Jack. "Followed? By who?"

"By some kids."

"What kids?"

"What's the difference? I ditched them."

"What did they look like?"

"They just looked like kids."

Roco roared, "Did you sell us out, Jack?"

"I didn't, I swear."

"Leave Jack alone," Elkie said.

Gabe cried, "Stop arguing."

Roco and Jack stood cheek to jowl.

Roco said, "You know who was following you. Why don't you tell us?"

"Get off my case. Leave me alone."

"There's something you're not telling us. What is it?"

"Don't mess with me again, Roco. I didn't recognize them." Jack looked around. "Don't anybody believe me?"

"I believe you," Ari said.

"I got another dollar." Jack waved the bill. "Look, Roco, I don't want to fight with you."

"Then don't act like a jerk."

"You too." Jack said. "I'm sorry if I was a jerk. I know I am sometimes. But so are you. I don't want to fight with you. You're the closest thing I got to brother."

Roco stopped short, then said in a smaller voice, "You too."

"Then we're good again?"

Jack held out his palm, Roco hesitantly slapped it, then they reversed, and Jack slapped Roco's palm.

Preston entered the Stoloff living room, carrying a paper bag, followed by Jim and Rory. On one end of the room stood Blinka, and at the other end Detective Rendorf. In the middle, Technician Garson was busy at his tubes and dials.

Preston asked Garson, "Have you seen my dad?"

"Try the kitchen."

Preston said to the other two boys, "Wait here."

Stoloff was at the table, pouring over some papers. Before Preston could open his mouth, Stoloff said, "Don't bother me."

"It's important."

"It will just have to wait."

"What if it's about the girls?"

Stoloff looked up. "What about them?"

"All the kids in the neighborhood are out looking for them. What if one of them finds a clue?"

"For God's sake, you guys aren't still running around out there playing detective again, are you?"

"No, no. But what if one of the kids finds a clue and gives it to me, and I give it to you? Then who gets the reward?"

"Do you want me to lose my job? Stop that immediately. Get it out of your head. You can't collect any reward. My family can't collect a reward on one of my cases. I don't want to hear another word about it. What in the world are you thinking?"

Stoloff turned back to his work on the table.

Preston stared at him, then left.

Back in the living room, Preston said to Blinka, "I got a question."

Blinka was on his walkie-talkie with one of the helicopters, and snorted, "What do you want? I'm busy."

"I got a clue. What should I do with it."

"This is not a kid's game. Just stay out of my hair." Blinka glanced over at Senior Analyst Rebecca Unter-Tractole, who was standing at the window, looking out at the river. Then he motioned toward Galush and Rendorf. "Go bother them."

Preston walked over to Chief Detective Rendorf.

Rendorf looked up from her notes. "What is it, Preston?"

He handed her the paper bag. "I got a clue."

She looked inside. "Two kids' caps. Where'd you get them?"

"Some kid gave them to me. He said he found them in Fort Tryon Park. Can I get the reward?"

"What kid?"

"I don't know him. He doesn't go to my school."

Rendorf said, "Commander, look at this." She held open the bag. "Preston just brought it in. Some kid found them in the park."

Galush shrugged. "No big deal. Kids lose their caps every day."

Rendorf exclaimed, "Not usually two in the same place. And that one's a Dodgers cap. One of the girls was known to wear a Dodgers cap, which they say is unusual in this neighborhood. You never know. This might be a break. Let's give them to the dogs."

U-T overheard and rushed over. "What's that?"

Galush said, "Just a possible clue. Stoloff's kid brought it in. We're putting our dogs on it."

U-T said, "If Stoloff's kid brought that evidence in, it's ours, so we'll put our dogs on it. They're better than yours."

"You got to be kidding," Galush snapped.

U-T turned and shouted, "Blinka, hang up that contraption and get over here."

Blinka was still on the walkie-talkie. "This is an important call, U-T."

"Sign off now."

Blinka mumbled hurriedly into the receiver, "Sorry, duty calls. Over and out."

U-T snapped at Preston, "Why didn't you give that evidence to your dad or to Mr Blinka?"

"I tried. They wouldn't take it." Preston grinned. "First I tried to give it to my dad, and then I tried to give it to Mr Blinka too, but neither one of them wanted it. They wouldn't take it."

Galush chuckled, "They wouldn't take it!"

"He's lying," Blinka protested. "Why are you lying like that?"

Preston said, "Can I get the reward now?"

U-T stuck her finger in Blinka's face and said, "Out in the hall. Now."

"U-T, just give me a minute, I can explain."

"Now!"

He'd seen that look on her face before, and knew there was no arguing. He slouched toward the foyer, toward the front door, U-T marching close behind him.

In the hall, she slammed the door behind them. "That's it, Blinka. You turned down evidence. You made us look like idiots, rookies, rank amateurs one time too many. In front of those losers. You're off the case. You're out."

He was dumbfounded. "For what?"

"Incompetence."

His jaw dropped. "What did I do? Everything's going fine. We're just on the verge of making a breakthrough. Don't joke, U-T."

"This is no joke. I warned you."

Blinka said, "Just give me a chance, U-T, I'll pull it out of the fire. We'll come out smelling like roses. Guarantee. Just one last chance."

"Nobody makes me look like an idiot in front of these hacks."

"Why me? What about Stoloff? You don't believe his badmouth garbage, do you? Don't listen to it. He's just got it in for me. He just dumps on me to cover his tracks. It's all slander." Blinka looked deep into her face. "Oh, I see, maybe all those rumors are right. Stoloff can do no wrong. What has he got on you? What is he, your golden boy?"

As soon as the words passed his lips, Blinka knew he had voiced the unspeakable, he had overreached, and wished desperately he could pull the words back.

U-T said, "You're suspended. Relieved of duty."

"I'm sorry, U-T, I didn't mean anything, I was just joking. Don't make me beg. I just need fourteen more months to early retirement."

"Hand me your badge and get the hell out of here."

Back inside Stoloff's apartment, U-T took a few deep breaths and cautiously approached Galush. "How about we compromise, Commander. There are two kids' caps in that bag. How about I take one and you take one, I give one of those caps to my dogs and you give the other one to yours. First dogs to sniff out the perps get bragging rights."

•

Ari and Kelly were up on the lookout station. A ways down the platform, Roco was at the surveyor's scope, watching through the other set of slits.

Ari yelled, "They're here!"

"They got big dogs," Kelly exclaimed, dread in his voice.

"They're staring at us," Roco said. "They got binoculars."

Jack and Elkie scrambled up the ladder and onto the makeshift planks alongside Roco. Gabe clambered up the ladder after them. His shoulder throbbed when he moved it. Gabe found a space next to Ari and Kelly, and gazed out through the slits. Down by the highway stood six men in uniforms and five dogs—three German Shepherds and two Dobermans—straining at their leashes, panting and whining.

"They're just standing there," Kelly blurted. "Why are they just standing there?"

Something in the sky caught Gabe's eye, birds soaring over the river, swooping through the bridge suspension cables, heading toward the rocky heights on the other side, over the Palisades, beyond the cliffs.

Henry, lying on the rug near the foot of the ladder, with his foot propped up, pushed himself up on one elbow, holding his ankle. "What do you see? Tell me everything you see." He took a deep breath.

Jack sniggered. "They're probably waiting for their big guns to arrive."

Elkie said, "Keep your head down, they'll see you!"

"They're going to sic those dogs on us," Roco muttered through his teeth.

Kelly said, "This is the end. We're finished. They got us."

Gabe shuddered at the thought.

With difficulty Henry pushed himself to his feet. "If not for me, we'd be in Maroon now. I let you all down. I'm sorry."

Jack said, "Shut up, Henry. It's not your fault. We're all in this together."

Gabe thought of the little house at Maroon, surrounded by trees and fields, the forest beyond, with his family in front, smiling for the camera, and wondered, *Is this how I'm going to die?*

Ari gasped. "Those dogs can get in."

Gabe realized she was right. The dogs could crawl right in through the secret entrance.

*We need to block up the entrance hole,* he thought. It's so obvious, why doesn't somebody say to do it? Then he wondered why he himself wasn't saying it, since nobody else was. He was just standing there. Why do I always want somebody else to say it? Why don't I just say it myself? What am I always waiting for? Out of nowhere, he remembered the words of Miss C.: *Don't hold yourself back. Always say what's on your mind.*

Gabe exclaimed, "Everybody, stuff up everything up in the secret hole." He scrambled down the lookout ladder. "I mean, stuff up everything and block it up with stuff so the dogs can't get in."

He was surprised to hear himself saying that, it sounded almost like he really knew what he was talking about.

Ari, Roco, Elkie, and Jack scrambled down the ladder right behind him.

Kelly stayed on the platform. "I'll keep chickie."

As fast as they could, they carried and dragged over chairs and bikes and toys and rugs and junk.

"Don't anybody throw our backpacks in there," Ari said.

They filled up the secret entrance, and piled the rest of the stuff against the metal door as a barricade.

•

Up in the living room of Stoloff's apartment, Chief Detective Rendorf exclaimed into the handset, "Are you out of your mind?"

Commander Galush, who had been nodding off after swallowing a bologna sandwich, was suddenly alert. "What's going on?"

"They've got to be wrong."

"What?"

"The dogs think they've found the girls."

"Where?"

"According to the field officer, they're... in this building," she stammered.

"Give me that." He grabbed the receiver from her hand. "This is Commander Galush. What's going on?"

The line crackled. "The dogs have got a match. We're right down here at the highway, straight down from the command center, where the parking garage juts out. If you look out the window, you can see us. There's a metal door down here."

Galush glanced out the window, saw them waving up at him. "Don't move. We're coming down."

At the other end of the living room, Unter-Tractole exclaimed, "Your dogs found them?"

Stoloff rushed out from the office. "What's happening?"

Galush ignored them both, and barked at Rendorf, "We're going down to the highway and take charge. Let's move!" He yelled into his walkie-talkie, "Send every available man immediately down to the West Side Highway behind Monarch Towers." Then he turned to U-T and Stoloff. "Stay here, we got this."

U-T blew her top. "No way, Galush. This is a hostage situation. We're in charge."

Galush said, "You just continue directing your people from up here. We don't need you down there."

U-T said, "Stoloff, follow me."

"Should I bring the hostage negotiation handbook?"

"Of course."

"I've got to look for it."

"We don't have time."

All four rushed to the elevators and got into the same car. They didn't say a word to each other on the way down. When the door opened into the parking garage, the two pairs rushed to their separate vehicles and sped off, screeching their tires.

•

Elkie whispered to Ari, "Are we going to die here?"

"Maybe."

Elkie entwined her fingers with hers. "I don't want to die."

"This is the end," Kelly said. "They got us."

Roco said, "Kelly, do the worms song."

"That's not even funny," Kelly said.

"Yes it is, it's very funny," Roco said. "You're always shooting your mouth about how much you want to be dead. Now's your big chance. How does it go?" He continued in a sing-song voice, *"The worms crawl in, the worms crawl out, they eat your guts and spit it out."*

"Shut up, Roco," Kelly said. "Maybe I changed my mind."

Ari put her arms around Kelly. "We love you, Kelly."

Elkie wrapped her arms around the two of them. "I love you both."

"I love you too, Elkie," Ari said.

Ari, Elkie, and Kelly hugged. One by one the others joined in, until they were all hugging each other in a circle.

"So what are we going to do?" Henry looked around. "Kelly's right. This is the end. What does everybody want to do? They probably won't kill us if we just walk out there. Anybody got a white flag?"

No one responded.

Finally Ari said, "You can do that if you want to, Henry."

"I don't want to, but what else can we do?"

She said, "All I know is, I didn't do this just for nothing. We didn't do all this just for nothing. Let them come in and get us."

Henry said, "I feel like I got you all into this."

Ari said, "You didn't get us into this. We got you into it."

Henry said, "I just want to get you all out of here okay. You're my family. I don't want them to hurt you."

Ari said, "I rather be dead here than go back to my uncle. I'm not going back."

"I'm staying with Ari," Elkie said.

Gabe said, "If Ari and Elkie are going to stay, I'm staying too."

Roco said, "I'm in."

Jack said, "I'm in."

Kelly said, "You're all my family too. I'm in."

271

Henry said, "Then we stick together, no matter what."

Nobody said anything for a while.

Sirens in the distance. Everyone except Henry sprinted up the lookout tower, crowded onto the platforms around the two sets of slits in the bricks overlooking the highway.

Gabe's shoulder still twinged, but he didn't pay it much mind. Henry hobbled along in the rear and pulled and pushed himself slowly up the ladder, until he was now on the platform with the others.

In the distance down the highway under the bridge, Gabe saw flashing red lights, police cars and vans hurtling toward them.

Roco, said, "Here they come."

Henry said, "Everybody grab your signal mirror."

Gabe felt his pocket where he always kept it. His little mirror was there.

Across the river, the sun was preparing to set behind the Palisades, and beams of sunlight burst through the fiery clouds.

"The sun's at a good angle. Everybody keep your head back, so they don't see your face," Henry said. "Watch the angle of the sun. Get your mirror ready. Everybody ready? Here they come!"

Sirens, flashing lights, police cars speeding toward them from under the bridge.

"Now!" Henry shouted.

Sunbeam blasts of glaring light bounced off their mirrors and hit the windshields.

"Got him!" Jack yelled.

The first drivers stomped their brakes. The cars behind plowed into them.

A police van spun across the highway. One by one each of the others ricocheted and plowed into the one before.

"I hope nobody got hurt," Elkie said.

"Now they're really going to be mad," Kelly exclaimed.

•

# CHAPTER EIGHTEEN

Commander Galush and Detective Rendorf were stuck far back in the traffic jam, their sirens blaring to no avail. The shoulder wasn't wide enough here to drive on. They got out of the car, hurried along the side of the highway. Two motorcycle patrolmen quickly pulled up alongside. Galush and Rendorf hopped on, and sped to the front.

They jumped off and joined the officers crouched behind the leading police car. All the officers and dogs were waiting there, using the police cars and vans as shields.

"What the hell happened?" The commander bellowed.

"They hit us with something! They've got some kind of weaponry."

"Ambulances on their way. Any officer seriously hurt?"

"I don't think so."

"The hostage team is six minutes out. Proceed with top caution. Assume they're extremely dangerous. We'll get an entire battalion out here if we need to."

One lane of the highway was cleared, and the traffic was slowly proceeding.

"We can't take any chances. Shut down the highway. Shut it down now."

A fleet of dark IPA vans roared towards them from the opposite direction, from the north, driving the wrong way down the highway. They screeched to a stop. The two fleets—IPA and NYPD—were facing each other from opposite directions, separated by only about ten feet.

Unter-Tractole, Stoloff, a group of armed men, and a pack of dogs jumped out and took up positions behind the IPA vehicles.

U-T yelled to Galush. "We're in charge here now."

"Go home, we don't need you here."

The two packs of dogs growled at each other, straining at their leashes.

"I'm not messing around," U-T shouted. "The IPA rescue team is here with me to get those hostages out, and if I were you, I wouldn't stand in our way."

"Who in the devil do you think you are?" Galush spouted back. "Maybe you can play those games in DC, but not here. Our dogs beat yours fair and square. Get those puppy mutts out of here."

"Dream on."

Galush lifted a megaphone and spoke into it in a deep tone. "We know you're in there. We just want to talk about why you took those kids."

No response.

U-T yelled at Galush, "Put down that bullhorn. You're interfering with our rescue operation."

Galush said, "Go tell it to your spooks."

U-T picked up her own megaphone, blew into it, then jawed in as tough a voice as she could muster, "We know who you are and why you're doing this. It won't work."

Galush shouted into his bullhorn, "No matter what your goals are, this is not the way to achieve them. Release those girls now."

U-T: "The leaders of your group are already in custody and are cooperating. They have made full confessions and have named names."

Galush: "Release the kids now, and I assure you on my personal honor that you'll be treated fairly, with all your constitutional rights."

U-T: "One way or another, those kids are going home tonight."

It went on like that for quite a while, with dueling bullhorns, but still no response.

Galush: "You can trust me. I know you must be in pain, and I can empathize with that. I just want us all to go home."

U-T: "We all want the best for those kids, don't we? We want the best for you too. We're trying to help you."

Galush: "Don't make us come in and get you. This could get ugly. "

U-T yelled across at Galush, "Don't threaten like that, not yet."

Galush yelled back, "Maybe you play footsy with perps, but we don't."

"It's counterproductive."

"I'm giving them one last warning, and then we're going in."

U-T yelled, "Wait, Galush, wait. We don't even know what we're up against. We don't know what to expect in there. We got resources you don't. We can get some eyes in there. We know how to do it."

"How are you going to get eyes in there?"

"See those slots in the brick? We can get in there and see everything that's going on inside. We got a secret weapon. The army used it to great effect in the war, to get eyes behind enemy lines. We've been using it in domestic operations. Mobile lab delivers photo prints in seconds. They're already on the way here, we'll be ready to launch in ten minutes."

Elkie said, "Look, there's a bird in one of the slits."

She and Kelly climbed up to where the pigeon was.

Elkie said, "The poor thing is stuck. I'll help it."

It looked like it was trying to squeeze through, but the space was a little too narrow. Pigeons often gazed curiously into the slits, but none had ever tried to squeeze through before. The bird was very persistent.

Elkie reached in and helped it through the bricks. She held it in her hands. "It's got something around it's neck. It looks like a tiny little camera!"

It wriggled out of her hands and took off, circling the room.

Jack said, "Look, there's another one." A second pigeon had somehow gotten in through another slit, and both flew around and around.

"Grab them," Roco exclaimed.

Henry shouted, "Get the butterfly nets!"

Gabe and Elkie chased the birds around with the nets, and Elkie caught one in her net. The other pigeon flew in a big circle a few times, then landed up in one of the brick slits and tried to squeeze back out. Kelly grabbed it, but it wriggled away. Gabe caught it in his net.

They unbuckled the little cameras from their necks, and examined them.

"I love these little cameras," Ari said. "I wonder where they sell that little film."

Gabe said, "What'll we do with the birds?"

"They're so cute," Elkie replied. "Just let them go."

Gabe and Elkie released the pigeons. They flew in circles, tried to squeeze through the slits again, gave up, fluttered to the ground and walked about, bobbing their heads and pecking the dirt.

Kelly said, "Let's throw them some bread crumbs."

•

Over on the highway, Commander Galush, crouching behind the police van, yelled to Agent U-T, who was ducked behind the IPA van ten feet away, "How'd you train those pigeons to fly into those slits?"

She shouted back, "We got the best bird trainers in the world."

Ten long minutes passed, with no sign of the birds.

"What happened to your secret weapons?" Galush yelled. "They get lost?"

"They'll be back," U-T responded.

"You already said that."

"Give them another two minutes." U-T flashed an impatient dirty look at Stoloff. He was her point man to the pigeon unit, he had set this up, and he was sweating.

"Maybe they got distracted by a peanut," Galush mocked.

Stoloff started to fume, and couldn't restrain himself any more. "Don't badmouth those pigeons," he shouted. "They know what they're doing. Nothing's going to stop those birds. They'll be back."

Galush couldn't restrain a chuckle.

Stoloff yelled, "You probably wouldn't appreciate it, but thirty-two pigeons got medals for bravery in the war. Thirty two."

"Bravery? For flying home? That's what pigeons do. It's instinct."

"Instinct doesn't get them flying out there in the dark over enemy lines, risking their lives."

"Then what does?"

"Training, discipline, dedication, that's their motto. I mean, that's their unit's motto, the IPA pigeon trainers. You wouldn't understand."

They all fell silent.

Another ten minutes passed, with no sign of the pigeons returning.

Finally Galush muttered to Chief Detective Rendorf in a low voice, "I was hoping it wouldn't come to this."

"So was I," she replied.

"We're going to have to make a blind frontal assault. Are the dogs ready?"

"Waiting."

"Tell the battering rams to stand by. Everybody on high alert."

Rendorf said, "Aren't you going to tell the feds what we're doing?"

"I suppose I have to. But they'll just try to sabotage it."

•

Ari noticed Jack and Roco doing something with their bows and arrows, and came over to where they were working.

"What are you guys doing?" Ari asked.

"What does it looks like?" Jack replied.

They were taping cherry bombs onto the arrow heads.

"Why are you doing that?"

Roco said, "Why do you think?"

Jack said, "You got to fire fight with fire."

"That's not how it goes," Roco said.

"Since you know everything, then how does it go?"

Ari shook her head. "Do you want to be just like them? That's what they do, they explode things at people and hurt them and scare them."

Roco said, "If I'm going down, I'm taking some of them with me."

Ari said, "That's how you're going to wind up, just like them."

•

James J. Blinka crouched over his narrow kitchen table. Behind him his wife Emma popped an occasional small dry cracker into her mouth as she watched a quiz show.

He carefully spread a kitchen towel over the patterned oilcloth cover, and set his favorite handgun on it. He opened the lid of his small tool box, and laid out a number of items in a row.

"Come watch TV and keep me company," she called to him.

"I'm busy."

"Doing what?"

"Cleaning my Colt."

"You just cleaned it yesterday."

"I'm stressed out. It relaxes me."

He extracted the magazine, pulled back the slide, sighted down the barrel, released the slide, squeezed the trigger, smiled when he heard the click. He drew the slide back again, pulled down on the stop, slid it off the housing. He lifted the frame, dipped a cotton swab in cleaning solvent, worked it into the small spaces and crevasses around the trigger. He removed the recoil spring and barrel, then methodically wiped down the slide, recoil spring, and outside of the barrel with lubricant. He fed the patch through the barrel with the bore punch, sighted down the barrel but didn't see any residue.

"Someone just won a trip on a cruise ship. We should go too."

He pushed the striker back until it locked into place, pushed down on the release button, moved the back plate off the slide, slid the striker out, removed the extractor plunger, pushed the safety pin out, wiped down, cleaned, and lubricated all the parts.

"Are you listening? Someone just won a Caribbean cruise," she repeated. "Why don't we go too?"

"On a quiz show?"

"On a cruise. We haven't gone anywhere in so long."

"I was fired."

"Seriously, let's go on a cruise. The Caribbean or Hawaii. They even have cruises now to Alaska."

"I was fired."

"You're not serious."

"I'm serious."

The gravity of the situation hit Emma like a brick to the head. "Beg her."

"I begged her."

Desperation suddenly overwhelmed her. "I'll go. I'll beg her."

Blinka moaned, "What are we going to do?"

With a sweep of his arm, he scattered the gun parts across the floor, and lay his head on the table sobbing.

The highway was crowded with police cars, fire trucks, ambulances. Helicopters kept circling overhead.

Commander Galush barked into his walkie-talkie, "Evacuate the building. Send officers to every apartment. We'll begin the assault after the evacuation is complete and the last person is out."

Rendorf and Galush spoke in low tones.

"We still don't know what weaponry they've got," she said. "They haven't shown their hand since that first attack when the fleet arrived."

He replied, "They're waiting. They'll spring their arsenal when we begin the assault."

"If we just storm them blind, we're risking the girls' safety."

"If those girls are harmed, I swear by all that's holy they'll get what they deserve, if I have to do it myself, and I'll do it in the line of duty. No judge's going to get a chance to let those perps walk."

Ten feet away, U-T and Stoloff were still hunkered behind the IPA convoy. When she heard Galush taking the initiative, a cold chill shuddered through her. She muttered to Stoloff, "Mayday. Follow me. Stick close."

Throwing caution to the wind, U-T rushed across the open space, Stoloff close behind, over to the NYPD fleet. They ducked in next to Galush and Rendorf.

"Keep out of my operation!" Galush spat.

U-T responded, "You keep out of mine!"

Galush said, "We can't use both teams of dogs and battering rams and sharpshooters for the assault. And we've already got two different helicopter teams circling."

U-T said, "So back off."

"You back off."

Rendorf intervened. "We have to work this out. Immediately. We're partners. There's got to be room for compromise."

U-T said, "Let's flip a coin. Whoever wins, is the lead team and goes first. The other is backup if needed."

Reluctantly Galush agreed. Rendorf pulled out a buffalo nickel and tossed it.

"Tails!" U-T called.

Tails it was. "Yes!" She gloated in triumph.

Galush said, "All this means is that we'll use your personnel in the first assault."

U-T replied, "You can bet your family jewels we're not going to need a second assault."

"Let's at least agree on the game plan. How about we soften them up first with some gas? Our water cannon can blast out some of those bricks, make the hole big enough to shoot canisters through."

"And gas the girls? That's bush league, Galush. Rookie mistake. Maybe you need a refresher course. We won the toss. We're doing it our way."

Within a half hour, Monarch Towers was evacuated. Hundreds of people crowded along Cabrini Boulevard between police cordons. Word spread quickly, a swelling crowd gathered. News vans appeared, reporters walked through the throng interviewing people.

U-T was satisfied that everything was in place, gave the signal, and twenty heavily armed, helmeted Special Forces officers in battle armor stormed up the hill and set up their positions about ten yards away from the metal door. Six more followed, led by the Dobermans and German shepherds growling and tugging at their leashes. Finally, four officers in body armor rushed up the hill shouldering a

283

large battering ram. A group of sharpshooters arrayed behind various vehicles kept them covered.

U-T enunciated into the bullhorn: "This is your final warning. Come out with your hands up. Surrender and no one will be hurt. You will receive a fair trial. This is your choice. We are coming in to get you. There is no escape. Surrender. You have five minutes to make up your mind."

•

# CHAPTER NINETEEN

Inside the hideout, Henry said, "Everybody grab a handful of rocks."

Roco said. "What are we going to do, toss stones at them?"

Henry hobbled over to the metal door, climbed the ladder to the platform by the slits, with Jack and Roco and the others right behind. Through the slits they could see the forces arrayed against them.

Henry said, "Ready?"

He began throwing stones through the ventilation slits. One, two rocks hit the log. The others joined in. Three, four, five, six rocks bounced off the log.

A huge swarm of bees burst out. They appeared to hesitate an instant, then hurled themselves on the men and dogs.

At first the attackers didn't understand what was happening. The air all around them was suddenly dark with bees, uncountable thousands swarming everywhere, all over their bodies.

"Retreat!" the lead battering ram officer roared, angry bees covering his face.

They dropped the battering ram and ran. The dogs and handlers howled and yelped in pain, scattered in every direction. The sharpshooters leaped up from their positions, clutching their faces, dropping their rifles. They tripped and fell and screamed and rolled on the ground. The panic and rout was total.

Down at the fleet of cars, at first they couldn't figure out what was happening, but as some of the panicking officers and dogs approached, followed by the huge angry swarm, they all ran back to their cars as fast as they could, and desperately rolled up their windows. It was too late in most instances, and they only succeed in locking the angry bees inside their cars with them.

Galush, Rendorf, U-T and Stoloff all took shelter together in the NYPD command vehicle, where only a few bees penetrated.

Meanwhile, inside the hideout, the group watched through the slits. Several bees flew lazily around.

"Let's not celebrate," Ari said. "They'll be back."

Jack said, "I got stung. It really burns."

"Show me where he got you," Henry said. "I know how to pull out the stinger."

They stood on the ladders and platforms, watched the defeated forces hunkering down on the highway, as the sun set over the river behind banks of crimson cumulous clouds.

It quickly darkened. Long shadows swept across the hideout like clouds of dread. The atmosphere was tense and gloomy. They didn't talk much. Some sat alone and some held each other.

With darkness, most of the bees calmed down and returned home.

The little army encamping along the highway regrouped. Fresh troops poured in, replacing the many who had been rushed to the hospital.

The NYPD van became the de-facto joint command center, since U-T and Stoloff had taken refuge from the bees there with Galush and Rendorf, although none of them much liked being in such close quarters with the others.

Galush and Rendorf were in the front seat, Unter-Tractole and Stoloff in the rear.

As they'd agreed, Galush took over command when the first assault failed, and was waiting for a communication from one of his helicopters.

U-T, in the back seat, had spent the last hour trying to cover up her failure with a barrage of words. She kept chattering, and it was getting on Galush's nerves.

Galush said, "Excuse me," and slid the soundproof glass partition shut between the front and back seats. The sliding panel was meant to facilitate confidential communications when needed.

Rendorf said to him, "Something you want to talk about, Commander?" She always felt a little uncomfortable when she was in close quarters with Galush, because of his reputation. Although he was always such a gentleman toward her, she had seen the consequences of offending him and, to avoid any misunderstanding, she needed to navigate the space carefully.

Galush replied, "I just need some rest from that jabber. It's none of my business, of course, but I hear she's already buried three husbands."

"Really? She doesn't look old enough. Now that we've got a minute alone, Commander, can I be frank?"

"I always expect frankness from you, Chief Detective."

"What if we've been proceeding in this operation under false assumptions?"

"Such as?"

"Such as what we're going to find when we get inside."

"How so?"

"I don't really know. I just keep getting this feeling that our friends in the back seat are taking us for a ride. We've got to watch our back. Now that we're the assault force, we'll be taking the brunt of whatever we find inside."

"That's just the way it is," Commander Galush responded. "We'll find out when we get in. It's too late to turn back now."

"If this goes bad, if things go south, they'll throw us right under the bus. We should prepare for that."

Commander Galush said, "You know what they say, turnabout's fair play. We can always do a preemptive strike, throw them under first."

"No great loss."

Meanwhile in the back seat, U-T and Stoloff sat in an awkward silence, watching Galush and Rendorf through the glass, curious about what they were talking about, and at the same time glad that the partition was closed.

Finally Stoloff said, "Do you ever think about getting out?"

U-T was momentarily taken aback. "To tell you the God's honest truth, I can barely force myself to come to work any more."

"Then why do you stay?"

"I don't know what else to do, I guess. How about you?"

"Most of the time I don't mind it much. I only wish I didn't know as much as I do."

"What do you mean?"

"Sometimes I think back to how the Agency looked to me when I first got started. I wish I could see things like that now. I was so... naive."

U-T said, "It's a shithouse world, Stoloff, but what can we do but keep on with the work, put in our time, enjoy some brief vices, and hope for a few final years drunk in the Caymans or wherever it is that people like us go to die."

Galush slid the partition open again. "The whirlybird's ready. We're good to go."

U-T said, "I advise against a helicopter assault. Too close quarters."

"You people have had your chance. It's our turn now."

"Don't say I didn't warn you."

Galush spoke into the handset. "Turn on the floodlights."

Intensely bright lights flashed on from several of the trucks in the fleet. The building was suddenly in full light.

Galush enunciated, "Gasmasks on. Teargas canisters ready."

U-T said, "You're going to gas the girls along with the perps."

Galush turned to her. "Those girls are going to sleep in their beds tonight. Now you spooks are going to see what a real rescue operation look like." He grit his teeth and spoke into the handset again, "Prepare to storm the target. Five minutes to zero. Bring in the bird."

Around the side of the building a small police helicopter appeared, slowly lowering until it hovered twenty feet above the log. It released a long canister from its underside, which exploded as it hit, a large cloud of grey-black smoke and gas billowing in every direction. The explosion rocked and shook the walls of the hideout.

The whirlybird rose up the side of the building, engulfed in the fumes. As it reached the top and ascended above the roof, a larger IPA helicopter that had been circling, suddenly emerged from the other side. One veered as the other dipped, and in an instant the two were entangled, spinning out of control. The IPA helicopter crashed on top of the roof and burst into flames, while the police whirlybird fluttered down the side of the building and crashed onto the lawn.

Rendorf, watching from the command vehicle, gasped. "The building's on fire!"

Inside the hideout, Roco yelled, "They bombed the bees!"

A cloud of gas billowed into the hideout through the slits.

In the command vehicle, Galush shouted, "Hit those brick slots with the water cannon! Master stream!"

A high pressure stream burst forth from the deck gun. The fire fighters struggled to control the hose and keep it aimed at the slits. Water poured into the hideout. Some of the bricks gave way and collapsed, widening the gap.

Galush cried, "Teargas!"

Canisters flew through the breach, exploding when they hit the ground, and filling the hideout with billows of gas.

Elkie shouted, "What should we do?"

"I don't know," Gabe groaned.

Kelly shouted, "Grab a water jar. I seen them do it in a Tales From The Crypt. Get your shirt wet. That makes it into a gas mask! Cover up your mouth and your nose!"

Gabe looked around for a water jar, but his eyes and nose burned. He fell backwards and tumbled down to the ground, hacking in spasms.

Everyone was coughing, puking, rubbing their eyes.

Jack exclaimed, "I can't see!"

Henry fell down, vomiting. Roco knelt by him, crying "You're okay, you're okay."

Ari shouted, "That place up on top. In the cobwebs! That metal box. We can hide in there!"

She and Elkie helped Henry to his feet. Ari led them all hobbling and clambering up the slope at the back wall.

Outside in the command vehicle, Galush enunciated into the handset, "Sharpshooters! Rams! Dogs! Ready!"

The sharpshooters, battering rams, and dog team rushed up the hill and took positions.

Galush counted down, "Ten seconds. Five seconds. Ram! Dogs! We're going in!"

The two Special Force battering ram teams, in full riot gear, with gas masks, rushed forward, stormed up to the metal door, began pummeling it, the sharpshooters keeping them covered, the snarling dogs leaping and straining, the battering rams smashing again and again, beating at the metal, the door dented and throbbed and creaked, the metal bent, the walls rattled.

Gabe and Henry and Ari and Elkie and Roco and Jack and Kelly all scrambled, pushed, and pulled each other up the dirt slope at the back of the hideout until they were all on the back ledge at the top. They crawled into the cobwebs, pushed aside the insulation, slid open the metal panel on the big air duct, all climbed inside, then slid the panel shut behind them.

In the command vehicle, Rendorf blurted, "The steel's too thick, it's not going to snap."

Galush grit his teeth and shouted, "Battering rams retreat. Dogs pull back. Sharpshooter One! Grenade! Now!"

As soon as the rams and dogs were out of the way, the sharpshooter steadied his launcher, squeezed the trigger. A grenade shot out and hit with tremendous impact, blowing the metal door off its top hinge, driving the barricade tumbling back into the hideout. The ram teams leaped back into action and pummeled what was left of the door.

Henry pushed up against the cast iron grate above them. Coal dust fell in their faces.

Henry said, "It's heavy, help me!"

They squeezed in next to him, pushed up on the grate, pushed and strained. It gave way. Coal dust poured in all over. They shoved it up and out of the way.

Roco climbed through into the furnace room, and gave Ari his hand.

One by one they helped each other climb up into the furnace room, alongside the coal pile and boiler. They replaced the grate.

"This way," Henry said.

He led them crawling up the coal chute, pushed open the metal access doors. They stepped into the parking garage of Monarch Towers.

They stole up the driveway. A large crowd filled the street. Hundreds of people, fire trucks, police cordons. They were all looking up, watching the fire trucks drenching the upper floors of the building. No one noticed a group of small kids sneaking past.

They slipped over to Cabrini and down the hill.

Back at the hideout, the last hinge snapped, the door collapsed, the commandos, gas masks on, kicked the twisted metal out of the way, rushed inside, rifles on the ready, followed by the dogs. The atmosphere was so filled with teargas and grenade smoke they could hardly see. As the air slowly cleared, the commandos stood looking around, bewildered.

Meanwhile, down at the highway, which was still jammed and closed, James J. Blinka stalked along the shoulder, under the bridge, up the back of the long line of vehicles, all with their lights flashing, police, fire, ambulance, and other emergency vans. He brandished a card to the officer in charge, who noticed the staring look in his eyes, but credentials are credentials.

Blinka walked slowly, with determination. He looked into every car, smiled and nodded, and perused every group of officers and officials.

He finally saw what he was looking for, and walked slowly over to the vehicle.

Inside the car, the four occupants were all looking the other way, fixated on the assault on the burning building before them. None of them noticed the grinning man on the far side.

Blinka tapped on the window until finally he caught the attention of Senior Analyst Unter-Tractole, and she turned.

At first she barely recognize the face, then slowly realized it was Blinka. What's he doing here, she wondered.

Then she saw the Colt .38 Special pointed at her.

Shots rang out as Blinka was tackled from behind.

•

# CHAPTER TWENTY

In the crowd on Cabrini Boulevard, Mrs Anita Stoloff and Mrs Irma Golman stood wrapped in blankets, with Jim, Preston, and Rory.

Explosions ripped the air.

"What was that?" Anita Stoloff exclaimed with alarm.

Mrs Golman replied tensely, "It sounded like gunshots."

Preston said, "Maybe they're shooting at the kidnappers."

Jim pulled at his mother's sleeve. "Where's Dad?"

Mrs Stoloff replied, "He's working."

"But he's all right, isn't he?"

"Yes, of course he's all right. I hope no innocent people got hurt."

Four fire trucks poured water on the blaze, and the flames turned to dark smoke.

Irma Golman stared at the building and kept shaking her head. "Thank God, they've got it under control."

"Count your blessings," Anita Stoloff said. "We both have resources."

"Mom," Rory asked, "Where will we live?"

"We're going back to our old house."

"Then we'll be back at Hilldale next year instead of this stupid school?"

"Yes."

"Us too?" Preston asked his mom.

"Absolutely."

"Hooray! Then I'm glad it's burning down."

"Don't say that. Some people here may have lost everything."

Preston replied, "You're the one who always says that we're the important people. Make up your mind."

In another part of the crowd, Selene Odelia and Jeffrey Daumer were huddling.

"I pray for those beautiful girls. They are both so nice and smart. Their families must be devastated."

They subtly squeezed hands.

Daumer said, "I've decided, Selene, let's go away together this summer."

"Now's not the time to talk about that."

"To Oaxaca. Let's try it. Let's just try it together, and see how it goes."

"It's too much, Jeff. I think I need to just spend time by myself this summer."

"Let's just give it a try."

Further down the block, toward the back of the throng, next to an ambulance flashing its warning lights, stood Helen Hopper and Laurrinto Foxx.

A wave of fatigue washed through her. "At this point I just want to do the right thing. This is all my responsibility. I probably should give them what they want, and resign."

"Don't even talk like that."

"Do you think we're far enough away from the school? That restraining order's still in place, isn't it?" she asked.

"At least until tomorrow, according to the attorney," Foxx replied.

"I don't want to give them an excuse to detain me again. I'm not very good at spatial estimates. How much is a hundred yards?"

"The length of a football field."

"I feel so discouraged. Disheartened. How do we prepare the children for a world like this?"

"I wish I knew."

"I used to think we were winning, but I think we let it all slip away."

"Nonsense, Helen," Foxx said, "We're going to win this thing."

In another part of the crowd, the Drannily sisters were speaking in low tones.

"I can't help but think I somehow brought this down on us all. I'm sorry."

"It's too late for that, Maude. The damage is done."

"All I wanted was to make things better, like they ought to be, like they used to be."

"I know you meant well," Chloe said.

"I've made a mess of everything, haven't I?"

"Yes, you have, Maude dear."

Tears welled into Miss M. Drannily eyes, something which even Miss C. Drannily had not seen in many years. "At least we have each other."

Miss C. said, "Maude, I've decided to go back to Iowa."

•

As the first hints of dawn lit the horizon behind them, a tired little group slipped past the toll booths and started across the long bridge. Only a few cars passed. Rush hour would not begin for several hours.

Henry was still limping badly. "I got to take a break. My foot hurts too much."

They stopped. Gabe looked down at the little red lighthouse and the mighty river flowing lazily below them.

Henry leaned against the railing. "I can't do it."

Gabe said, "We can't stop now."

"Leave me here. You go on. I'll catch up."

Ari took his hand. "We're not going without you."

"We'll carry you," Elkie said.

Jack said, "Hop onto my back."

"I'm not letting anybody carry me," Henry said.

Roco said, "That's the only way we'll get there."

"We'll take turns," Kelly said.

"Just let me lean on somebody. I'll be okay."

Gabe put his arm around Henry, and Henry reciprocated.

"I'll take your other side," Ari said. "It'll be faster."

"I'll take your back pack," Elkie said.

Henry slung his other arm over Ari's shoulder. They trudged along, Henry hopping on one foot. They reached the first tower.

A great cargo ship passed below them, headed to the sea.

A police car in the far lane. They hunkered down behind the barrier fence.

When it was past, Ari said, "Let's go."

Roco said, "We can do it."

Elkie said, "We're almost there."

Gabe said, "We can do anything."

"To Maroon!" Henry said.

"To Maroon!"

They started across the main span, the giant cables swooping down alongside them. They approached the middle of the bridge, where the cables joined the roadway.

Right in the center of the bridge was a sign with a line in the middle. On one side was written New York, and on the other side New Jersey.

A sharp breeze pinched Gabe's cheeks. Banks of cumulus clouds swooped across the sky. The Palisades cliffs rose before them, lush with forests.

A flock of birds in V-formation glided on wind currents over the river, huge white pelicans with dark wingtips. They hovered as if suspended in the air alongside them.

Suddenly a police car pulled over.

Henry yelled, "Run!"

They took off running.

Two cops leaped out, jumped the rail to the walkway.

Gabe glanced back over his shoulder, the cops were almost on top of him. He stumbled, tripped and went flying. His head hit the railing. A blinding flash of light. He grabbed onto a pelican's neck, and suddenly he was soaring on air currents up above the bridge's towers. Henry was with him, and Elkie and Ari and the others, all on the backs of enormous pelicans as they sailed high over the towers, banking on air currents, their wings hardly moving, in a great circle over the Palisade cliffs in V-formation, then veering south, the pine forests spreading endlessly below them.

•

When Gabe opened his eyes again, vague shapes were moving around him, muffled voices. He felt very tired. He couldn't keep his head up. His eyelids drooped. He didn't know where he was.

The room came slowly into focus.

Mom and Dad and Benjo were there.

Mom said, "We're just happy you're safe."

He was in bed.

Benjo winked. Dad cracked a pained smile.

He was in a hospital.

"Where's Henry?"

Mom said, "Henry's right over there."

Henry was propped up on pillows in another bed across the room, his mom and gramma alongside him, his foot in a cast. His eyes were shut. He looked asleep.

"Where are my other friends?

Mom said, "Your other friends are all back with their families."

"Are they okay?"

She shook her head side to side. "Of course. A lot of people are going to be keeping an eye on them from now on." She smiled, sadness in her eyes.

"Don't forget to tell him," Benjo said.

Mom said, "Oh yes. You know what? That Mr Foxx friend of Grampa from his old union got us some real good lawyers. After all that grief they put us through, they ruled in our favor. It looks like we're getting the land back. They're letting us keep Maroon. They're not going to let them knock it all down and build a mall after all."

"Really?" Gabe burst out.

Benjo said, "It's not over yet, but we're winning, at least we haven't lost yet, and we're going to keep on fighting."

Gabe's eyes widened. "And the house and the pines and the creek are all still there?"

"Of course," Mom said. "So maybe there's a little justice once in a while in this old world after all."

Gabe looked over at Henry.

Henry slowly opened his eyes. Their gaze met. A communication passed between them that neither could have put into words.

Gabe turned his eyes to Mom. "So can we go there this summer? We can go to Maroon?" Gabe exclaimed.

Mom said, "Probably. Once you're better. We can probably go to Maroon this summer after all. It will do us all good to get out of the city. I think we all miss that fresh pine forest air and clean country living and hiking and wild huckleberry picking."

"Can I bring my friends?"

•

OTHER WORKS BY JOHN CURL

NOVEL

The Co-op Conspiracy (2014)

MEMOIR

Memories of Drop City: The first hippie commune of the 1960s and the Summer of Love (2008)

HISTORY

Indigenous Peoples Day: Documentary History and Handbook for Activists (2017)

For All The People: Uncovering the hidden history of cooperation, cooperative movements, and communalism in America (2009, 2012)

History of Collectivity in the San Francisco Bay Area (1982)

History of Work Cooperation in America (1980)

TRANSLATION

Ancient American Poets: The Flower Songs of Nezahualcoyotl, The Songs of Dzitbalche, The Sacred Hymns of Pachacuti (2005)

POETRY

Yoga Sutras of Fidel Castro (2013, 2014)
Revolutionary Alchemy: Collected poems 1967-2012 (2012)
Scorched Birth (2004)
Columbus in the Bay of Pigs (1991)
Decade (1987)
Tidal News (1982)
Cosmic Athletics (1980)
Ride the Wind (1979)
Spring Ritual (1978)
Insurrection/Resurrection (1975)
Commu 1 (1971)
Change/Tears (1967)

THEATER

The Trial of Christopher Columbus (2009)

## ABOUT JOHN CURL

The Outlaws of Maroon is John Curl's second novel. His translations Ancient American Poets won an Artists Embassy International Book Award. His transliterations from Quechua formed the libretto for Tania León's Ancient (2009). His play The Trial of Columbus was produced by PEN Oakland's Writers Theater in 2009. He represented the USA at the World Poetry Festival in 2010 in Caracas, Venezuela. He is an editor of the annual poetry anthology Overthrowing Capitalism, published by the Revolutionary Poets Brigade, and a long time board member of PEN Oakland.

Born and raised in Manhattan, John Curl has a degree in Comparative Literature from New York City College. He currently resides in Berkeley, California, and has one daughter. He was a professional woodworker by trade at Heartwood Cooperative Woodshop, served on the steering committee of West Berkeley Artisans and Industrial Companies, on the board of the Network of Bay Area Worker Cooperatives, and as a Berkeley planning commissioner. He is a founding member the Berkeley Indigenous Peoples Day pow wow committee.

www.ingramcontent.com/pod-product-compliance
Lightning Source LLC
Chambersburg PA
CBHW030345020726
47493CB00003B/689